KATARAINA

KATARAINA
BECKY MANAWATU

SCRIBE
Melbourne | London | Minneapolis

Scribe Publications
18–20 Edward St, Brunswick, Victoria 3056, Australia
2 John St, Clerkenwell, London, WC1N 2ES, United Kingdom
3754 Pleasant Ave, Suite 223w, Minneapolis, Minnesota 55409, USA

First published by Mākaro Press 2024
Published by Scribe 2025

Copyright © Becky Manawatu 2024

All rights reserved. Without limiting the rights under copyright reserved above, no part of this publication may be reproduced, stored in or introduced into a retrieval system, or transmitted, in any form or by any means (electronic, mechanical, photocopying, recording or otherwise) without the prior written permission of the publishers of this book.

The moral rights of the author have been asserted.

This is a work of fiction. All of the characters, organisations, and events portrayed in this novel are either products of the author's imagination or are used fictitiously.

Text design by Paul Stewart, Mākaro Press

Printed and bound in the UK by CPI Group (UK) Ltd, Croydon CR0 4YY

Scribe is committed to the sustainable use of natural resources and the use of paper products made responsibly from those resources.

978 1 761381 45 4 (Australian edition)
978 1 917189 19 4 (UK edition)
978 1 964992 18 1 (US edition)
978 1 761386 17 6 (ebook)

Catalogue records for this book are available from the National Library of Australia and the British Library.

scribepublications.com.au
scribepublications.co.uk
scribepublications.com

to Tim

Run, baby

I tell the children they can
wear their shoes in the house if they ever
sense they'll have to run.

It would be easier if I could just tell them
not to go into the house if they sense
they'll have to run.

But maybe they can't help but go close
to the fire, or run their fingers against
the split mirror. Some people name the small animal

clinging to the ceiling, despite it
scaring our dogs and cats, eating all the birds,
discarding beaks and bones and we can hardly think

with that gentle noise, with it crouched there
watching the suds
latch on to our hands, grey bracelets.

It thinks we feel too beautiful wearing them.
It's not breaking tikanga, baby, to wear your shoes
in the house, where the mirrors are yawning open.

You don't have to say goodbye to the people
who are happy there scowling. You can just run, baby,
you can just run in your shoes, to water, or trees or me.

Just get to the road and call out all our names.

Who we are

Tikumu
c.1871–c.1890

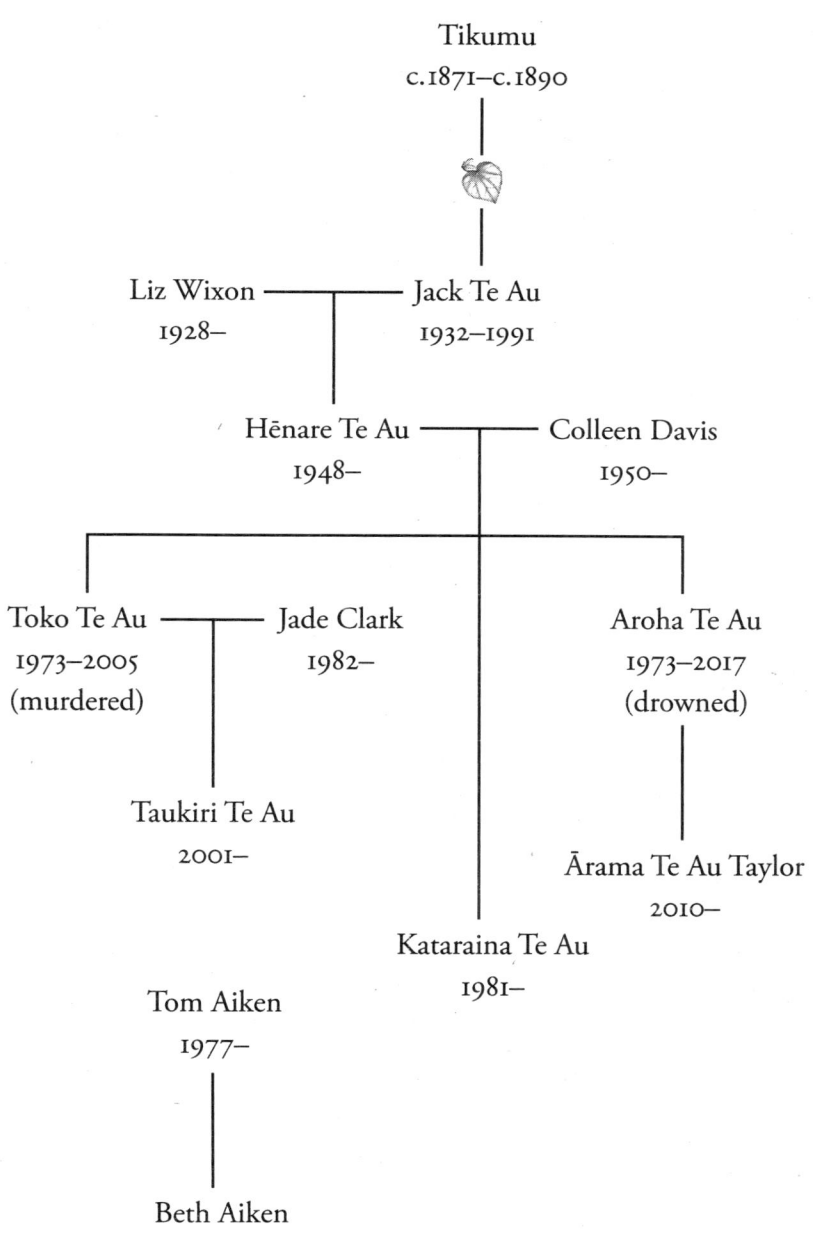

Liz Wixon —————— Jack Te Au
1928–   1932–1991

Hēnare Te Au —————— Colleen Davis
1948–   1950–

Toko Te Au ———— Jade Clark   Aroha Te Au
1973–2005   1982–   1973–2017
(murdered)   (drowned)

Taukiri Te Au
2001–

                                    Ārama Te Au Taylor
                                    2010–

                    Kataraina Te Au
Tom Aiken   1981–
1977–

Beth Aiken
2010–

Our ancestor once lived close to the house where he was shot. She was at the river when a man approached her and offered her some peaches from a can, but then he attacked her.

Many years after the girl shot the man

We are telling this story. A clambering of vines seeking up towards the sun, then wanting, again, the groundwater.

Sometimes after telling more we walk into the bush, towards the bulging part of the river behind a series of grassy hills, remnants of what was our life here. It was a place we'd lay down plastic, squirt Sunlight liquid and slide and slide under the hot pale sun, never imagining that one day we'd shoot the man who owned the land. We'd walk over those hills, a day of telling behind us, take off our clothes, go into the cold quick awa, let it rush over our face and hair.

When you shoot a man something inside you wants to be repulsed by who you are. You can't ever manufacture – through deeds or words or service or prayer – a certain goodness again.

Telling allows us to live in the plain and pointless space of proving the moving, flailing, contesting and yielding parts of a contradiction to all be true, or at the very least honest. Tika. Pono. Together we listen. One of us might sometimes create the whistle, scratch, whistle, scratch of lead on paper. Who even does that anymore? She does. Kataraina.

Hear us rush towards each other, blue and green and silver and brown and murky and chalky and clear tributaries coming down different sides of our mauka, to find each other, flow through and over each other. We meet at the growing beast, to pull up our history, the impressions left of an existence, life drawn in the earth preserved as mātātoka – as fossils.

If our stories are vines, are we the sun coaxing them up, out of their whenua, or are we their whenua?

No. We are the rinsing. We crave the rinsing and we are the rinsing.

Ko wai tātou?

Ko wai tātou.

One month after the girl shot the man

Almost a week before we left Rakiura we walked into Māori Beach for a night's camp-out. Jade wanted to say goodbye to the island, and even if she could have said it anywhere, from the ferry even, she wanted it to be Māori Beach.

Colleen and Hēnare stayed behind, while we went: Ārama, Beth, Taukiri, Jade and Kataraina. We were still not ourselves. One month is nothing to murder. And some of us – Ārama and Beth – sometimes forgot that Stuart Johnson was not even the first victim; he was not even the second. And if we went right back through our whakapapa, his murder could be deemed quite unremarkable, par for the Te Au course, even. Maybe that's what made it worse. Made us feebly wonder in each of our own inner worlds who was next?

So at Māori Beach, with its great curving band of pale sand encircled by low forested hills and the soft fat water of Wooding Bay, and under the southern sky, we wondered if this place was to be our end. Each place we went we wondered if this supermarket, street, dream, pie, drive, walk, morning, afternoon, evening, night, kiss was to be our end. Māori Beach, isolated and pretty, was only one of the more poetic possibilities, soaking our wonderings, giving it a disconcerting weight.

Māori Beach was not our end.

Taukiri lit a fire and around it we ate buttered bread and small salted venison steaks. Ārama and Beth ran up the beach to find the river mouth, a vivid blue channel of the freshest water we had ever seen, pouring quick into the southwest Pacific. We returned to the camp and the rest of us were arranged as if posing for a Department of Conservation tramping brochure. Taukiri crouched at the fire, which glowed on his handsome face. Jade resting on a picnic blanket she'd brought. (She had patted it, asking Kataraina to sit with her, but Kataraina, Kat, Aunty Kat could not sit.)

Kat was standing near the shore, her arms folded tight across her chest, impenetrable, even to the beauty of the Rakiura twilight. A snapshot of any one of us would have made for a great tramping brochure. No one would have guessed how consumed by violence we were.

Of us all, Ārama – our little Ari – was the most willing to pretend. He was the one who believed pretending everything was okay, seeded okayness. The rest of us were of the whakaaro that pretending encouraged more pretending. Especially Kat.

But camping! What a precious memory. And so, to stop pacing and stop Jade from patting at the picnic blanket, Kat suggested camping activities. We played spotlight in the grassy backshore. We took a torch up to the river to see if we could spot an eel, though we didn't. We drank warm Milo around the fire before bed. Then it was Ari patting at the picnic blanket. 'Come sit here by me, Aunty,' he said.

'I'm all goods,' she said, standing, her lower body at odds with gravity, her upper body battling its many selves for the right to peace.

'But come on,' he whined.

'Knock it off,' she said.

Ari's eyes watered.

'Don't be a sook,' she said. 'Surely, you're harder now. "Django", wasn't it?'

And we felt this was quite mean, even Kat, who decided it was time to take her Zopiclone, go get a moe in, on a bloody camp mat, yeah right eh, hahaha.

Tomorrow she could start her day over the same way she had for a month. Forgiving us all for shooting him before she'd gotten to the bottom of a secret question that had barely bothered her before he died, but since he was shot tormented her. The question, once a dog barking somewhere distant, was now a shrill bird busting its head bloody against the glass pane of her heart.

Two years after the girl shot the man

Nothing much was ever happening on the grass oasis, near, and yet away from the swamp. Maybe the grass place was safe from that growing beast. It was hard to doubt it would be eaten up, too, the way fences, roads, sheds were being consumed around it.

This was what we returned to, after the camping trip at Māori Beach and the ferry ride across Te Ara a Kiwa. We'd stood together, to say bye again, or at least see-ya-later from the catamaran's stern. And on this grey day, we could see the ghostly outline of our mauka, Hananui.

'One day we could climb it,' Kat said, as if the confinement of the ferry was making her restless.

'Yuck,' Jade said. 'That looks high.'

Back in Kaikōura we were reunited with Tom Aiken. We pulled up and there he was, in gumboots and a green hunter's polar fleece, pulling a vine away from a window frame. The house looked as if it had been picked up and plonked where it was. So much budding about it. Bare patches were now tendrilled. The birdsong was a chorus. It was dusk when we arrived home; the autumn air was cool and damp. We crossed his green yard, which had not long ago been wood chip and pale brown mud, some grass.

Tom Aiken stopped pulling the vine. We stared at one another, and no one knew what to say. Blue swamp hens crossed the yard in front of us, as if we were not there. They disappeared into the dense bush and headed towards the swamp.

Holding up the blade in his hand, he said, 'I wanted to leave it, but … we need this house.'

'I missed it,' Beth said.

'Welcome home.' He looked around the property. 'Hard to believe eh.'

'How long were we gone?' Kat said.

Not very long ago it had been summer, a summer when Beth and Ārama went back and forwards between the two houses. They'd walked the dry gravel road or cut under the fences and darted through paddocks to reach each other and press sticks into each other's backs and say, hands up, ya hear. Now, the entire landscape of farmland appeared to have reverted, wild with life: mānuka, rimu, kōwhai, nīkau, ponga. Some grew overnight. Bold. Hungry. Obscenely generous, the air was so fresh and rich.

This evening, though, two of us were on the grass: Jade resting, Kataraina restless.

'Always wished for grass, to sit on, lie on, read on,' Jade said.

'It's the dream,' Kataraina said, pulling weeds from our herb garden.

'We should also eat our kai out here tonight.'

'This bloody mint is strangling the thyme.'

'Taukiri can play his guitar. We could light candles.'

You could sit? thought Jade, and she put her head back onto the picnic blanket.

Kataraina continued pulling up weeds. The sun was bright on her face and hair. She paused and looked out past the trees to the kūkūwai, the water almost red in the late-afternoon light. She could hear the youngest of us, Beth and Ārama, bursting through the ponga and mānuka, spilling out to the grass armed with sticks of toetoe, the sun's light attracted to the soft translucent plumes above their heads.

Beth whipped Ari and luminous toetoe particles scattered then floated, making time look slower, harnessed. She tripped on her own too-big gumboots and fell. Taukiri stepped out of the house with his guitar, sat down beside Jade, his face red from napping in the sunroom.

'What should we do for kai?' he said, tuning his guitar, spurring time on again with the question, which made Aunty check it on her phone.

'A picnic.'

He started strumming, and singing, '*A picnic before she leaves us before she goes, before she breaks our hearts. So much going and leaving, who will keep us from drowning ourselves in the swamp ...*'

'Oi. What's with all the songs about being left.'

'Mummy issues. *We will keep from drowning ourselves in the swamp we will keep ourselves from wanting to look inside the taniwha's mouth ...*'

'Fish wraps? The leftover butterfish.'

'*Make us butterfish wraps, my aunty, my aunty.*'

'You want me to sing a verse?'

'No one wants that. You have not been blessed with the Te Au voice.'

'I got some Te Au fight though – you want that?'

He laughed, but we were gone again to the water to dip the toetoe in it, and watch it come away and float on the too-dark, too-deep water. Taukiri stood up. 'Fish wraps can't be that hard to make. I'll sort dinner eh.'

'And the boy is a man,' his mother said.

He flexed his muscles.

'And the man is a boy,' his aunty said, thrusting some dill and parsley at him. 'Chop it fine. Mix it in with our mayo.'

Tom Aiken returned, and all six of us ate butterfish wraps with young watercress leaves, sliced tomato and a fresh dill and parsley mayonnaise on the grass – Kat pacing, her food in her hands. 'Great choice, wraps!' – until it got damp, and the sun disappeared, then the candles we'd lit were not enough to comfort us, and when the moon came up and the strange quiet began, as if a silent movie was being projected onto an invisible screen, we retreated into the house to play gin rummy.

Beth and Ari watched a cartoon in our lounge. We were so lucky they had found a path back to childhood after it all. As if they trod a path back through the dark trees of what happened, we said. He only put one plaster on his knee today, we said. Beth squeezed her eye shut and pointed her fingers at a bird and pretended to shoot it only twice today – that we saw, we said.

In the lounge, Beth unscrewed the cap from the imaginary bottle again. She passed it to Ari. He took the imaginary bottle, and we drank imaginary courage from it.

4 January 2020, field study day one, 5.30–6.30am

The scientist would pray at the Waiau-toa before she worked.

Her karakia revered te taiao – what karakia wouldn't?

It was dawn and she welcomed it. 'Haea te ata, ka hāpara te ata.' She acknowledged the waking birds, especially the wrybill that used its crooked beak to scavenge beneath the river rocks. 'Ka korokī te manu, ka wairori te kutu.'

The morning, so important. 'Ko te ata nui.'

How it spread into the day. 'Ka horaina.'

The dawn chorus. 'Ka taki te umere. He pō, he pō. He ao, he ao, ka awatea.'

She knew the braided river to be part of an ancient pounamu trail tying Kaikōura coast with Lewis Pass and on to the West Coast; the ara tawhito was how her ancestors once brought the children of Waitaiki – the pieces of pounamu broken from her – across to trade with her eastern ancestors.

Cairo was the name of this scientist and she was a descendant of the pounamu trail. It was as if she'd been loosened from the melted snow and had tumbled through the Arahura gorge to be folded in harakeke and trekked over the alps herself.

She'd made the journey east to study a swamp. When she first saw the deep green lagoon, oxygen poured into her lungs, pulling her ribcage up, separating the bones, and she didn't want to let the breath go. This had all been pasture – square patches in different shades of brown and green – now it was harakeke and raupō, wīwī and water. The ferns, grasses, mosses, trees, birds and insects, which grew there and flew over, under and around the kūkūwai, were a spectacle. Its mauri, its life force, hummed with original energy.

Her visit to the braided river that morning was not only spiritual. She was interested in seeing the place where a botanist had rediscovered pygmy goosefoot.

Pygmy goosefoot. Wild spinach. The land starfish. Parahia. A plant her ancestors might have ripped by the handful from the kūmara crops as a weed, presumed extinct.

She scoured the dryland. This was the same place the botanist had rediscovered the herb, after no recorded sightings in more than fifty years. She continued walking, her eyes becoming sore. She needed to see the plant, dubbed a phoenix risen from the ashes. A Lazarus. The seeds – she wanted to pocket some. But she would not. The seeds could remain dormant for years and years. Then when conditions were right for the herb, the seed would sprout its leaves and roots, and churn out thousands of seeds to be carried away by water. Moved by the braided river, moved by the wind and birds.

She spotted the plant. It was small and unremarkable. She squatted to look. It was, as she expected, like a scruffy, sprawling land starfish with small green leaves. 'Tēnā koe i tēnei ata,' she said to the plant, and laughed. 'You're not much to look at, are you?'

The river flowed silver beside her, parallel timelines merging near the rising sun.

Cairo had studied the aerial shots of Waiau-toa. Braided rivers fascinated her. She thought if she were ever to build a time machine, she would model it on a braided river. Somehow. She laughed quietly to herself. Time machines. A morning search for a resurrected plant. She snapped her fingers about the corner of her left eye. The logical side of the brain. 'Wakey, wakey,' she said.

She took out her pencil and notebook and began work. She described the edges of the phenomenon. The distinction between the old and the new was plain. Beyond the spectacle, a drear of gorse, weeping and cracked willow. She walked further upstream. Bog pine and weeds and willow and gorse and broom.

She saw two people on the stone island, a diamond in the braid of the river. They were up against the edge, cutting gorse. She wrote about them in her notebook. *Two people, a young man and a woman, cutting gorse growing on the riverbed. They are at the line between ...*

She paused writing, unsure how to log what she was seeing – and indeed if she should – so she could decipher it later in the study when she would go through her observations.

They are at the line between ... what has happened and what hasn't happened.

She questioned using figurative language but could not produce a more succinct analysis. She reminded herself that their field study had recently begun, and once she understood more she might better describe the kūkūwai and its borders. She followed the river back downstream, cut into a recently built track, reached the saltmarsh and crossed it all the way back to the swamp.

Thirty-seven years before the girl shot the man

Kataraina Te Au is born on a chilly November night in 1981. These are facts that can't be changed. Not then, not now. Nanny Liz comes to her son's house, to her daughter-in-law's house, to the house soon of her granddaughter Kat. It's an old story, and we can see it all as if we are there. Nanny Liz comes from the pub. Hēnare called her there and asked to speak to Lizzy Te Au. The bartender shouted, 'Who?' into the phone, yelling over the noise in the bar.
'Lizzy.'
'Oh,' he said, and then shouted, 'Oi, Lippy Lizzy, you got a man asking for you.'
'Hello,' Nanny Liz shouted back.
'Ma,' said Hēnare down the phone, 'Colleen's having contractions. We'll head to hospital soon.'
'Early? Auē. Okay, I'm getting in a taxi now,' she said and hung up the phone.
Nanny Liz arrived soon after to her son's little cottage by the sea. She walked in with rain falling off her face and hands and strands of hair. She was wearing a red Angora jersey and black velvet leggings.
'Where is she?'
Aroha came to the room, rubbing her eyes. 'Nanny,' she said.
Hēnare picked up the girl and kissed her. 'You should be asleep, like Toko.'
Nanny Liz walked to the father and his daughter and kissed them both on their cheeks and Hēnare said, 'I'll make you coffee, Ma. The old man still there?'

'Āe.'

Hēnare went to the kitchen with Aroha on his hip. Nanny Liz followed. She opened the coal range and scooped a shovel into it. She hovered her hands there for heat. Hēnare put his daughter down. 'Go and get Nan a towel, baby girl.' He put the kettle onto the hot iron.

Aroha skipped away for the towel.

'George was up from the island,' he said, opening the fridge. 'He brought fresh birds and cod and livers.' The man turned to look at his mother.

'Some fried livers would be lovely. Where is she?'

'In the bath. She sent me out. She's okay for now. You didn't have to rush.'

'I was ready to leave.'

'Hmm.'

Aroha returned with the towel. Her grandmother took it, kissed her, then dabbed at her neck and hair. Hēnare dusted the small livers in flour and fried them in oil and butter. The kettle whistled. Nanny Liz made herself an instant coffee with no milk. Aroha touched the velvet leggings, rubbing nanny's thighs, watching the change in the way the fabric caught the light. Hēnare gave Nanny Liz a small plate of fried liver and a piece of buttered wholemeal toast. She pressed the livers onto the toast, salted them and ate.

'Mmm, delicious, son. Thank you.'

Colleen came into the kitchen. She was wearing slippers, tights and an oversized cotton shirt. 'Tēnā koe Whaea,' she said.

Nanny Liz went to her daughter-in-law. She gave her a hongi. With noses pressed they held each other.

Nanny Liz said, 'Kei te pēhea koe?'

Colleen nodded. 'Kei te pai au.'

Nanny had been a little sad that Colleen was afraid to birth at home, but she understood. Soon Hēnare and Colleen would go to the maternity unit, and Nanny Liz would look after Toko and Aroha. She would wait up all night to hear her mokopuna had arrived safe.

She put Aroha back to bed in the little room she shared with her twin. She whispered to her that the world was changing tonight, the whole world, because a whole new one was arriving, just like the two arrivals the day she and Toko were born. It was perfect. It was raining.

When the little girl was asleep, and the rain had stopped, she went and sat out on the porch of the cottage by the sea and watched the moon climb into the sky. She smoked a rollie and drank a second cup of coffee. She went to the kitchen and looked for the ingredients to bake something lovely to eat with Toko and Aroha in the morning. There was a big paper bag of apples in the pantry.

Bright light spilled into the kitchen. There was the sound of a car door slamming. Her heart raced. She looked out the window and Jack was walking up the path, with his hands hardly in his pockets and his head hanging loose from his shoulders. She walked to the door and opened it. 'The bubbas are asleep.'

'Ha! Wake them up,' he said. 'Grandad's home.'

'No, Jack, let's leave them.'

He grinned, and he stepped past her into their son's house.

'Stop,' she said. 'Take off your shoes.'

'Ahhh.' He stepped backwards, eyeing her, though she kept her face down. He stepped back outside and stood, swaying. He went to bend and untie his laces and stumbled. 'Help me.'

She bent and untied them, and he kicked his shoes off and stepped back inside.

He sat on his son's couch, and he looked around the room like he was seeing it for the first time. Liz examined him quietly, unsure. When she realised his breathing was deep and mood was fine, she asked, 'Coffee?'

'Sure.'

She went to the kitchen.

He stayed in the lounge and she wondered what he was thinking, looking around at the tidy little room, with the pictures on the walls and the books in the shelves and the woollen throw there for anyone who might need it, and polished carved wood and potted plants, and the sound of the sea that was just beyond the pane of glass. She wondered what he was thinking looking at all the things placed in the room with a certain sort of care, a care they never quite managed because of their energy, their vortex. She put a heaped teaspoon of instant coffee into a mug and imagined Jack in the lounge. Then he was at the kitchen doorway. And he looked at the apples out on the bench and the paring knife. Again, the kettle came to a whistle. She rushed to it because she worried the sound might agitate his peace. Beautiful when he was peaceful.

'Did you have a good night?' she said, pouring steaming water into the mug. She added milk and one teaspoon of sugar, and he did not answer.

Finally, he said, 'You left.'

'Āe,' she said. 'I told them I'd be here in a flash if she went into labour.'

'Is she in labour?'

Nanny Liz laughed nervously. 'Well, that's why we are here.' She handed him the mug of coffee.

'Bunch of dickheads down there.'

She stirred the coffee. She pushed it a little closer to him. She picked up an apple and began peeling it. Her heart was pounding; she worried he'd hear it thudthudthud. She controlled her breathing.

'I'm going to surprise the kids with a sponge. Dessert for brekky. And cream. Icing sugar.' She rushed to the pantry. 'God, I hope there is icing sugar.'

She stayed in the pantry, looking at the icing sugar, but making noises like she was still searching for the icing sugar. She picked up packets and dumped them down.

She heard a chair squeak, and his footsteps. She held her breath, slowly picked up the icing sugar and held the packet at her chest and closed her eyes and stepped out of the pantry. He was holding the paring knife. He looked at her, his face sagging, and he took an apple.

He began cutting it. He took a sip of his coffee, put down the mug and carried on cutting. 'My mother used to fill her crumbles with stars,' he said.

'I know,' Liz said, walking to her husband at their son's kitchen bench, their mokopuna asleep in little cosy beds down the hall, the smell of jasmine coming down the short hall from the bathroom, a fridge filled with salad leaves and carrots and cheese and milk and cream and cod and livers and three fresh muttonbirds. Pictures on the walls and books on the shelf, and her son's nylon and hooks and sinkers and filleting knives out there, outside on the nice wooden table.

The man held up a star, cut from an apple.

Liz took another apple, and she found another knife, and they cut stars from apples for an hour, in a drunken silence she'd never shared with this man. The confounding depths of peace and the exquisite current of hope she felt as she watched him layer a ceramic dish with stars they'd cut from apples. To stop herself staring at the man, she lightly whisked the batter.

The phone rang.

The baby was born, and both she and her mother were strong and well, and her name was Kataraina, after Nanny Liz's dead baby sister, and they would need a few days, and Hēnare would stay with his wife, if that was okay, which it was of course, of course.

Jack sprinkled brown sugar over the stars, then cinnamon from a small glass jar, and the sun was up then, the two grandparents had stayed awake all night long, and she poured the batter over the stars and put the dish in the hot oven. And while it was baking the man fell asleep on his son's clean and comfortable couch, and Lizzy pulled the woollen throw over him, and she kneeled on the floor and almost cried. The small children tiptoed into the room and Toko said, 'Mmm, what smells yum, Nanny?'

Nanny Liz opened her arms, and the children ran to her, warily eyeing Grandad Jack on the couch like he was a sleeping bear.

'Grandad Jack is tired from baking for you. You wait and see, he stayed up all night baking for you.'

And they stayed several days baking and cleaning and smiling and sleeping and looking at the little details of their son's gentle existence in the world. On the second night Jack lit a candle and sat out on the deck listening to the sea. During the days he made jugs of Raro and poured the sweet drink into little amber glasses for the twins. He put out plates and knives and forks for kai. He took books from the shelves and turned their pages. His son or his daughter-in-law had a book of poetry by Hone Tūwhare, and he read the very short one called 'Desdemona' to his wife while she folded the children's clean T-shirts, and she kept folding, afraid to draw too much attention to the new thing that happened. He had read her a poem. Even if it was just six lines and two of those lines were a single word each – 'flexing' and 'necking' – it was a poem.

When Liz took the children to the beach, Jack opened a beer and put a cassette tape into the player. He watched it spin and there was a rustling sound, and then an indistinct strumming of a guitar. Hēnare's voice. Their son was singing a song Jack had not heard, and he could tell his son wrote it, because it was about being small and on his father's shoulders and his mother was yelling out.

'... don't stumble on the stone shore, my love,
with our son on your shoulders,
my love.
Don't ever fall,
don't fall on the stone shore.
Your pāpā's blood is on the stone shore.
Like your pāpā's pāpā's blood.
The cuts from their fingers and hands.
But don't fall.
On this stone shore.
Find the sea now, and cry there,
my love ...'

Jack rewound the song and listened again, then once more, and then he rewound it and took it out of the player and put it back where it was.

Jack was agitated or calmed or mystified by a scent in the bathroom – jasmine – and when he saw the bush through the open window he wanted to plant some at his house and he wanted to never plant one at his house. His son had a cottage by the sea, with jasmine in the garden and a porch to listen to the waves and watch the moon and a couch with a woollen throw for whoever might need it and a coal range that the twins hovered their hands over. The cinnamon was jarred and had a handwritten sticker on it, telling what was inside. There was a cassette tape with his son singing a song about the day Jack took him to the peninsula after he'd been to the pub, and his mother fretted, and yelled out to take the boy down from his shoulders, but his son didn't want to get down and Jack did not stumble. There were novels and history books and poetry books, and books on cooking, and folders with song sheets, and instruction books on first aid, knitting, rainy-day crafts, lead lighting.

The things were placed about the house thoughtfully and in a house like this you chose the words you used and the way you used them carefully, here in this seaside cottage. Jack sensed it; Jack knew it. You cleaned the fish outside out of respect for how nice it was inside. You left your nylon, your hooks outside, and you always took your shoes off at the door even when you'd had too much to drink.

This was the place we were raised.

For the three days after the birth, and the subsequent creation of the new world, Jack fell asleep on the couch every afternoon and the children finally climbed on him on the third and final evening of the world's creation. That evening Hēnare brought his wife and the baby who made it all happen back to the little cottage by the sea. And though Nanny Liz thought of it as a new world, she also understood it was the undoing of something.

It was Lizzy and Jack, but Lizzy and Jack if some of the things that had happened to them hadn't happened to them.

It was Lizzy and Jack, but Lizzy and Jack if some of the things that had been stolen from them hadn't been stolen from them.

How ancient this new world that came with their youngest mokopuna.

She was a worried baby, unlike the twins. Her expression was perplexed, like she had arrived at the wrong place, at the wrong time. She looked like she wanted another term in the dark. Unlike the twins – so inquisitive, already socialised – when they were born, she did not want to look at people, and found dark creases at people's necks to focus on. Aroha kissed and kissed her and wanted to feed her ice cream. Grandad Jack held the baby, and everyone watched him hold the baby, and Hēnare stared. No one had ever seen him without a weight making an avalanche of his face until he held Kataraina.

Then later, Liz was outside hanging up a load of washing on the line when Jack walked by her, and he said, 'Going to wet baby's head.'

She said, 'Take Hēnare.'

He spun around, the taxi was there now, and he said, 'He doesn't want to come.'

Who should she be upset with: her son or her husband?

Had Hēnare not felt the magic? The charge in the air, a new ancient world the baby brought with her – that things were different now? Did he not understand it needed acknowledgement of how different things were now? Magic had come and saved them, saved her. If no one acknowledged it, why should Jack bother to maintain it, and without Jack maintaining it, the new ancient world would become again what it had been before Kataraina was born: dormant potential, a 'what if' in their story.

How did Hēnare not see it was safe to go with his father to wet the baby's head?

Jack got in the taxi, and she hung the last sheet, and the newborn baby girl cried out from inside the house, soft and worried.

The new ancient world did not dissipate entirely. In fact, the magic that was the love between Grandad Jack and Nanny Liz and Kataraina only grew and grew.

Thirty years before the girl shot the man

Together, on the old green couch. Kat and her grandparents.

Kataraina wanted to be at her nanny and grandad's house, where things were not put about thoughtfully, where a certain sort of chaos had taken root and seemed to confuse even Nanny Liz and Grandad Jack. They could not see how they might make something small like a tiny jug with a koru painted on it appear larger and precious, by being careful about where it was placed and what was allowed to gather around it.

If only pamphlets and a bottle of fly spray were not so close to the pretty little jug, Kataraina thought. Nothing was precious in the house, except Kataraina. Nothing looked like it belonged in there and nothing belonged to the people in it, and no one would ever fall asleep easily on the couch, except Kataraina. And Kataraina wanted to be there as often as she could. She wanted to sit and watch rugby and rip the coupons from the coupon book and pretend the leaves were money and eat ice cream and look at a new comic book and stay up late watching movies her mum and dad would not let her watch.

Sometimes she ate warm sesame seeds on honey-and-buttered toast at nine or ten or even eleven at night. And sometimes she would be allowed to sip on Grandad Jack's beer, and sometimes Grandad Jack would yell out from the old green couch to ask Nanny Liz if dinner was ready yet, or was there another flagon in the fridge? And she would yell back that it wasn't quite ready yet, my loves, or that was the last of it, darling, and he would usually say nothing but sometimes he would say something, and though it might be a something her pāpā would never say, Kataraina knew Grandad Jack was restraining himself, which was a good thing. And her pāpā would come to pick her up, and he would come inside but not for long.

Alone in the car he would ask her, 'Was everything okay there?' And she would nod.

'Are you sure, they didn't get upset with each other, did they?' And she would shake and shake her head. 'We had fun.'

'Okay,' Hēnare'd say. 'Isn't it funny, how you bring out something lovely in them.'

Kataraina understood in a way that was beyond language, beyond this description: she was absorbing something for her grandparents, she was buffering something for them, and this was not hurting her at all, no, not one bit. In fact, it interested her; whatever her role was in this new ancient world, the new ancient world Nanny Liz whispered about and thanked her for, thanked and thanked her for, bought her ice cream and stickers and comic books for, let her stay up late watching TV for, it all interested her. The way she could absorb other people's mamae without being hurt one bit – that was her power.

Three years before the girl shot the man

Her old friend, new friend, one friend, found friend Pare arrives. She brings a twenty-four-box of Steinlager, a pack of tailies, a loaf of white sandwich bread, some butter and three scoops of hot chips wrapped in creamy paper. Kat goes outside and walks to the car, opens the back door.

'Chips are still hot!' she says, taking the chips under one arm, the bread and butter in the other.

At the table Pare says, 'You live here in the wops and shit. You a farmer's wifey, far.'

'Got me a pair of Red Bands.'

'Your mother must be very proud.'

'Loves the home kill, does our Colleen.'

Half a dozen deep and Kat's turn to choose a song. She gets a text from Stu to put the oven on for a pie, home-kill pork. She sing-songs her way to the oven, laughing, almost tripping over.

Pare lifts her beer. 'Put on the oven, good woman, Stu has a pie. Put on the oven, good woman, what a life, what a life.'

'Shut up,' Kat squawks and hiffs a cold chip at her friend's head.

Stu comes home, and he's happy. He's got a pie in his hand and his sleeves are rolled up. He sets down his pie, kisses his missus's head, opens a beer and sits at the table. She puts the pie in the oven for him smiling, opens another beer for herself, falls into her own seat, puts an arm around Pare.

'You,' she says, glowing.

'You,' Pare glows back.

Stu does not seethe, until a sharp smell fills the kitchen. His eyes contort.

Kat rushes to the oven, pulls open the door, and a cloud of white smoke pours out. 'Shit,' she says. 'Shit, shit, shit.'

Stu investigates. He takes the black-topped pie in his hand and holds it up, though it must be very hot. He stares at Kat, throws it into the bin, stomps out of the kitchen. Such restraint. (We remember that restraint, in our memory his restraint was charged enough to warp flooring, ceilings, walls and spines, to attract swarms of wasps.)

Pare mouths, 'A pie?'

Kat whispers back, 'Oven was on grill.' And she shrugs, drinks her drink, but knows it's the inherent rejection that's scalded him.

It's not the first time he's been hurt by her attention being diverted from him to another person. She gets like this, doesn't she? Thoughtless, selfish. She can get like that around her friends. Carefree, careless.

Our ancestor once lived close
to the house where he was shot.
She was at the river when a man
approached her and offered her
some peaches from a can, then
attacked her. Offered food, then
attacked. As if he were luring some
small beast into some savage trap.

5 January 2020, field study day two, 7.30am–2.30pm

Cairo read her late-night ramblings about her awful sleep then exited her tent.

Her notebook. Eric had scoffed at it when they were studying kanakana in Mataura last year. He didn't approve of the poetical nature of some of her notetaking. The habitat of the lamprey was a serious business, apparently, and poetry wasn't appropriate. But when it came to their team's final presentation to funders, Eric opened and closed it with writing from Cairo's notebook. She'd described a kuia on the riverbank early one morning, walking towards Te Au Nui with three tamariki in tow. Each of them held empty tītī buckets, except for the small girl who cradled an ice-cream container – humble tools for the humble work. The day was pale grey and a bitter wind was tunnelling down the river. The kuia had her hair wrapped in a scarf. The children wore beanies and bright polar fleeces. They picked up stranded kanakana one by one and walked them upstream of the falls, putting them back into the river to continue their journey.

This time, though, her notebook already contained much stranger details.

The silence at night makes me feel hollow, even Hana seems hollow, my sleeping bag feels thinner, the tent fabric feels transparent. We could fall right into the earth, the land is on the cusp of churning to quicksand.

In the tent, in the dark beside Hana, the watchful night-silence had made Cairo imagine the swamp bulging out of its weedy bed, like it was straining from a socket, and despite what Eric thought, she'd written this down, because it felt important to record it. It was a fact, too, just like measurements and water testing.

The research group of five – Hana, Cairo, Jordy, Eric and June – had stated in their application for funding this project that connecting with the whenua and the kūkūwai would be prioritised, interference minimised. Only small samples would be taken, most returned.

Both Hana and Cairo having Kāti Kuri whakapapa – their memories of running the length of grass from Takahanga wharenui to the point with a single grave – made this study singularly compelling for them. It was, in many ways, a study of their own mauri. The mountains, farmland, highway, streets, houses, sea, boats. You could see it all from their marae.

Like many whānau, they'd left the area for work. Hana's family went to Christchurch when she was seven. Cairo's family left when she was eight, her father going to work in the mines at Stockton, north of Westport. They'd all returned for holidays, tangihanga, birthdays, weddings. They each understood the whenua – their own placentas were buried here – but both felt humbled to be returning this time in a different role.

The group's impetus question was simple: *What was the main water source contributing to the massive increase in both the circumference and depth of Johnson's Swamp?*

It wasn't an hour after they'd arrived that Eric Green said, right out loud, staring at where a length of gravel road disappeared into the swamp, his eyes resting on the lip of water, not seeing the yellow eyes of a kāhu concealed in the grass: 'Should this water be stopped?'

The rest of them turned to him, June Baker's mouth open and her eyes alight, as if she was about to praise him for such a bold suggestion: *stop nature*. But it was an ugly question. Especially in contrast to their simple mission statement constructed around the words 'to understand'.

Eric stood there looking embarrassed – his face hot and rosy – and then his mouth contorted with anger at this embarrassment. He had a sun-worn face with a prematurely greying goatee. Skinny limbs. He wore his thick red hair long and loose, a black obsidian stone in a string net around his neck.

'Well,' June said, glancing at Cairo and Hana to make sure they were paying attention to what *June* was about to say, on their behalf. 'That's a dangerous thing to suggest, Eric. This swamp is taoka,' she looked to Hana again, as if for approval. 'And whatever it's doing, is ātaahua.'

Somewhere near the water a kererū threw itself into the sky, its wings made a noise that sounded like hahahahahahahahahaha.

Hana rolled her eyes, smirked at Cairo. Cairo felt lucky to have her here. They'd met during a research trip to Ōkārito on the West Coast, bonding quickly over early-morning excursions to watch the kōtuku stalking the lagoon. They'd walked there together, along the beach, with the roar of a wild sea crashing on the shore, to the lagoon. One morning they saw a large kōtuku at the edge. Its reflection on the water was perfect and they walked closer and closer, wondering when it would fly off. It didn't.

They'd stopped just metres from it and watched the magnificent bird until it left for the hills. They watched it leave in the reflection on the lagoon, holding their breaths. Then they bonded over a cigarette on the beach, which Hana – a non-smoker now – had only brought with her because she had fantasised about smoking a tobacco pipe or cigarillo in Ōkārito like Kerewin. Turned out they'd both re-read *the bone people* before going there: art informed their work, whakapapa informed their work. Stories of people's lives on the whenua, fictional or non-fictional, kept them looking always for the connection, in a field that could make them feel isolated from the natural world, villainous even. It was unhelpful to feel like a villain if you wanted to attain symbiosis.

That's what irked them now about Eric's question: *Should this water be stopped?*

Then June's aaataaahuaaa.

Cairo stood up and walked away from the group because she wanted to laugh. 'Fucken beeeauuutiful,' she said, and went to the tent, took off her boots and zipped the tent open, climbed in and shut it.

Cairo could hear Hana: 'Not everything has to be ugly or …' it seemed she struggled to feel connected to her own kupu, or maybe she didn't want to use them around June anymore '… otherwise.'

'I know,' June said, 'but—'

Hana cut her off. 'Nah. Let's just not label this, all right. Let's keep our mission statement in mind. Not throw around words because we're approaching this project differently.'

Other research groups and individuals had been to the swamp, though none – or so they understood – had opted to sleep so close to the swamp's edge. This, Eric said, making his usual joke, would be the one – he'd make the discovery and finally get something named after him.

'Name the lily *Nymphaea erico braggus*, maybe. Or a frog – *Anura erico braggaritus*.' He laughed loudly, turning red.

Hana retorted, 'You're destined to discover a perennial, Eric. Hmmm, how about *Narcissus alban hominis ericus*?'

'That's mean,' he said, laughing louder.

'*Ruber inconcinnus.*'

'What?' Eric said.

'*Lame red*. Eric, hate to break it to you. If something is discovered on this whenua, your dream still won't be coming true.'

'Bugger,' he said, laughing some more. 'Ah well. My name'll still get in the history books.'

'Our names?'

'I suppose.'

Cairo, though she'd been enthusiastic about spending plenty of time close to the kūkūwai, was doubtful now. She lay in the tent, holding her eyes closed to refresh them. It didn't work. The kūkūwai was tapu – it was poor judgement to sleep near it. She felt embarrassed.

She could hear Eric wanking on about kaitiakitanga. Just as June had earlier – he was wringing the kupu dry. After all the years they'd worked together, and all they'd learned and discovered together, sometimes words came up and out of him from some shallow arrogant place.

She felt restless and climbed back out of the tent. In the makeshift kitchen, under a tarpaulin, she made herself a coffee.

Hana came up behind her. 'In one of his moods. Just go drink away from him,' she whispered to Cairo. 'Can't have you two fighting.'

Cairo didn't go drink her coffee away from Eric. She took it and sat next to him. She cared for Eric's work ethic; she empathised with his fear of loosening the reins. An unprecedented number of scientists would be presenting their projects for funding to study Johnson's Swamp. As Eric specialised in wetland ecology, it had come as no surprise his research group gained one of the first seed grants, but it was the next grant they needed. He was very aware how competitive people were. This was their opportunity to find the fresh angle. And they had just two weeks to do it.

'Saw a tennis court in town,' she said to Eric. 'Want to go for a hit?'

'I don't know, Cairo. I think we need to work.'

'Come on. It's helped us plenty of times before.' She looked towards the swamp. 'It ain't going anywhere.'

'Let me get a bit of work done first,' he said.

'I'll wait for you at the lagoon.' She took her coffee and went.

A small body of mist drifted out from some trees onto the dark lagoon, looking lost. It surrounded a kahikatea tree. A kāhu dived and raked up a silver fish from the water then headed west towards the mountains. The sunlight was bright in the east and the saltmarsh would be gleaming, water like satin ribbons across the sand, tiny pink crabs scuttling from rock to rock.

Cairo thought she saw a shadow in the water in front of the kahikatea tree. It looked like something large had broken the surface. She blinked again. Must have imagined it. The light became cleaner, crisper, and a wind unsettled the still water like a hand rubbing a dog's coat the wrong way.

She wrapped her hands tight around the mug and blew at the steam. The urge to run away hit her heart with a double beat, small hairs on her thighs and arms pricked up. She looked at the lush expanse of raupō, the rich greens and browns. Water dark as a night on a moonless planet. She wanted to eat the swamp. She wanted to chew on its moss and grass, its fish and birds. She wanted to slurp it up and let it take root in her belly. She was no one looking at that swamp. She had never been anyone.

'Hey,' Eric said behind her.

She returned like his voice was quicksand. 'Let's go then.'

Cairo drove. On the way to town Eric put on the radio. The bushfire in Australia was staining the skies above Tāmaki Makaurau a rose-gold. The southern glaciers were rouged with an apocalyptic ash. Australian Prime Minister Scott Morrison was holidaying somewhere; people were crowding a beach to avoid the fire. There was a fireman yelling out that Scott Morrison could get fucked.

'Useless bastards, all of them,' Eric said.

'The swamp's caused some distraction though, here.'
'Swamp mania.'
'Kūkūwai cuckoo.'
Eric laughed. 'Who is the current champ anyway?'
'That'd be me. Gore. 6–3, 3–6, 6–4?'
'Shit, it was cold.'
'Shit, it was.'
'Ugly suckers, weren't they?'
'The paper mill and the meat works?'
'Mataura's landmarks.'
'Do you think we'll find any in the tributaries here?'
'Mills? Meat works? Surely not.'
'Good one. Kanakana.'
'Too secretive. And not our question.'
'The question is generic. Swamp's full of distractions. Agree?'
Eric tapped his tennis racquet. 'Don't answer it. We need to focus or we won't see the pūtea. The competition's going to be intense.'
'None of the tributaries could have done this.'
'Cairo, really? Two days in. You haven't come close to putting eyes on a quarter of the possible tributaries.'
'Still,' said Cairo, 'the thing is enormous. At two years old it looks prehistoric.'
Cairo turned onto Kaikōura's main street; shopkeepers were putting out signs. Their car scared a flock of gulls from the road. Joggers ran Marine Parade, with the sea like bright green glass beside them.
She pulled up at the tennis court. The tear in the fence was still there, which they used to squeeze through: her father and his brothers playing in the heat in stubbies and worn runners, Cairo fetching the tennis balls.
They started the match the same way they always did in a new place with a fresh project, with Eric tying back his red hair,

Cairo's hair already in a low bun. Server shouting, 'Eye on the ball.' Receiver replying, 'Mind on the pātai.'

The tennis match did not clear her head as she'd hoped. Eric won and did not celebrate or mock her. He just shook her hand in his old-fashioned way and they drove back to the swamp in a chaotic silence, both struggling to order their thoughts. They pulled up on the high section of the broken road, where it seemed safe to park, and hiked back towards the swamp and their camp.

Cairo headed again for the lagoon and Eric, tapping his thigh with his racket, started towards the communal tent. He stopped. 'Cairo.'

She turned.

He said, 'Our objectives are good. Simple.'

'I know.'

Near the lagoon a pūkeko stalked through the shallow then disappeared into the rushes. The wīwī rattled as the bird made its way along the grassy edge. The white sky cut by thin trees was mirrored on the water like a set of loose teeth. Another kāhu plunged into the grass and went back to the sky with a small animal. All the birds that hunted here rose up with a catch.

The smell came. A dense cloud of rot. The damp of her sweat from the tennis match chilled her.

Cairo backed away from the water, went looking for Hana. She found her at the wooden table under the blue tarpaulin. Still in her sweaty tennis clothes, Cairo put down her racquet and sat down.

'Tennis help?' Hana asked, without looking up.

'Not at all.'

Hana was looking at the photographs she'd collected of the wetland. The pictures were taken two years ago by someone unnamed, when the ground at the centre of the kūkūwai was smeared with a greenish-black substance, tarry like meconium.

Hana shuffled through the photographs slowly. One by one she held them up to compare, using landmarks – the distant mountain range, the old kahikatea, the broken road – to gauge what she was looking at.

Jordy and June were walking to the saltmarsh today. Eric had already been to take some samples, test the water. 'Every hour on the hour' he wanted a sample to see how the tides were affecting the lagoon.

Cairo picked up one of Hana's pictures.

'I know what I'm looking for,' said Hana. 'What are you looking for?'

'I don't know,' Cairo said. 'Maybe I just like the difference. That,' she said nodding at the water and then at the picture, 'compared to this. The power of it. How it's gone and done something like it has a mind of its own.'

Cairo held on to the single picture while Hana shuffled through the others. Then Cairo saw something she hadn't noticed before: a hard edge jutting out from behind the kahikatea tree. A corner. Almost silver. A fingernail-sized piece of iron. She looked from the photograph to the kahikatea tree. No iron there, nothing man-made. She turned the picture to show Hana. 'Look,' she said. 'Is that a corner of a roof. A shed or house maybe?'

Hana leaned and squinted. 'Could be. Yeah, definitely could be eh. Out of it.'

'How'd we miss that?'

'Hard to say what it is.'

'Imagine,' Cairo said, pointing to a deep section of swamp, close to where it tapered and some of the water escaped into a small creek, 'putting a building there.'

Hana tapped the picture. 'Well, it sure would've looked safe enough a few years ago.'

'Safe as houses.'

'What a whakataukī.'

'That's got to be corrugated iron.'

Cairo had been sitting with a kuia at the marae, and the old woman had said, 'That kūkūwai is all roimata. Tears.'

'Whose, Whaea?'

Then Eric had come over and introduced himself to the kuia, a distant aunty of Cairo's she'd not met before. Eric offered his hand and the kuia shook it, smirking. He stayed standing, leaning over her, talking excitedly about their project.

'I can only hope we can answer some questions for the hapū,' he said. 'It's all very interesting. Cannot wait to roll up my sleeves and start the mahi.' He would have continued if Cairo hadn't given him a look. 'Right,' he said, pinkly, composing himself. 'Um, how long have you lived here, Whaea?'

'Since before we were born.'

Eric sat down.

'What were you saying, Whaea, about tears?' said Cairo.

'Oh.' She laughed. 'Kā roimata o te wahine, auē. Yeah.' And left the statement to hang there, then Hana sat down beside them, June too.

Cairo said, 'Which woman, Whaea?'

'Ah. Yes,' she'd said, nodding. 'He pātai nui.'

Now, holding the photograph in front of her, looking out at the dark water, Cairo said, 'This swamp's tapu.'

'Yeah,' Hana said.

'Keen for a mish?'

A bowl of mussels was in the middle of the table as well as a jug of cold beer and a basket of hot chips. The kuia, Cairo's distant aunty Moira Stirling, was wearing a green Hunting & Fishing polar fleece and black tights. On her feet she wore wool socks and scuffs. She took a mussel, pried it from its shell and ate the meat. 'It's my niecey's recipe, this sauce.' She took the mussel shell and filled it, dropped her head back, poured the sauce down her throat. 'Mmm, mmm, mmm.'

A group came into the bar and started playing darts nearby. Moira ate another mussel then skulled her beer. She fished in her pockets and came up with a two-dollar coin. She went to the pokie room. Soon after, she was out again and she sat back down. Her aunty was a different woman than Cairo remembered at the marae, less ethereal. Moira pulled a pouch from her pocket, started rolling a smoke. Twisting the end she stood up and stuck a finger in Cairo's arm. 'Come have a smoke with me.'

'Yeah,' she said. 'All right.'

They sat under a plastic corrugated roof. There were ferns in mossy pots around them, a stag's head bolted to a wall, a pāua shell on the only table filled with butts and ash.

'Can't remember what I said to you up Takahanga.'

'Swamp is made of tears, you said. Kā roimata o te wahine.'

She took a drag on her rollie. Slapped her own thigh. 'How mysterious,' she said, laughing. 'No wonder you've come looking for me. Now that's a story.' She tapped her foot. 'I've been in trouble with my sister for saying the swamp's made of tears. My sister would tell me to get a grip, even though she was the one who said it first. She was pissed of course. Pissed as a fart. She says to me, it's tears, like the fulla said, and I say, *it fucken is*. Next time we're out I say it's tears and she says it's fucken not and I need to shut the fuck up about the swamp. Excuse my French, you know. The only time she says fuck is when we talk about the swamp.'

Cairo put her hand out for a puff. Moira passed the smoke. Cairo took one drag and her head lightened.

'Why though?'

'Why what?'

'Why say it's tears in the first place.'

'Because her daughter – my niece – was in a coma when the swamp started doing what it ended up doing. He'd hit her hard in the temple and it was one time too many. She was out of it. Then a girl shot him. The swamp was on their land, but it was drained originally about a century ago.'

'Originally?'

'It was an ongoing thing. It wasn't one action or one event. Never done and dusted.'

'How very colonial.'

'Ha, yeah.'

Cairo rummaged in a tote, pulled out the photos. 'This is what made us leave today.' She took out the picture with the tiny corner of roof and showed Moira.

Her aunty squinted. 'Mmm.'

Cairo pointed to the corner. 'Is that a roof?'

'Can't say without my glasses on, but if you're looking at what I think you are looking at, it's the house.'

'What house – whose?'

'Belongs to Stuart Johnson, of – what do people go around bloody calling it – Johnson's Swamp, and while she was out to it in the hospital the whole thing kicked off.'

'When?'

'Just over two years ago. There was a farmer there at the time, Tommy Aiken. His daughter was the one who shot this guy. He said my niece might be in a coma, but she's busy all the same. She's busy as in that coma. She's *bawling* in that coma, he said. No one believed him because everyone knew he was into her. Some of the whānau even had the cheek to blame him for her getting the beating she did. They were off together, you know. Her, him, the two kids.'

'Two kids?'

'Yeah, our Ārama was with her.'

'Ka aroha,' Cairo said.

'She was in a coma almost two weeks, before they all headed to Rakiura, to heal, I guess. Te Au whānau, you see, whakapapa to here and the island. Colleen and me, Kāti Kuri. And her husband's mother was born on the neck at the motu. Waitaha, Ngāti Hinetewai, Moriori. Kaiks wasn't easy on them. They went to the island. To hide. For quiet. While they were gone the swamp kept doing this.' She tapped on one of Cairo's pictures.

'And this guy said the swamp, like, started its thing when she went into the coma?'

'Āe, Tommy Aiken said that, but because he was into Kat no one believed him, except for everyone.' She laughed then. 'Everyone believed him, and everyone pretended not to. Because his girl shot the man, and he was in love and running away, and no one wanted to know too much.'

'So how did this Tom fulla notice the swamp was growing?'

'Noise first, a sort of howling sound. Then a roaring, or a sort of grinding sound. He said it was like it was raining hard in another world, so poetic for a bloody farmer, ha! And he said the land was getting damp. That land had been septic, he said. Johnsons spent more than a bloody century draining it. Like, man, let it be. All around was humped and hollowed, except this bit in the middle that seemed to, well, seemed – excuse the poetry shit again – to slip into chaos. It's hard to describe, but just looking at the ground made you feel confused, like you were looking at something you shouldn't be looking at. My sister, the devout Catholic, said it was like a bit of land wasn't fully formed in the seven creation days, a glitch, like, there, on the first day light was almost created, second day sky was almost created, then dry land, seas, plants and trees successfully created, but lawless because the rest wasn't sorted, I dunno, she said it better.'

'Where is your niece? Kataraina?'

'Like, today?' Moira shrugged.

June's phone rang. She nodded as she listened to the caller.

'Eric's found something.'

'What then?'

'A body.'

'Jesus Christ,' Moira said.

Our ancestor once lived close to the house where he was shot. She was at the river when a man approached her and offered her some peaches from a can, then attacked her. Offer food, then attack. As if he were luring some small beast into some savage steel trap. Instead of entering his trap, she drove his own industrial tool into his own chest.

Two years after the girl shot the man

Just one of us was there, up to nothing much.

It was Ārama and he was resting on a picnic blanket, his arms back and his skull cradled on the palms of his hands, and he was wondering how he might look to the gods. He watched bright white clouds drift across the pale blue sky. Then he wondered if his mum and dad were in those clouds, and if they could see him, and if they saw him now would they think he was perfectly happy without them. He moved his arms down to his side, then he turned onto his side and curled up, to try to feel sad instead.

The sun was warm on him. This spot on the grass was perfect in the afternoon, protected from the wind, the heat trapped. He closed his eyes and soon he was having a good dream. Nothing much happened in it, only he was running so fast, and then he just floated up off the ground and flew into the sky, and he was flying over rivers and mountains, until he woke because Taukiri nudged him and put a bowl of chips and some onion dip on the picnic blanket.

'You sad?' Taukiri said.

Ari shook his head. 'I'm happy.'

'You're allowed to be.'

The boy sat up and dipped a chip and crunched on it. The chips were salty; the dip was creamy, cold, a bit tart. Taukiri had used lemon juice.

'This is really good,' Ari said.

Taukiri dipped a chip and ate it. Ari dipped another and ate it. They ate dip with chips sitting on the picnic blanket on the lawn and watched the clouds pass, one brother's head on the other brother's chest. Taukiri's bone carving soft and cool against Ārama's ear.

From where they were sitting they couldn't see the people arriving at the edge of the swamp, the eel writhing about the preserved body, greedy for the greedy water.

Taukiri picked a bit of chip off his brother's chin.

'Hey!' Ārama said. 'I was saving that for later.'

Taukiri laughed, just as a large toebiter used its many legs to abandon an ancestor's weedy hair.

Thirty years before the girl shot the man

We like this story. When she was just seven years old, her mother, Colleen, came home from church with a large glass jar, and inside it, floating in water, was a scoby for making kombucha.

Colleen set her handbag on the chair, and the jar on the table. Seven-year-old Kataraina Te Au said, 'What's that?'

'It's to make a drink.'

'What drink?'

'A drink to make us strong and healthy.'

'Where did you get it?'

'A woman from church.'

Hēnare came into the kitchen. 'What's that?' he said.

'A scoby.'

'That thing Ingrid was going on about?' he said.

'Āe,' Colleen said.

Hēnare sat beside his daughter, her eyes wide, looking at the floating jellyfish shaped like a disc. 'It's making us a drink,' Kataraina whispered to her dad.

Colleen sat at the table. 'You know Nanny Liz's rēwena bread, that bug in the fridge she sometimes feeds?'

'Yes,' Kataraina said.

'This is like that. The drink is fermenting. Bacteria will turn the sugar into something like fizzy, like when the holes form in Nanny's dough.'

Kataraina looked at the mushroom floating on the rose-coloured water. 'I like Nanny's bread.'

Colleen put the jar in the pantry.

One day Toko, Aroha and Kataraina sat at the table and Colleen handed them little glasses and Kataraina, the smallest, had both hands around her glass, because she was excited to try the drink Peachy the jellyfish had made her.

Toko drank his first. He spat and said, 'Eww, it's vinegar.' He turned to Aroha, whispered to his twin sister, 'It tastes like shit.'

Colleen clipped his ear. 'Did you just say what I think you said? Are you just swearing at our table now? Might as well just sit your bum on it eh.'

'Sorry, Māmā,' Toko said.

Colleen looked at Kataraina, who had opened the pantry door every day to visit Peachy. 'If you swear around Peachy, it will die,' she said.

Kataraina gasped.

Toko and Aroha frowned. They were just at the age where they were dropping off the precipice of the believing-in-things-that-had-no-logic world, whirling away from magic. Disbelief bullied the wonder from their faces, but Kataraina stared at Peachy with her eyes wide and said to Toko, 'Say sorry.'

'Sorry,' he said, frowning.

Kataraina sipped her drink and shuddered, her lips curling and her eyes watering. She opened her mouth to say something, then looked at the gluey disc and closed her mouth.

'It's good for you,' Colleen said, then she took the jar and put it back in the cupboard. 'Drink it all up.'

Every few days Colleen would pull out the jar and sit her children at the table and they would drink their drink, which would make their gut strong and fire up their immune systems. Kataraina stopped feeling so fascinated by the jellyfish and dreaded the ritual. She said if Nanny's rēwena did the same thing, why couldn't they just have slices of that with jam.

'This is stronger, and uncooked, so it's better,' Colleen said.

Colleen left the room and Toko whispered, 'Can't wait till I'm old enough to move out, won't have to drink this shit.'

'Oi, you'll kill Peachy,' Kataraina said, and then she grinned, the little girl grinned because she had a great idea, and she went to the kitchen door and closed it and then she hopped back up onto her chair, and she leaned, her chubby arms like small loaves on the table and she stared at the jellyfish and she said, 'You're shit, Peachy.'

Aroha gasped and Toko grabbed his mouth with his fist and whistled into it; he rocked back on his chair. 'No!' he said.

'Shit,' Kataraina said, one eye on the door and one eye on the jellyfish.

She looked up at her brother. 'Don't worry, Toko, you won't got to move out. I will kill it.' She looked back at the jellyfish, then she closed her eyes tight, ready to make her final blow. 'Yucky bitch,' the little girl said, and Toko and Aroha were laughing with tears running down their faces. But Kataraina was taking no notice – she was staring at Peachy, willing it to bleed out rust-coloured blood, explode, or at the very least disappear.

Realising the jellyfish was stronger than she'd expected, she took in a deep breath and, imitating her mother, made the sign of the cross. As the door opened she said, 'Fuck … you.'

It was Nanny Liz who had opened the door, and she stood there looking at her three moko, wondering where her daughter-in-law was and if she'd heard Kataraina say that word, that un-Christian word. Nanny Liz had a rollie hanging out the corner of her mouth and a loaf of rēwena wrapped in a tea towel under one arm and a small jar of freshly toasted sesame seeds in her hand. She shuffled into the room and set down the bread and jar, closed the door, took the rollie out and went to the little girl, whose lip was trembling now.

'What's just come out of that mouth?'

'Sorry, Nanny,' Kataraina said.

'It's my fault,' Toko said.

Nanny Liz held up her hand then re-lit her smoke and sat at the end of the table. 'You were trying to kill it, weren't you? I know this one. Your mother said bad words would kill it, didn't she?'

Kataraina nodded and hid her eyes from her darling nanny, but some tears rolled away down her cheeks onto her scraped knees.

'Bad words will kill it,' Nanny Liz said. 'But it depends on the person.'

'How?' Kataraina asked.

'Gotta be a witch.' Nanny Liz winked. 'Get out, go on, go out and play so I can have a coffee and smoke my smoke.'

They left the old woman alone with her smoke and Peachy in the kitchen, and a few days later the jar was black with mould and the water was ballooning with milky, sour-looking clouds. Colleen tipped the water and dead Peachy down the sink. Kataraina leaned over to see a furry piece of membrane trapped in the drain. Fresh cold water was rushing over it; Colleen was scrubbing the jar. Little Kataraina whispered, 'Sorry, Peachy,' and she held a large and pure bubble of joy in her belly, pressing her magic tongue lightly between her teeth. She ran to tell her brother about the miracle death, but kept her status secret.

Two years after the girl shot the man

'Go on, sit,' she tells her son. Taukiri sits on the picnic blanket.

Jade likes to sit. Kataraina likes to move. The rest of us manage a balance of both, and this makes us believe we have a better command of our grief, our bodies, our ghosts.

We burst from the trees, we were always bursting from the trees, two of us, just Beth and Ari this time, in gumboots, thermal socks, shorts, T-shirts, with hoodies wrapped around our waists. The mother, the widow, Jade, closes her eyes and those two of us who are small fall on the picnic blanket, and before we've even caught our breath, we are off again – something about tadpoles.

We know that it comforts them. The tadpoles. The plaster on Ari's leg, the way Beth pretends to shoot birds. Though they are comforted that we do these things less and less, they are still comforted we do these things at all. Adults are strange, we say.

'Are you tired of pretending?' Beth asks, screwing the imaginary metal cap back on the imaginary glass bottle.

'I think so,' Ari replies, staring out at a black swan sitting on the dark water. He studies the hook of the large bird's neck. He peels the plaster from his knee.

Kat comes out with a plate of toasted cheese-and-tomato sandwiches in one hand, a plate of sausage rolls in the other and a bag of chips under her arm. Busy, busy bee.

'Aunty,' Taukiri whines, 'come on! Why don't you yell out for me to help?'

'Shut up,' she says, but smiles.

A rooster trots towards them. Taukiri breaks up a piece of sausage roll and feeds it to him. The chickens come for pastry too.

'Where'd the kids go?' says Kat.

'The lagoon, something urgent about tadpoles. I should have gone with them.'

'We can.' She's grateful for another thing to do, a place to go.

Taukiri stands and offers his hand to his mum. She shakes her head. 'I'll wait here. Go with Aunty.'

Kat and Taukiri take sausage rolls to share with the children and the ducks and eels and black swans. Jade curls up on the picnic blanket and imagines a trajectory that lets Toko be with her now.

Twenty-two years before the girl shot the man

We're in the kitchen. There's no 'dinner' tonight because of all the leftovers: boil up, quarter of a meatloaf, some ham, some cold steamed potatoes, three mussel fritters, a generous spoonful of surimi and shrimp salad, half a packet of questionable bacon. Hēnare is frying mustard seeds in sunflower oil. They crack and pop. Hēnare sprinkles in mustard powder, and the oil foams yellow. He adds the cold potatoes and grinds black pepper over the pan.

Aroha is rinsing a pot and Kataraina waits with the tea towel. Why she is not twisting it and whipping them is a large shining question hooked in the room.

Kataraina almost whispers to Aroha; she almost says, 'Sis?' But she knows her voice will give the greenness away, her secret greenness. We have not told where it came from yet, but we will tell. This pale greenness, a kawakawa leaf leeched of almost all colour.

Kataraina almost says, 'Sis?' Instead, she watches her sister spin the soapy water in the pot to a vortex, pulling the pieces of watercress from the silver. The water, the vortex and the dark green watercress make her feel cold. The eczema near Kataraina's mouth itches. She rubs it with the back of her arm.

The potatoes are fried now, and Hēnare takes them from the pan and puts them onto the plate with the paper towels. He throws on two of the mussel fritters. He grinds more pepper and shakes over more salt and takes them to sit with Nanny Liz and snack on them. Nanny Liz used to like to call evening snacks like this supper, when words came easier to her.

Aroha steps closer to Kataraina. She puts an arm around her and rests her chin on her sister's shoulder. 'What's up, my baby sis?' she says.

'Ha, nothing. Nah, nothing.'

Kataraina begins drying intently now. A piece of watercress has pinned itself to the pot – it looks splayed there – and refuses to shift.

'Give it back. I'll wash it properly.'

'No.'

Aroha's wrists glisten with pork fat.

When the dishes are done, Kataraina goes to her room and puts on a hoodie, beanie and some thick socks. Aroha is already waiting out on the porch when she steps outside. Meaty rain clouds wring the mountains' necks, but the sky near the coast is bright white and light gold. Kataraina picks up her shoes. Someone has worn them without putting their feet in properly. The heels are pressed down, and the laces are still tied.

'Bloody Toko,' she huffs, untying the laces.

Kataraina sees his shoes and chucks them on the shed roof. 'There, ha.'

In the car Aroha turns on the radio. She likes the radio. She likes that other people might be listening to the same song, and some days that's all the sense of community she can get, she says. And laughs. Hēnare had the car last so the station is one that plays old-fashioned love songs. The Righteous Brothers, 'You've Lost That Lovin' Feelin''.

Aroha sings too. Her voice is husky and strong, soft and worried, but happy like she lives in a village near the sea, because she does – we do. We drive through town, the sisters. Seagulls scatter from the main road when the car approaches. A group of women is sitting around a table outside a restaurant. They're dressed in bright dresses and shirts, with earrings and lipstick, and they laugh loudly.

'*Baby, baby,*' Aroha sings.

The sea at Gooch's is a chalky blue. The tide is low. Around the corner, past the pier the white rocks are bared like teeth. At the car park a seal is sleeping on the footpath. They head up the hill, along the concrete path, both puffing before they reach the top. They catch their breath and look across the cliffs, down at the stone shore. Four people are crossing it, walking towards the sea. Kat counts the boats. There are three coming in – one is not coming in or going out.

'Haere mai,' Aroha says.

Kat follows her big sister, thinking of things to say, practising them in her head to make sure they sound natural and normal, perfectly natural and normal. Aroha has applied for a scholarship to study midwifery. It's a good safe thing to talk about on the walk.

'Have you heard back on the application?'

'Not yet.'

'Soon then?'

'Hopefully.'

'You'll get it.'

'What about you – is school going okay?'

Kataraina practises answers in her head. Then she remembers the essay she is writing. Despite the greenness in her, writing still feels honest and decent. 'I'm doing this sort of essay but giving it an edge.' There's energy in her voice, but the dusk is soft and lilac, which takes the sting out of the shame of enthusiasm.

'You sound … into it.'

'I am eh. Learning heaps doing the research. You know like, almost ninety per cent of our wetlands have been drained.'

'Far out.'

'Yeah. It's massive.'

'I heard there's a farmer near Gore Bay who has been regenerating some swampland. Maybe we could go for a drive?'

'That'd be choice.'

They walk along the cliff, beside the paddocks. The grass is long and brown and haloed by late sun. A pīwakawaka flits near, cutting in front of them, then flying off a little way ahead, waiting to cut across their path again. The rain clouds wring the mountains.

'Sis?' Kataraina says.

'What is it?' Aroha says, like she has been waiting, needing to understand something about her baby sister. She is worried about her baby sister.

Kataraina hears that and it spooks her. If Aroha's been worried, and Kataraina confirms she has good reason, it makes it true. She wants to hold on to the ability to deny what she's done; who she is.

'What's up though, sis?' Aroha says, more casually.

'Any chance you'd give the essay a read?'

Aroha holds her eyes ahead, on a large tree in the distance; there's a tightness in her neck. 'Course,' she says. 'We should go see Aunty Moira, get some cream for your eczema.'

Kat lifts her hand to her nose, self-consciously covering her mouth.

Aroha looks at her. 'No, don't … It's not bad, just looks a little sore. Anyway,' she brightens, 'I'll race you to the tree. One, two, three … go!'

'Cheat!'

Kataraina's legs feel weak, but something ignites in her belly and under the sky darkening to purple, the smell of coming rain in the air, the sound of her sister's ragged breathing beside her, she runs and runs towards the large tree. As she runs, she's reminded how lethargic her secrets have made her.

Aroha gets ahead, Kat chasing. Aroha doesn't run fast but she keeps her lead. She reaches the tree first, turns back and watches her sister coming towards her. Kat sees Aroha force triumph into her face, pretend there is nothing strange about beating the teenager at her own game. Kat's the runner, the athlete, the quickest Te Au.

'Toko's been wearing my shoes,' Kataraina laughs. 'Bloody heels are all pushed forward, given me a blister.'

Aroha appreciates the excuse, is comforted by it, but mustn't spook her sister again. 'Just admit, kicked your arse.'

Kat plonks down in the grass, takes off her shoe, adjusts her sock. She sees a first star in the twilight. Old emotions flood her, of being small and excited to see the night's first star. Images of Nanny Liz cutting apples to stars come to her. The wishes Kat could make overwhelming her. She searches for one single wish in the torrent of them now and when she can't cut one loose from the other, when she can't choose just one without feeling ugly or selfish, neglectful or needy, she looks away from the single star in the sky and puts on her shoe, ties her laces slowly to hide her eyes from Aroha a little longer.

In bed, she lies awake looking at the ceiling. She turns on a bedside lamp, picks up her school folder and opens it. She starts reading the essay. On the pages, she sees what she has been doing – it glares out at her like it's sprouted eyes – and it embarrasses her. She has been trying to escape persistent nausea through other people, through their stories, sees Nanny Liz in the piece she is forming. Nanny Liz's secrets are there, out in the wide open, fuelling the narrative.

Kataraina has enjoyed writing the essay because she has been searching for something that will make her feel less like a person. She'd rather be words strung together than this nervous system held up by bones and muscles, kept warm by fat, firing on oxygen and glucose.

Ashamed, she tucks the essay under her bed.

Late the next morning Colleen comes into her bedroom and says, 'Nanny Liz is very sick, e kare. Your dad has taken her to the hospital.'

Kat launches from her bed in anger. 'You should've woke me, though.'

'Tried. You were out to it.'

'Sure,' Kat says, but knows it's probably true.

At the hospital they wait in a small bright room. Kat can breathe deeply here in this room. The terrible bleached smell soothes her. No smell of wet grass, no greenness, nothing green, just light blues and bright whites and boundaries everywhere: stern doctors and nurses, people bowing their heads when they pass open doors. She's comforted by the dry sounds: squeaking wheels and shoes. Anything wet or dripping or oozing is a consequence of someone's lack of vigilance. You would not stare at anything wet or dripping and oozing and do nothing here in a hospital. You would attend. People would attend.

A doctor takes them to Nanny Liz's room. The bed's sheets look nice. Nanny Liz's face looks different.

When it is Kat's turn to be close to Nanny Liz she takes the kuia's dry hand, and she is probably the only one comforted by how papery and bloodless it feels.

That evening we came together. Aunties and uncles and cousins came to hui.

Some of the young cousins crossed the saltmarsh to light a fire on the beach. Aroha and Kataraina came too. Toko stayed to play darts in the garage with his cousins, Isaac and Kaleb.

There were about ten of us. We moved together away from the lighted windows, the shouting and laughing of the adults, and towards the sea. One of the boys screwed up some newspaper he'd brought. The rest of us went for driftwood.

'Who's got a lighter?' someone yelled.

'Me,' someone replied.

Stacey was there. Stacey was cool. Stacey didn't laugh at everyone's jokes, so if she did it meant you were funny. Kat had taken some of her dad's beer from the fridge. At the beach, she took two cans from the plastic supermarket New World bag. She could feel Stacey looking at her. She liked it. Kat held a can out to her cousin, and she took it.

The fire was already burning bright. It glowed on all our faces. We were laughing, talking. Someone threw a stick at someone and then they were chasing each other, kicking up sand, shrieking. Kat drank from her beer quickly. It stung the dry corner of her mouth. Aroha took one from the bag too. Kat shot her a greedy look. Aroha shot one back, like who are you today?

After Kat's second beer, she said, 'Nanny Liz put up with so much bullshit from Grandad Jack. He's fucken gone, and now she gets this.'

Aroha said, 'Kat!'

'What? She did.'

'Not now though.'

'When she's dead then?'

Stacey leaned over and tapped her can against Kat's. 'Nah, cuz, cheers to that. Cheers for Nanny Liz.'

Kat was emboldened. If Stacey agreed then Kat was right. The warm fire and the cold beer loosened her tongue. 'To be honest—'

'Really? To be *honest*? Go on then,' Aroha said.

There had been moments where Kataraina believed her family was one entity, one body, moving towards something so incredible, and she was both in awe and afraid. Nanny Liz was the reason. She was connective tissue, and the third eye and the heart of that one body. Although Hēnare said she was actually the kidney of it.

'People like to describe leaders as being at the *heart* of an operation or a grand idea,' he'd say, 'but your grandmother is the throat and kidney of ours. Tell her something that's causing an ache for you, and she'll run it through her own flesh. She'll let it clunk about in her own blood for a bit, purify it for you.' Then Hēnare would chuckle and say, 'Pour you a drink to help you piss out the rubbish.'

Beside the fire, Aroha glaring at her, Kataraina continued: 'She let us down, putting up with his shit.'

And suddenly there they were, her regretful words, and they hissed around the fire, weaving across the sand and stones, sliding over the driftwood, onto people's legs, up their torsos, onto their shoulders, their necks.

'Nah, cuz,' Stacey said. 'She didn't let us down one fucking bit.'

Someone threw a stick in the fire. Bony Tommy appeared from behind some rocks. He'd been sitting under a kitchen window minutes before, attracted to the smell of frying onions and people talking over one another. He had with him half a big bag of salt-and-vinegar chips. He sat beside Ra Junior without saying hello. The boy opened the bag of chips and offered it to Ra, who took some and, on the boy's urging, passed it on.

When the bag was empty and its foil burned on the fire, Kat stood up. 'Nanny Liz told us the story about Hine Rukutia like she was her.'

Kataraina looked around the fire and saw all her cousins were remembering the story that was based at the long limestone headland south of Goose Bay.

Stacey nodded. 'I remember that story,' she said.

'Me too,' Aroha said, quietly.

Others around the fire said they remembered too.

Yeah, yeah, yeah, we said. We remembered the way she told it, more than what happened in the story. We remembered how black her eyes turned.

Hine Rukutia had betrayed her tāne with another man. After the betrayal he tricked her to come back to him; he tricked her into the sea to walk to his waka. He told her to take her piri off, which she did, because she was flooded with newfound love for him. As she was walking into the sea to return to him, he used a pounamu mere to cut her down the middle, splitting her from the crown of her head into two pieces. He kept half of her body for him and left half behind for her lover.

When Nanny Liz told the story she would raise her arm and strike down and spittle would sometimes fly from her mouth. She would stop speaking like she was telling a legend from the past, and she would describe an agony, the mamae of being torn into two pieces, like it was a real gushing bloody thing, happening and happening and happening. The story was always happening. Hine Rukutia was always walking into the water, trusting and hopeful, then forever trapped, tricked, looking up at the green glinting mere, split from the crown of her head over and over.

'He split her,' Kat said.

Aroha glared at Kataraina. Maybe a cloud covered the moon, or maybe it turned its face from the loud thoughtless teenager, who was sipping on beer and talking shit about her nanny.

'I don't know what's going on with you lately,' Aroha said, 'but if you're going to be like this, instead of just telling me – telling someone – what the fuck's up …'

Kat could not quite pinpoint how she had pissed off Aroha. She depended on her sister's patience. She felt alone without it now, as if no one would search by torchlight if she didn't come home. No one would shout her name.

Early the next morning, Kat climbed out of bed and dressed in trackpants, her Swanndri and gumboots. She walked around the saltmarsh, rather than crossing it, and went to the cold fire pit. She sat down nearby and looked at the scaly charred sticks, the white ash. She liked the sulfurous smell. Nothing could grow here; no caterpillar could survive. Not that caterpillars lived at the beach, but if they did they would die here. Good.

Tommy was down on the shore, and she couldn't tell if he'd gone home at all. She walked to him to say hello. He was busy sharpening a stick with a mussel shell. She said to him, 'Tommy, my sister is upset with me.'

He asked if she'd tell him the story of Hine Rukutia, but properly. Kat squirmed. And that's when she might have got the lightest grasp of something, might have for a fleeting moment understood why her sister was so upset. It wasn't for what Kat had said. It was her growing brazenness at telling. The way her confidence and ability to tell her stories was greater than her understanding of them. She left out facts, she missed context, she flapped around chaotically, tipping stories this way and that, making others feel as nauseous as she did.

'Or maybe something else. Tell me about something else, Kat.'

'My grandfather could be very mean.'

Tommy walked towards the saltmarsh, with his pointed stick gripped tight in his hand. 'Come on,' he said. 'Let's go look for things. Crabs.'

Kat did not want to go digging in wet mud. She didn't want the marshes to slurp at her gumboots. 'No,' she said. 'I'm going home. And aren't you too old for this crap?'

'I don't think so,' he said. 'I don't think you can be.' Tommy followed her. 'I'll come too. I'll come visit Toko.'

'Whatever,' she said.

She walked along the beach, scrambling over the rocks, wanting to take the path home on the dry dirt or tarseal road. Tommy scrambled behind her.

'I'll see if Toko wants to come fishing this afternoon, or maybe he wants my dad to take us hunting tonight. I'll ask my dad. Toko loved when we went hunting a few weeks back. Did he tell you about it?'

Kataraina shook her head.

'Yeah, he loved it. We didn't shoot anything though.'

'Shame.'

'Nah, it was good though. He loved it.'

'He hasn't mentioned it.'

'I'll ask him.'

Kat wanted to avoid the marsh again, so she crossed the stones heading inland, towards home and he followed talking and talking. She didn't mind his talking. She liked his voice and she liked to hear his plans and ideas. He liked to sketch, he told her, and she told him that she liked to write.

'*Write?*'

'Yes. Does that surprise you?'

'Yes.'

'Why?'

'I don't know. You're so fast.'

'Do you mean I run fast?'

'Yes, you are the fastest fourth former.'

God, he sounded like a boy, thought Kat. God it was annoying. Couldn't he act his age – why was he so bony and stupid?

'And what does that have to do with writing.'

'Well ... exactly.'

'You're good at more than sketching.'

'Not really.'

'This is boring.'

'I think of writers as slow. Like if they were an animal, they'd be a snail or butterfly, even though a butterfly flies fast it won't find its way to a place directly like a tiger, or a shark, or horse, which are the animals I think of when I think of a sprinter like you.'

She spun to him. 'A sketcher would be a ruru, but you don't remind me of a ruru. You are not thoughtful or sceptical. You talk and talk. Your sketching must be shit.'

Tommy walked on behind her, quietly now. Not sulky, though, he was not heavy behind her. He just walked on, tapping his sharp stick against his thigh.

Kat felt sorry. 'Do you think my writing must be shit?'

'No. I thought maybe it would be better than writing I've read before. I thought maybe it was a good thing. I'm sorry you thought I meant it different.'

'Maybe it's me. Maybe you made me realise something I was thinking.'

'I've drawn a picture of you.'

'Is it a good picture?'

'I think so.'

'Did you draw me with legs, or did you cut me at the neck, or waist, or something?'

'I didn't cut you,' he said.

Then Tommy tripped on a large rock. His sharpened stick went into his side, and he cried out. It was not deep, Kat saw, but it was ugly and dripping and awful to see.

She lifted him. He started to cry, the boy, and then he went pale and quiet like the chalky sea. She veered back, across the saltmarsh again, his arm over her shoulder, the slurping of mud on her gumboots, blood on his shirt. Birds above stitched the sky and tiny raindrops fell. Kat held her breath.

She walked up along the lane and steps that led to the Anglican church and picked daffodils from the church garden. She planned to split them between Nanny Liz, and Tommy, whose cut had become infected. At the hospital door she realised she would need to ask for water for them, so she threw them behind a shrub.

The next time instead of bringing flowers, she brought newspapers from home for Nanny Liz and read her the articles, and for Tommy she brought pencils and sheets of sketching paper.

She felt stoic there in the hospital, and good, like she needed nothing much. She ate biscuits and toast and sipped on water. She ate ready-salted chips. At home, in the morning, she ate cornflakes without milk. She ate crackers and once she spooned Milo right into her mouth from the can.

Kataraina occasionally showered and she did not reuse her towels. She would not reach for the one on the bathroom floor, not even if the hand towel was missing and she needed to dry her hands. In that case she would dry her hands on her shirt and change it quickly. She put headphones on when it rained. She did not go with the twins for tuatua or pāua or kōura or for fires on the beach across from the saltmarsh. Toko and Aroha would do that on their own. At school she looked at her essay whenever she could, exchanging the words on the page for other words, even in maths, but not in science. Because even if she thought there was something missing in the science taught at school – a narrative, or a thread, or some deeper understanding – she liked science.

She visited her Nanny Liz and Tommy in the hospital with devotion, and people praised this devotion. While Kat revelled in the distraction and the excuse to go to the clean dry place, Colleen revelled in how different her teenage daughter was in the face of a family illness and an injured young man, how tame other people's pain had made her.

'It's fascinating,' Kat heard her mother say to her father, 'what can be the making of people.'

He said, 'You think Nanny Liz's illness has been the making of her?'

'No. It has brought out the best in her, made her reflective.'

'Quieter is better?'

'Safer,' Colleen said.

Kataraina was happy her mother wanted to believe that her safe quietness was a symptom of reflection. In fact she liked the idea so much she convinced herself it was too. 'I'm just reflecting,' she'd say.

She sat in her nanny's room at the hospital and read from the local newspaper. The stories she chose to read her grandmother were often quirky and usually cute. They celebrated local people's achievements: a silver medal in the South Island judo competition, a woman's self-published book of poetry, a man pictured with three bags of rubbish he collected in just one week off Peketā Beach. As she read them, she saw they were not quite the veinless, fleshless stories she thought they were.

As the days went on and her reading to Nanny Liz continued, she noticed small patterns in the print. Not only the clichés and puns and alliteration, but a sense of hunger to make something out of nothing. No, that wasn't it, the fifteen-year-old thought. There was an undercurrent of tension or frustration weaving through each story. The writers were either frustrated they were stuck covering the annual flower show again, or they were frustrated with how difficult it was to describe the way the hui at the marae had moved them. They were just supposed to simplify, state facts, tell the news plainly and effectively. Kat didn't like facts – she didn't know why. But she liked the stories. They filled something in her, like dry biscuits when she was hungry. Then they brought Nanny Liz back home, and Kataraina could no longer visit her.

The day Nanny Liz was discharged, Kat had been holding her hand and could feel something buzzing under the kuia's skin. A nurse came in with a trolley and Kat told her: 'She's busy.'

The nurse frowned. 'I just have to do a quick checkup.'

'Do what you need. I was just stating a fact.'

An ugly feeling had pulsed through her when she used that

word 'fact'. She winced. She'd decided it was a character flaw to have such little interest in facts and she was repulsed by each new character flaw she discovered in herself. She saw no hope in trying to become a better person; she saw that if she tried to be good, the goodness would want to grow, exposing where she was rotted.

When Nanny Liz's fingers moved Kataraina asked her, 'Did I let it happen? Please tell me.' Her question was about her grandfather. Had her presence silenced her grandmother, forced them to pretend.

Kataraina waited an hour for her grandmother to wake and answer the question. When she didn't, Kataraina left.

That evening her father and mother drove to the hospital and brought Nanny Liz home. They put a firm but comfortable chair near the window in the living room. They put a small table next to it for her cups of tea, or cans of beer once she was better.

Kataraina played games of patience on the floor in front of Nanny Liz. Behind the comfortable chair was a framed photo of Nanny Liz and Grandad Jack on their wedding day. Her grandfather was dead now. Five years ago. A sudden and violent stroke. Kat shuffled the cards, and her grandmother watched the movement, not like the movement either interested or bored her, but like she was absorbing movement. More and more often she would let movement come to her now. More and more she would swallow movement with her eyes, digest it in her brain, let it keep her alive.

Kat went to the hospital to see Tommy. He was sitting up in his bed, stiffly. He didn't turn his head to look at her when she came towards him, but she saw goosebumps come up on his skinny arms.

'I was lucky. The way I fell. Could have gone into my heart or neck.' He stared like he was imagining a stick in his heart or neck.

She grabbed her elbows.

'You saved me,' he said. Such a boy.

Aroha stepped into the room then. 'Hey, Tommy,' she said.

Kataraina looked up and said, 'Hey.'

Aroha was wearing Nanny Liz's faux-fur jacket and purple bell-bottoms, and a bone heru in her hair, which was pulled tight to her scalp in a low knot. Nanny Liz had given Aroha the jacket months ago – she wore it all the time, but Kat felt upset to see it on her sister today.

Kataraina was wearing a pair of old black trackpants, a navy blue hoody and suddenly she couldn't remember whether she'd washed her face that morning. She doubted she had brushed her teeth.

Aroha said, 'Mum and Dad told me to come get you, Kat. We're having a big kai and waiata at home tonight. We need help.'

There were three of us at the outdoor sink. Toko was at the bench bashing pāua, Hēnare was filleting a large butterfish, and Colleen was pulling beards and shelling the steaming mussels. The hot shells never bothered her.

Kat went to them.

Colleen said to her daughter, 'Can you carry on with them? I need to go in and do the pūhā.'

'Toroī tonight,' Toko said. He was grinning.

Kat looked at the open mussels, steam spilling from them; the running tap; black slimy ink splattered across the bench from Toko bashing the pāua without covering them properly with the stained tea towel. Her father was holding up a butterfish frame, its dark blue head flopped to the side. He threw it into the blue bin marked STOLEN FROM TALLEY'S. He looked at his daughter, not moving, just staring.

'Kat?' he said.

She blinked and went to the bench. Kat picked up a mussel. It was hot. She gripped it. The green of the shell was bright but dark. It was fine. She began pulling a beard from a steaming mussel. She put the beard in the compost bucket and the mussel in the colander. Freshly made toroī for tonight, and her mother would leave some of the jars to ferment. The thought of it made Kat feel sick. She used to love toroī, but now … Pūhā and mussel packed in a jar. It made her think of the caterpillar she had squashed on her leg in the grandstand. A sour chlorine taste in her mouth.

The grandstand.

The telling moves towards it, swirls around it, draws away like a tide.

The green was bright but dark. It was fine. She could manage this green wet work. She bearded another mussel. Another. Music came from the house. She bearded another and another. Hēnare sighed. Toko hugged him with his slimy black hands held up and open, holding him with his elbows. Toko went back to his work, then started to sing along, *sugarpiehoneybunch*.

It was fine.

Another.

Nanny Liz was back home. The green was bright but dark. There was black slimy ink splattered across the bench. The dead eye of a fish stared up at Kat. Her brother was singing, he was bouncing, he was looking at her like, come on, sis, come on. My sis, my sis. Come on.

It was fine.

Later, at the table covered in a feast, her father said a karakia, 'Nau mai e kā hua e hora nei o te ao, o te wai tai, o te wai Māori. Nā Roko, nā Tāne, nā Maru, nā Takaroa. Ko Rakinui e tū atu nei, ko Papatūānuku e takoto iho nei. Tūturu whakamaua kiatina …'

'Tina!' everyone said.

'Haumi ē, hui ē …'

'Taiki ē!' everyone said.

People reached for plates and put pāua and fresh mussel and pūhā and butterfish and kōura and dressed salad and bread and thousand-island dressing on them. Kat went to the bathroom. She looked in the mirror. Her eyes looked black and bright, dark green like the mussel shells. She splashed her face and washed her hands, she splashed her face and washed her hands, then she went to Nanny Liz and sat on the floor and played patience. Aunty Moira was there.

'Not hungry, bub?' Aunty Moira said.

Kat shook her head.

She played her solitary card game in front of her grandmother, who was nibbling at a mussel fritter, and Kataraina tried to stop seeing the pounamu mere being lifted, glinting in the sun, splitting Hine Rukutia in two.

The next night, Aunty Moira called people for dinner. Kat felt like people were always calling out that the next kai was ready. She wished she felt lucky that there was always kai, but she didn't. The constant presence of food was exposing. Kat opened her door and yelled she wasn't feeling well.

'Oh no, bub,' Aunty Moira said. 'I'll make you a cup of tea.'

Kat said, 'Nah, Aunty, I just need a sleep.'

'Okay, bub, okay.'

Kat listened out for the noise in the kitchen. Chairs scraped across the floor, a clattering of plates, and knives and forks, the happy humming murmur from throats readying themselves to swallow buttery mashed potatoes and corned beef and creamy parsley sauce.

She went to the bathroom, and Aroha's door was open. She saw Nanny Liz's jacket on her sister's bed. She went over and swung the jacket onto her shoulders. It was a little big for her, but it felt good and heavy on her body. It smelled like Nanny Liz and Aroha. She looked in the dressing-table mirror and spun. 'Stop it, Aroha,' she said frowning at her own reflection. 'Cut it out, Aroha Te Au. That's enough, you egg,' she said, smiling now, lying to herself, and it made her feel good.

She fished in the pocket and found something. She pulled it up already knowing it was a lighter. She pinched something dry between her fingers. Her teeth shone between her lips. She took off all her clothes except her bra and knickers. She did not look in the mirror in case she saw herself in the grandstand, her heart sluicing sweeter red blood through her veins. She remembered a time – just some short weeks ago – before the greenness, when she might have looked at her own body in the mirror with curiosity, admiration even. She didn't hide her body then, she didn't want to shrink it then, she didn't want a narrative instead of a life then, she didn't want to be a sketch then.

She pulled on her sister's bellbottoms. They weren't as snug as they might have been. Her thighs and butt were not thick like they were a few weeks ago. She was still mostly eating cereal straight from a box. With Nanny Liz being sick, no one had really noticed. She gagged at chicken soup, curried sausages, beef stew, even cream pāua, even fry bread. Only dry food could mop up the green bile in her belly.

Her legs were lost in the bellbottoms. Her legs were gone in them, like magic.

She saw Aroha's heru and hoop earrings on the dressing table. She looked at them longingly. She remembered dressing up pretty to go with Aunty Moira to be a lady in the kitchen at the clubrooms and fill the big wide trays with meat from the hāngī. People stared when she came into the room, and because she was holding the lovely steaming food and she was interested in her coming beauty then, she didn't mind; she liked it. There was no greenness.

Just magic. Just this thudding precious magic of what it meant to be her, so smart and crack-up and beautiful and alive.

Now her eczema was back and there were stinging cracks at the corner of her mouth.

She pulled her hair into a tight low bun. Her hair seemed thinner. She exchanged her studs for the hoops first because that was the easier decision. Much easier than what she did next: took her sister's taoka, the bone heru, and put it in her own hair. Maybe she wanted to feel repulsed by herself. Instead, she was intoxicated looking in the mirror and no longer seeing herself. She was soothed.

Out the door, away from the house, knowing she was a secret then, her movements now and in front of the dressing table only known to her, and with her nanny's jacket on and her sister's taoka and a nicked $10 (Aunt Joanie's) in her pocket she was just beyond her life. She'd just taken a step ahead of, and away from it – all of it – that powerful force was dazzled by her, was watching her, knowing it had to meet her, had to suck back against her, pull back towards *her*.

She headed up the hill, rather than along the main street. It was a darker stretch of road. She became uneasy because of the wind, and the trees swayed like tongues and she felt cold like she'd suddenly sobered up from the drunken minutes alone in front of the dressing-table mirror. Her head burned where the bone was touching her scalp. She braved a viscous rise of nausea. She needed to turn back and get home and take the heru out of her hair and take off Aroha's jacket and bellbottoms and hoops and climb into bed and wake up tomorrow and pretend this was a bad dream. If no one saw you, you could, couldn't you? You could pretend it never happened. Life had not been a step or two behind you, dazzled by you. No. Life had stepped back from you, and watched you, appalled.

The headlights on her then were accusing and bright. She turned away and walked on, even as the car slowed up and rolled along beside her.

'Hey,' said a voice from the opening window, bored but firm. 'Get in,' he said, and stepped out of the car.

She kept her head down and got in. He shut the door behind her and looked up and down the road, then he got in the driver's seat.

He was silent. It was the silence after someone has used words to trick another person. It was that cold pounding silence people sit in to reckon with their lies. To confirm to themselves the lie was a necessary thing, the only choice they had. The bellbottoms made her legs look miserably thin and powerless.

'Why are you all dressed up?' he said. 'What's going on?'

She felt wretched and thieving and worthless. The heru still burned her scalp, the hoops burned her lobes, the eczema itched something wicked. She didn't want her body anymore; the caterpillars climbed up her neck and into her hair to save themselves from his hands, from drowning, and he said she didn't need to explain herself, it was just surprising to find her out here in the dark, dressed up, 'looking so hot'.

Then Nanny Liz's faux-fur jacket watched like a cat.

She heard a can crack and sizzle. There was a crisp sweet smell of apple. She licked her dry lips. She had her hands folded in her lap. For a second her own poise impressed her. The feeling soured, reminding her of the root cause of her predicament: inaction, non-attendance. Two words that had arrived with her beauty, along with other words like hindsight, serendipitous, revolution, grooming, terra nullius and statutory rape.

He was upset.

'Are you going to tell people about us?' he said.

She'd rather he threw her out into a disgusting wet rain than talk to her, but it was not raining. The sound was coming from inside her head.

She took a reluctant sip of the apple juice. Then she skulled the whole can. The sweetness stung the dry cracks at the corner of her mouth. 'I want to go home.'

He kept driving. He drove her away from the houses. They were near farms now, and rivers. They were near bush. He just needed her to listen. In sudden attendance of the situation she told him he was 'a lying cunt'.

'You don't think that,' he said.

'I'm going to be sick,' she said.

He slammed on the brakes.

'Why apple juice?' she said and opened the door to vomit the sweet juice onto the grass. She climbed out of the car. She picked up a stick and smacked it against his window. Close by, a farmhouse light came on.

'You ran your finger along my hand,' she said. Because right now that's all she could deal with. His finger running along her hand, weeks ago, making her believe in magic.

She used the skin of car light to launch herself into a web of vines off the road.

He called out, 'I'll take you home. I'm sorry, Kat.'

The farmhouse light was on. She saw something far from the road and didn't know what she was looking at. She wanted to see it up close.

She was stepping away from herself again, and she was dazzled and frightened by the choice she was making, knowing that once he left, as he would, because he couldn't be caught chasing her through this bush she was disappearing into now, she would be alone in the dark. He couldn't be caught parked here, or wanting her, or calling her name. She had time to change her mind and step out from the bush, let him take her home. But she chose fuss. She chose trouble. She chose attention, even if she didn't really want it, even if she'd rather disappear. This was the mess, she realised now, when your survival instincts were tampered with. You might choose danger to remind people you exist or to defibrillate your own heart.

In the bush, far in the bush, late, late, late in the night, wearing her sister's bellbottoms and heru and hoops and Nanny Liz's watching jacket, she wondered if anyone would find her. She wondered if they would go to the grandstand and find her there instead. Then she became afraid, that she was not in the bush at all, that she was there, a dead body in the grandstand. And that's where she had been all this time, like Hine Rukutia, stuck in that awful moment over and over, there she was, there she was. And people would see.

Her sitting in the grandstand, holding something in her mouth, not knowing what to do with it, the smell of fresh-cut grass and mild chlorine soaking her, a single caterpillar crawling through a rip in her jeans, along her bare thigh, like his finger had slid along the edge of her palm and pinky. Him saying, 'Oh look, Kat, at the way it moves – it's actually cute.' Her slapping the caterpillar, squashing it dead. Him looking at her like she was not the sweetheart he thought she was after all, the creature's wet green guts a foamy consequence on her thigh, no one attending, the smells soaking her while she did nothing and nothing and nothing.

6 January 2020, field study day three

The discovery of an ancestor is enormous. The kāhu have come to the roost. A small island in the swamp with bow-shaped nests in the ground has been filled with the swamp harriers. At least one hundred, maybe more. Cairo has only read about such roosts in books. The largest roost of kāhu she has ever seen had thirty birds, and the sight stunned her.

Watching the birds she can feel the electricity of whānau behind her, come to claim the ancestor. She wants to turn and acknowledge them, but right now she can't pull her eyes from the roost. As if a spring has surged up out of the earth, questions threaten to overwhelm her. She silences them.

An ancestor. Her legs tremble. Her tongue feels tapu. She holds it tight in her mouth. Everything tapu. She closes her eyes.

A woman, then beside her, takes her hand.

'They called this Johnson's Swamp, and we let them, because we knew the name would come – she would come up and stake her claim.'

Cairo opens her mouth. The air on her tapu tongue burns. She closes it and turns to look at the woman, eyes a tawny brown. Long twists of black hair, a round face with high cheekbones. A bright purple scar on her temple. A scar Cairo doesn't trust. It doesn't happen often, these glimpses of a parallel timeline, but she's sure this scar is a trick, a coulda-been.

'Haere ki o tāua tīpuna wāhine.'

Cairo squeezes the woman's hand. The woman leads Cairo towards sound. Keening shafts of sorrow, eased in a bright arena of song. *You died*, the sound laments. *But we will bring you home now*, it celebrates.

Cairo holds her eyes shut, but not because she is afraid. She will look, she will look soon, but when she sees for the first time, she wants to see as a descendant. She is proud she is mātanga pūtaiao – a scientist. But she wants to acknowledge her lost ancestor for the first time, without her mind hounding her eyes to see only answers to questions.

When Cairo opens her eyes, she sees two children with packs and homemade hunting bows on their backs disappearing into a wall of harakeke.

Ghosts, she thinks.

'Beth, she thought we were ghosts.'
'Aren't we?'

Three days after the girl shot the man

We are telling this story. A clambering of vines seeking up towards the sun, then wanting, again, the groundwater.

Just one of us was in a hospital bed after the girl shot the man. Kataraina Te Au. The rest of us willed her to wake.

Kataraina's eyelids were the colour of the moon because an ocean was behind them. Her heart made the graph spike. Her body held up sheets. Somewhere in Ōtautahi a dog barked and barked.

One afternoon one of us stormed into the hospital's whānau house, where people waiting for her to wake were staying. Tom Aiken stormed in and kicked off. 'Her swamp!'

Colleen was there and her younger sister, Moira, was beside her. On the other side sat Father Joe. Outside on the porch two people were smoking. Before Tom arrived, Colleen had whispered, 'I'm glad, Moira. But he brought us pigs. We still have some in the freezer. I'm glad she shot him, but what will I do with all the pig?'

Moira put an arm around her sister, afraid the sadness in their skin would be combustible against itself. When she found it wasn't, she said, 'We will cook it, sis. When your girl wakes up, we will celebrate, and we'll cook the pig.'

Then Tom Aiken stepped into the small lounge and he said, 'Her swamp!'

What should Colleen say now he was bringing up the kūkūwai? She didn't want people talking about it. No. Not the swamp, not that godforsaken swamp again.

She flew up out of her chair. Rage in her wrists. Worry in her knees. Guilt in her ankles. Tīpuna in her throat. The church on her tongue. Her heart desperate for her daughter to wake up, and then everyone would shut the fuck up about all the things – the swamp, the man, the gun, the bruises, the angels in heaven and their loving, loving arms.

'We didn't mean for it to happen, Colleen,' Tom Aiken said, his forearms out like shields.

'You kept things from us!' Colleen yelled. 'You lied for him. You knew.'

She saw it in his eyes – they accused her. *You knew too, you knew too.*

'Now you're here talking shit about te kūkūwai. You shut the fuck up about that.' With Father Joe right there!

With rage in her wrists she said, 'You shut the fuck up about the swamp. My daughter might never wake up. You shut the fuck up about it.'

Tom Aiken wouldn't shut the fuck up. Instead, with his forearms like shields he told her, 'I might be going crazy, but the swamp is filling up. It's salty though. Is it ...?' he shook his head, laughed, like he knew he must be wrong. He whispered now, 'Are they ... tears?'

Colleen scoffed. 'For the love of god, man.'

As if he was talking to himself now, Tom said again, 'Tears? No.' Then to Colleen he asked, 'Are you not curious?'

'Curious? My daughter might not wake, and you want my curiosity?'

'Her swamp.'

'No. You kept quiet before. You might as well keep quiet again.'

We were all watching, waiting. At the window, two cigarettes were a pair of taniwha eyes, fire-orange; at the bench, a kuia's cup of tea had a snake's ghost spilling out to see the fuss. Father Joe was hiding his teeth, but his lips kept blinking. Throats held sentences and mouthfuls of supper. Suddenly Colleen Te Au and Tom Aiken were poised.

'You just pray for her, Tom Aiken. You love her so much, you just pray.'

'I will,' he said. 'I will go to the swamp. And pray.'

'*The swamp?* And pray?' she said, then pulled her hand back and slapped him in his face.

People murmured then, like they hadn't been paying attention and hadn't seen the slap. Didn't hear the words. All the pāua fritters and tubs of marinated mussels and a couple of secret cans of beer that had become holograms in the hum of watchfulness were things again.

A murmur moved around the room. People coughed up tickling sand in those holding throats. Some even went as far as standing or walking to where they were walking to before Tom kicked off. One person sent a watchful drawer to a rolling close, another sent a watchful card to trump another.

Father Joe crept close to Colleen. 'Can I help here, Whaea?'

'No,' she said.

Tom Aiken looked from him to her to him. He said he was sorry. She said nothing. She sat back down beside her sister, who said, 'I'll drive you out there when we get back. See what he's on about.'

'Go without me,' Colleen said. 'I shouldn't have come here. I shouldn't have left her alone in that bed. I should sleep at her side. Go without me, sis.'

'Kei te pai,' Moira said, and she settled back in her seat, composed herself. Another smoke, maybe a sleep first. The swamp was not going anywhere.

Tom Aiken left the whānau house then like he was wading through a swamp himself. He might have gone home to listen to the tears coming up out of the ground. Colleen thanked Father Joe for rallying the people to make food, and for coming to be with her and pray with her. She thanked him for the prayers and the money he gave her, so Hēnare wouldn't need to fish. Because of this Hēnare could take a nap, and that's what he was doing when Colleen left.

She said to her sister, 'When Hēnare wakes, tell him I'm at the hospital. And that's where I'll be until my daughter wakes up.'

Colleen took her handbag with her Bible, pounamu rosary beads and can of beer inside it, left the whānau house and walked down the road, to the hospital.

We don't remember exactly where we were, Beth and Ari, but we think, maybe, we were sitting on a step, looking up at the stars, holding each other's hands. Maybe Beth said, your grandmother just slapped my father, or maybe Ari said, I'm sorry my grandmother just slapped your father, or maybe we said nothing, maybe we just remembered again, watching a man die after Beth pulled the trigger – after we shot him.

7 January 2020, field study day four

'Tell me, Matua, how did you find her?'

Cairo, Hana and Eric sit at the picnic table in the open conservatory outside the wharekai at Takahanga Marae.

'How?'

'Āe.' The man with the new question has deep-set dark eyes and wears a whale tooth strung around his neck. 'Kōrero mai.' He smiles, and gestures with his hand. 'Tell us.'

Another man comes into the conservatory and sits close enough to listen, but not so close as to disturb, and a woman too – the woman who was holding Cairo's hand at the kūkūwai – and there are two children with her, who look around eleven. They are the two children Cairo thought were ghosts. Eric looks at them and then at the man with the new question. He nods.

'I'd gone up the northern section, I was taking water samples near the tussock sedge, and I saw further up, what appeared to be giant cane rush – that's an endangered wetland plant, once abundant, now only found north in the peat bogs in Waikato.' Eric laughed. 'I thought no way, can't be cane rush. Grows in peat. Peat is formed through accumulation of matter. This swamp is just too new.'

The man agreed. 'Āe. Ha, does time mean nothing there?'

Eric frowned. The man spoke too flippantly for him. Too much like he was saying to someone arrived late for dinner that they must be on island time.

'Yes, time. A strong tool to guide our work, means absolutely nothing there.'

'Right so, the giant cane rush? You walked closer?'

'Well, I couldn't. Too deep. I went up and got our canoe. I paddled out to look and blow me down – giant cane rush! A good two metres tall. Even drifts formed, wire rush growing. Stunning. I spent several hours out there, taking notes, clippings. Then I find evidence of a small peat dome. I make my way to the centre of the bog, where – so contrary is nature – the bog would be shallowest if a peat dome has formed. I see in the water, the dome has … pulled something up. First, I see a wooden crate. Intricately carved. I am spooked, I have to say. Afraid I'm looking at something I shouldn't be looking at. Not an unusual feeling in wetland work – a shy place. But still, I reached into the dark water and took it. Trapped in a gap was a hand. Dark, and wrinkled, partially encased in peat. I saw it just briefly. I dropped the crate.' Eric rubbed his hands on his pants as if attempting to rub the bog's water off. 'I speared in one of our marker flags a few metres from the dome and paddled off quick as I could.'

The day after the girl shot the man

We were not well. None of us were well. We'd shot him.

Tom Aiken was running on zero sleep. His girl pulled that trigger, it was her finger on it. But we all did it. There, we said it.

And after that Beth was gone.

In a flash.

We were not well.

Bags packed, and off Beth went to her aunty's apartment in Auckland – a place she'd always wanted to go, but not like this. Tom was with the cops rehashing what happened over and over, making sure it stayed the same over and over. Which it did, of course it did. He wasn't lying. He had nothing to hide. But it was full on. Stuart Johnson was shot! The kid's eyes were gone out of her head when she pulled that trigger. Tom could still see the bullet flying towards Stu. Though he never actually saw it. This was a memory he created in the hours after the shooting.

When he went into the hospital's whānau house, he felt crazy. Mrs Te Au slapped him right in the face. He left. Got home to the sound, this stormy sound, this mechanical sound. All this noise, he couldn't tell if it was rain or an engine. He went and put earmuffs on to get some sleep. He was in bed, stiff as a board, looking like a right dickhead with these earmuffs on. Begged a god, or gods, or whoever he needed to beg, for some relief because the sound was so consuming it could have crushed his brain.

The earmuffs didn't help, that's when he realised the noise was coming from inside his skull. Or both. He could not be sure.

He realised he'd been a right wanker, going over there and ranting and making a scene and distressing everyone, like he'd clearly lost the plot. But the next day he noticed more water. Shitloads more. All at that swamp she'd told Stu 'to leave well enough alone'. It had been an arsehole bit of land. Rotten, stinking, and Stuart Johnson couldn't let it go. It was a bone and Johnson was a starving mutt. Now, though, who was as dead as the dog he shot? Johnson was. Any other farmer would have written it off. He had more than enough. Not a Johnson though. Nah, he was offended that bit of land would not yield to him, so he'd kept going at it.

Animals died there. Animals died and died and died there. He fenced it off; still animals died there. Birds, lizards, cows, even eels were climbing out the river and dying there. And what did he do? Usually farmers just drain out the water, but he went mad. He got all sorts of technology pumping away any water that leaked up. He kept turning the foul ground over; he kept on digging drains, wasting his energy on it to prove a point.

Tom had thought (maybe even wished!) that one day we were gonna find Stu dead there, you know. That land was gonna kill him just like it was killing bees and rabbits and weka and calves. But nah, he went there to work it every day, not even letting it rest on Sundays. Like he knew: give it one day and it'll claw its way back. Tom saw him go there with fuel drums and wood – his pockets probably full of lighters and boxes of matches and white Little Lucifer cubes. He had passed the point where he even wanted it to be turned to pasture. If it wouldn't be pasture it could be nothing. It wouldn't even resemble earth by the time he was done with it.

The bastard didn't stop. He lit fires on it and poured diesel over it. Wouldn't leave the property for a weekend, or a trip to see his own mother anymore. Kat had told Tom that Stu needed to be on the property all the time because he was obsessed. And she'd said other things to Tom, too, about how it all started. Them even. How that swamp was where she'd decided Stu wasn't as bad as she thought he was. That he wasn't just ugly, that he was beautiful when he let his hands loose to rest on his thighs – even if for just a minute.

'Now he just won't go anywhere anymore, Tom,' she said.

Like he knew, if he left, the swamp would flood up and his missus, well, his missus ... If he left, the swamp would climb up out of the ground and *his* missus would jump the fence, and where would she go? She'd bound off to farmer fuckface Aiken.

Tom remembered when Stu saw. Tom went there to borrow something. Beth wanted to make pancakes. Tom had no lemons. Beth liked lemon juice on her pancakes. Kat and Stuart had a tree. He turned up and Kat and Stuart were at the kitchen table having coffee, and Kat said, 'Wanna coffee then?'

'Yeah, all right,' Tom said.

The sugar bowl was on the table, and Kat knew Tom liked sugar in his coffee because he came to have coffee with Kat more than Stu knew.

'Sugar?' she said to hide the knowledge.

'Yes,' he said, so she slid him the bowl.

That was fine, but there were also biscuits on the table. Kat's hand was near the plate. There was a noise, like a tractor starting, and Stuart said, 'I told him to bloody wait,' and his head spun towards the window. Tom reached for a biscuit then, letting his hand graze over Kat's. Her fingers, like a large and troubled spider's legs, lifted, and Stuart turned away from the window and saw the frightened delight in those lifted fingers. Tom said, 'Sorry, Kat,' and began eating the biscuit while Stu sat there translating the elation in his missus's fingers.

8 January 2020, field study day five, 1.30–1.45am

Cairo wakes startled from a dream in which her ancestor – found preserved in the swamp – is alive and roosts with the kāhu on an island in the swamp. Hana sleeps on beside her. Cairo looks up at the ceiling of the wharenui, the carvings. There is an image of a woman. She thinks about the woman who came to her at the kūkūwai and held her hand. She closes her eyes and imagines the woman's lips, jawline. She imagines kissing the woman's neck. Hana stirs.

    Cairo gets off her mattress and exits the wharenui. It's not just the scientists here, its everyone come for the ancestor. The room breathes; it snores and squirms. She walks down the hall, past the framed Crown apology and the pictures of relatives. She goes into the wharekai, then out the door. She goes to the right-hand corner of the property, from where she can see both the ocean and the māra kai. The sky is thick with stars, not a lick of cloud hides their brightness. The moon and star light turn the night an electric blue. Suddenly she smells taramea, the fragrant speargrass used by her ancestors to make perfume. The scent comes fresh, as if its resin had just now, close by, been collected. But there is no taramea around, no person to be seen. She returns to the wharenui, to her mattress, closes her eyes to trick herself to sleep.

Four years before the girl shot the man

Colleen Te Au had manufactured trust in Stuart Johnson and we let her. Some of us were not born when this began, but our 'we' has no beginning, will not end. We let her, maybe we even encouraged it. To manufacture this trust, Colleen churned some facts: he had filled their freezer with pig; he worked hard; her daughter was wild, wayward, fiery, had a tendency to put herself in harm's way and she was calmer now, quieter with him, therefore safer; she was like the girl we got to see when Nanny Liz and little Tommy Aiken (when he was less trouble) needed her; it was nice to have this girl back; Stu wanted to marry this girl (only good men wanted to get married); Colleen had not seen bruises; she had not been told about bruises (none of us had been told about bruises, none of us had seen bruises); we had no reason to even be thinking about bruises because no one had seen them or heard about them, even though bruises appeared on the daughter's skin in the mother's nightmares; there were no bruises for Christ's sake; he filled their freezer with pig; their freezer was filled with pig; he was not punching her at the table when they were eating his pig from their freezer; he was not belittling her or berating her or putting his hands round her throat (except in a mother's nightmares); Colleen needed him to be a good man; we needed to believe he was a good man; Father Joe smiled at Stuart in church; Father Joe said, 'Hello, Stuart!' and Stuart said, 'Hello, Father!'; she needed him to be a good man; we all needed him to be a good man; we all had the newspaper clipping of him being commended for his act of bravery; we were so very grateful.

One evening Colleen and Hēnare went to Stuart and Kat's for dinner and their daughter was of course roasting a shoulder of pig this man had killed for them, and he offered to help Hēnare out with the ongoing financial drama with his boat's engine and suddenly Kat kicked off about the swamp.

'He wants to sell the land – you know, the old swampland – to help. And to do that,' she said, slapping mash spud on her mother's plate so hard a little bit flew and landed on her mother's chin. 'He's got to really truly and finally drain it, he reckons. Worth more really truly and finally drained.'

Colleen wiped the spud from her chin and almost vomited in her own mouth, because a sudden image came to her of Kataraina's urine being drained into a catheter. It was hard for Colleen to discern if it was a memory or a vision, because her daughter's face was blurred.

Right there, right in front of Stuart, Colleen told Kat to just let the man do his bloody job for crying out loud and if that job included getting rid of that tiny, tiny little bit of swamp that's what's got to happen, Jesus H Christ!

Stuart, pretending he wasn't straining to hear the women, hid his face.

From behind a veil of steam lifting out of a pan of bubbling gravy Kat said quietly, 'It wasn't always a tiny, tiny little bit of swamp.'

Colleen said, 'Well it fucking is now.' (She only ever said fuck about the swamp.)

'You believe the lie now don't you, Ma?'

'What lie?'

Kat let the question hang in the air to soak the room, flood it, so Colleen would have to wonder about all the lies, everywhere. Kat wanted to watch her mother try and pinpoint which particular lie it was for this particular kōrero.

'Kataraina?'

'The main one.'

'Stop being dramatic, stop talking in riddles.'

Kat poured the pale pork gravy into a gravy boat and whispered so Stuart couldn't hear her. 'This man can't own land, a man can't, like he thinks he can.'

'We're not living *back then*. And we won't ever again.'

'That's not what I'm saying though.'

'The swamp you are trying to save is long gone and what's left is symbolic at best, a bone for you to playfight over at worst.'

There was a loud, almost violent, clicking noise. Kat and Colleen turned to look at Stuart. Right there – right at the dinner table! – he was showing Hēnare a handsome new rifle. Hēnare had an expression on his face. Kat needed time, probably the whole night staring at the ceiling to translate this expression to understand what her father might have been thinking or even feeling when he was asked to admire a gun at the dinner table, but Colleen knew in a second. And she refused to acknowledge the cloud of concern this translation pulled up from the absolute pits of her stomach, refused it for plain facts: the man was a hunter, for god's sake. And in this day and age, people *did* own land, and those people had money, wealth even.

People who had wealth lived longer. And better. She wanted her children to live longer and better, and she and Hēnare were broke, and her husband would die working to pay off that boat's debt, so she needed this man to be good because, for god's sake, her daughter could use a little discipline, something to devote herself to, like a home, this home.

Stuart shot the pig. The pig on Kataraina's fork and now in her mouth. Her warm breathing mouth – and did they have Stuart to thank for her warm, breathing mouth? Well, yes, they did now, in a way, they did. He'd saved her!

Pig smothered in gravy. Don't bite the hand that feeds you. Freezer was filled with his pig. This pig. Getting rid of the swamp was a good thing, that godforsaken swamp, and he must want the swamp gone because of how much he loved her, and his wanting the swamp gone, making the swamp gone showed the lengths he would go to protect her. And god knows. God knows. Colleen's daughter could use a little protection; she was just like her Nanny Liz and look what had happened to her. He had a gun at the table because he was a farmer and a hunter and a provider. How else you get home kill, huh?

Our ancestor once lived close to the house where he was shot. She was at the river when a man approached her and offered her some peaches from a can, then attacked her. Offer food, then attack. As if he were luring some small beast into some savage steel trap. Instead of entering his trap, she drove his own industrial tool into his own chest. Afraid for herself and her family, she escaped along the coast, eventually finding her way to a swamp.

Five days after the girl shot the man

Like she'd promised us at the whānau house, Kat's aunty Moira went to see the kūkūwai for us. It was summer and the day was hot and we were suffering for the heat. She mopped sweat from her forehead with a handkerchief and swatted flies from her arms and face.

She'd driven to Aiken's place and he'd taken her to the swamp, and the flies, the flies, the flies. It was not a swamp, she thought, so much as an infection. She could see where raupō and wīwī might have once grown. Some harakeke was surviving. There was a single kahikatea towering over the wound and a broadleaf was folding over the whenua like it was on its knees, mourning.

She could smell rot.

Tom Aiken pointed. 'See there – see the water.'

There was water, maybe as much as a decent-sized paddling pool could hold.

'Āe,' she said, unconvinced she needed to come here.

'Hasn't been water here for a couple of years now. I mean, he ain't here to fight it like he was, but shit it's a fair bit in just a few days, and in summer – hasn't rained in weeks.'

'So, this land is his, and that,' Moira pointed to a fence a hundred metres back from what could be described as a bog, 'is yours.'

Tom Aiken nodded.

'You know how big it used to be?'

'The swamp?'

'If you want to call it that.'

'What would you call it?'

She swatted at the flies, lifted her shirt over her nose. The smell was intense. Unnatural. Frightening. 'A bog, Tom. A foul bog is what I'd call it. Certainly nothing worth coming to the whānau house and upsetting everyone about.'

'Colleen.'

'Yes, my *sister*. Yes, I think upsetting her was ...' she swatted at a persistent fly ' ... unnecessarily cruel.'

Tom Aiken was quiet for a time. Then he took a stick and hit at the ground.

'Soft,' he said. 'When I started farming here it was already gone off my land but there was a small bit holding on, maybe the size of our town pool. It seemed bigger when we were kids. The Te Au kids used to sneak over to play around it. Their dad said it was tapu and to stay away but they'd sneak here. We'd all sneak here. Once it was enormous. About a hundred years ago it came up to the land below that terrace there, even as far as the saltmarsh, and see those trees?' He pointed across paddock after paddock after paddock of grass to a small clump of kahikatea. 'It reached those trees. Eels used to come down from the river using the ditch and we'd feed them in there. That was when Stuart Johnson was just a kid too. His dad owned the farm then. So, Stuart'd be with us all sometimes.'

'Stuart's dad never tried to get rid of it?'

'His grandfather had done all that needed – if that's the right word – to be done. And there was no reason for Stuart to want that little bit gone. It was never going to be good for his cows. He knew that.'

Moira walked away from Tom and wandered the edge. It took her longer than she thought it would to reach the kahikatea. The size of the thing was an illusion. She felt dizzy. She saw the skeleton of a dead possum. She looked at the sky and she started to pray for her niece, for us, for all of us.

In the hospital Kataraina's eyelids were the colour of the moon because an ocean was behind them. Her heart made the graph spike. Her body held up sheets. Somewhere a dog barked and barked.

Two years after the girl shot the man

Fishing, we say. We are going fishing. *Fishing*, we say. We have hooks, sinkers, lines, knives.
'Bait?' Taukiri asks.
'Bait!'
'Here.' He wraps a few slices of bacon in tinfoil. 'Herring like bacon.'
'Cool,' Beth says, and nudges Ārama. 'Hey, Ari, what other things could we use for bait?'
Taukiri searches the fridge and Ārama disappears to rummage through his brother's stuff. He fishes in the pockets of his jeans. Nothing, nothing, nothing. He goes into the sock drawer. A lighter, a condom. The end of a broom, cut and hollowed for Taukiri to smoke weed out his window at night. They think we're silly, Ari thinks. Take the pipe? It smells sweet. But Ari is not silly. The pipe gone, Tauk will notice. Then he finds what Beth wanted. His tobacco packet. Taukiri does not vape. Too artificial. He likes weed, and tobacco, and playing his guitar and surfing, and taking his car to pick up girls who smoke weed and sing and swim naked in the sea.
Ari takes one of the rollies Tauk has ready-rolled. He puts it carefully into his pocket and slinks back to the kitchen, where his brother has found an old box of squid in the freezer.
Beth points. 'More bait.'
Ari nods, smiling.
They put on their backpacks loaded with handlines, hooks, sinkers, bacon wrapped in tinfoil, old frozen squid plastic-wrapped,

an ice-cream container full of peanut butter sandwiches, a bottle of water laced with vodka, a lighter and now a rollie. They walk into the bush, towards a murky stream, smirking. Ready to see what waits on the other side of pretending.

One year before the girl shot the man

It had been a shameful thing to wake up to, to go into the kitchen and be reminded – by the cold autumn wind in the kitchen, the broken glass, the unwashed dishes – that they were cruel, violent people. As she swept up some glass, she tried to remember what she'd said. She hadn't been drinking, but it was difficult to remember who kicked off first. She remembered swearing, that's right. Laughing? No, surely not. Then he threw something. Why was she swearing, though?

The King can opener had spun by her head, and so close that her temple felt like it puckered, and her brain shrank away from the walls of her skull like half an orange having its juice squeezed. (Maybe that was where the memory of what happened now was, juiced and soaking into the whenua?) She held up her hand then, gritted her teeth, balled her fist so tight the tendons around her wrist popped out. The shards exploded out into the day and the can opener landed in a patch of grass outside *his* house. (After she moved her stuff in, it went from being his house to *his* house.)

She didn't know it was her can opener that tore by her skull until lunchtime the day after.

It was shortly before his lunchtime when she made the choice that later aggravated her. It was meant to be a choice about peace, because Tina Turner was on the radio singing about not fighting no more, which made tears rise quick, causing Kat to make a decision. It was a small decision, hardly noteworthy: open a tin of creamed corn, make toasted sammies for the man who smashed that window.

She had pushed him to his limits after all, and she didn't want to fight no more.

She searched the drawers for the can opener. She checked the sink, pot cupboard, junk drawer, even went to the shed and looked in the man's toolbox because he'd hidden her mascara there once, her Eftpos card another time, and her treasured photo of her dead brother another, but she did not find the utensil.

Alone in the house, she ransacked the kitchen. She had not yet called anyone to come and fix the window because she was embarrassed. It was the third window Stu had broken. On one of those occasions another man came to fix the window and she had to speak to him with her lip all cut to fuck, swollen to shit, and though the window-fixer didn't say so, she could see in his eyes he put two and two together and made a sum that seemed to be – after looking her over – palatable to him.

A can of creamed corn before her and the window still smashed and letting in a cold autumn wind, she took up a serrated knife and drove it into the tin and the tin turned to bone and the yellow mash inside turned to brains then those brains were specifically the man's brains, and even when she had the tin open she couldn't stop going at the matter, fruitlessly stabbing creamed corn until it was all loose like vomit across her kitchen counter. Then she threw her knife, made a fist and thumped it. The knife was like her King can opener anyway, one of those old-fashioned ones, engraved with the word KING and a crown on it. It didn't have a cog like a clock. It had a sort of crescent-moon blade.

You had to get the knack of it. Kat had. She liked the bladed can opener – it had given her a nuanced strength. It fired different muscles in her hands and arms.

She'd found the can opener inside the wall of Stuart Johnson's house a few years before, after Stu punched a hole in the wall beside her head. Alone the next day she had played with the broken wall.

She'd examined it. She'd punched her own hand against it and hurt her knuckles. She'd pulled broken pieces of wall away and rolled them in her palm and considered their strength like she was comparing her own structure, the strength of her skin and muscle, to the material. That was his aim, wasn't it? By punching the wall, and breaking it, he was explaining to her something about his capability, and there she was, letting him tell and tell and tell her.

She imagined her ribcage with a fist-sized hole in it just like the wall. And then she looked inside the wall, like she was hoping to see her own punctured lungs there, because she was having trouble breathing and she had no good explanation for any breathing difficulties, because he'd missed. *Hadn't touched a hair on her pretty head.*

There was no fist-sized hole in her ribcage, nor her head. Then she saw silver, rusted silver. She reached into the wall and pulled the thing out. She pressed the sharp claw against her wrist. Then she went to the drawer and took out the modern can opener with neon-blue plastic handles and put it in the rubbish. She took a tin of fruit salad from the cupboard and stuck the crescent blade into the tin. She tore the smooth tin to a ragged, dangerous opening and poured the fruit salad into a bowl. She sat in front of the TV and watched Oprah while eating fruit salad, the King can opener beside her on the armrest.

But now it was gone. Tommy's kid's dog turned up at the door. Lupo stood there looking at Kat, turning his head this way and that. 'Come on then,' Kat said.

The dog stepped timidly into the house. Kat cut a piece of cheese from the block and threw it to him. He caught it and swallowed it whole. She kneeled to pet him. He came to her and licked her face. She kissed him above his eye. 'You always show up at the right time, boy,' she said.

She went to the fridge took out a leftover lamb chop that Stu hadn't wanted because it was overcooked and gave it to the dog. He ate it, then lay on the kitchen floor, as Kat went about making the toasted sandwich.

She cleaned the bench and the sammie was ready the very second the man arrived home. The peace sandwich, the olive branch. Crisp, simple.

The dog barked and barked. Kat said, 'Get home then.'

When he came in the door, into the kitchen, dirty boots still on his feet, he said, 'What's Aiken's mutt doing here?' The dog stood between Stu and Kat, and Kat thought she heard him growl behind his teeth. She said again, 'Get home,' and the dog went for the door, swerving from the man, the sound of his nails scuttling across the linoleum floor like the mutt anticipated a kick to the guts. She set the peace sandwich on the table and while he was still standing poised to sit, knees about to bend, heavy with satisfaction at Kat's crisp apology, she asked him if he had seen the can opener. 'I've searched high and low and it's nowhere. It's gone walkabouts.'

And he looked at her, and the smashed window behind her probably looked like she was the bullseye at the centre of his crafted chaos, and he stopped stooping, stopped bending his knees to sit. Glared at her. Let his plate with the hoiked-in sammie fall to the table, and the plate rolled and rolled and rolled like a tossed coin.

Stuart Johnson stood, rod straight. 'Can't help yourself, can you, Kat?'

'What ...?' she said, but already, as her brain pulled further in from its walls – like it was shrugging into a cloak, like it was a well-juiced orange and a fist was trying to get just one more drop, like it was a creature, a grub, trying to burrow down to hide in her throat – an image executed itself, threw its shadows onto the bone walls of her skull. It was a can opener that tore past her yesterday evening.

Kat saw the King spin past her head. She saw it bust through the window. She saw how her innocuous question was skipping lightly, innocently, but thoroughly disturbing the peace before it found the ground to settle.

She pursued this elusive peace. 'It's just I was looking for it today, to open the corn. Had to use a knife.'

But her newly found knowledge gave itself up in her eyes, in the way she spoke, in the way she shifted her feet. The man – with no interest in poetry or the way a lyric in a song could declare love without using the actual word, and no interest in land too wet to fatten cows – could not see it was *newly found* knowledge. Stuart Johnson could only see that, right then as he looked at her, she knew exactly where the can opener might be.

He lunged towards her. And as she tried to step away from him, she tripped and fell. When she fell, she knocked her face into the kitchen bench, lodging the sharp edge of it between her cheekbone and her jaw. 'Always shit-stirring,' he said. And he went back to the table, took the sandwich, threw it out the broken window and left. He slammed the door so hard, any glass left in the window frame fell from it.

She was left with the question: did she know he'd thrown the can opener? If she didn't have her suspicion that the can opener had been part of some violence between them, why would she even check his toolbox? That was crazy, checking his toolbox. She was crazy. And a stirrer. Obviously, she got into it. Stirring. Being crazy. If she hadn't asked him where the can opener was she would have stirred some other way, because one of her wanted peace and the other wanted trouble, the other was aggrieved, the other was watchful and conniving and hated the peace the first one craved, because it left her disarmed, it worried her. Beasts rose up in the silence.

The window was broken eight days before a single but monstrous bruise from where her face had hit the bench finally drew back beneath her skin and beneath her bone, the blood back into her head, returning the juice, now poisoned, to the drying cells in her brain, and those cells were grateful for the juice, any juice, poisoned, acidic, numbing, whatever. So starved, the thirsty cells slurped that bruise-juice right up, though some parts were windswept deserts now, enormous windswept deserts, and any juice returned there was quickly lost in the dry.

She walked past the can opener outside in the grass when she went to the washing line, or the pumpkin patch, or to his shed to find things she had sometimes lost all by herself. She watched it rust over the weeks and eventually it was hidden in the grass and weeds that grew, and finally it slid into the dirt, not unlike the bruise on her cheekbone, until one day the utensil was gone, and she no longer had to see it, be reminded of it, be forced into the thought pattern, the dead-end memories, which refused to reveal to her who kicked off first, or why, and how she'd found the can opener in the first place. It was better it was gone, she thought, because when they finally learned how to stop themselves being bad violent people, she didn't want to have to look at something that reminded her they once were. She didn't want to remember she had imagined cleaving him in two with that small blunted crescent moon.

She thought she'd found a cut to her temple that morning too. But it vanished minutes after she saw it. She decided it was probably her imagination or a smear of blood from maybe hacking at the tin (she didn't find that cut either). Crazy, she was.

But when she went to see Nanny Liz, Nanny Liz stared at her temple. She reached out and wanted to touch it, and Kat stood before her stunned, wondering if Nanny Liz was looking at a parallel world, one in which the can opener found its target. And she shivered at the thought that he had missed. It was her only comfort: that he'd not really wanted the can opener to hit her.

Three years before the girl shot the man

This was our last night before things changed.

Kat didn't know yet it would be her last night with Pare for a while; she didn't know the next time they'd be together, we would have already shot him.

It was three in the morning, and they were at the bar at the Strawberry Tree. The bar was like a long dark cave, and sitting there, at the bar on the high stools, they looked like witches. Pare, with her choker necklace and dark plum lipstick, smudged mascara and wide drunken eyes. Pare, who had just quit working at the fish-processing factory.

'Two sambuca,' she said. 'Black.'

The bartender set the violet shots in front of them.

'To unemployment.' Pare raised her shot glass and the two women downed the sambuca without a shudder.

'I'll bet Stu wants me to milk tomorrow,' said Kat. 'He never wants me to milk, but tomorrow. You wait.'

'Those moneyhungrywanks. You know Gina had two days she had to come in late to work 'cause the kids were sick and her ex couldn't get there till after he got some sleep after night shift, and she always works her fucken arse off but this week she's going to be five hours down. Five hours to her is the kids' school lunches, a pack of cigs and, I dunno, a day, what, two days' power? Let's go to the factory.'

The women walked out of the Strawberry Tree and onto the quiet Kaikōura street.

'She's worked there fifteen years. What was five hours to them?'

The night was cool. As they walked, Pare's indigo chiffon top trailed out behind her, her black hair. Kat followed with wonder, comforted to be with someone who still had it in them to pick a fight. The walk to the factory was long, and as they walked the sky began to lighten to plum, like her lips, then indigo, like her top. It was as if Kat was following Hinetītama.

At the factory Pare got them in using a key she had been entrusted with and had not returned. They didn't need to say shit to each other, they knew. Pare and Kat walked to the clock-in cards. They took them from the metal holder, then they marched out of the factory and towards the wharf. At the wharf they looked out at the boats docked there. Pare began tossing all the workers' clock-in cards – not just Gina's, Steph's, Axe's, Darren's, Miti's – into the water, one at a time.

'A waiata, kare?' Pare asked.

'I might be from a musical family but I can't help you.'

'Come on.'

Kat huffed. She remembered a Catholic hymn, 'Ko te Whaea'.

She sang the song for the Virgin Mary. 'Hine ngākau ... ko te whaea o te ao.'

Woman of great heart.

The mother of the world.

They looked into the water at the clock-in cards, floating there. 'We have taken our flax ropes, and we have reclaimed time.' Pare laughed.

She had a drunken theory. If there were no clock-in cards that week, people would have to be paid the hours they were rostered. (Next day Kat worried: who had been doing overtime to save up to fill some holes in their teeth, put down a hāngī for a wedding or a twenty-first or send a kid on a basketball trip?)

Pare lived near the wharf, in a small wooden house that faced the mountains. They walked there and Kat fell asleep on Pare's couch. She woke up to Stu looking at her, nudging her gently with his hand. 'Come on,' he said. 'Get you home.'

When she got home her bed did look lovely. And she climbed into it while Stu went to the kitchen, closed her eyes. Her heart was pumping hard out, all the nicotine, and sugar from too many Woodies in her blood. Still, she must have fallen asleep quick because she didn't hear him open the door or come to the bed, only woke as he ripped blankets off her.

He ripped them off, then he lifted her by her arm, then he took her to the bathroom, and her face flashed in the mirror and she saw the lipstick she'd put on before she went out and the sight of it made her feel disgusting, and he turned on the shower and threw her under the cold jets of water. 'You'll thank me later,' he said. 'Time to face the day.'

Later, Pare called and asked how Kat's head was, how Stu was, how funny was last night too, oi. Kat replied with a cackle: Stu was cracking up about that, he was cracking up, hard out, said he can't stand that fulla who manages the place, tosser he reckons, so good job, Stu reckoned. Like usual, these lies made her feel better for a few beats. They could be true; she hadn't had a chance to tell him these things yet, because he was upset, but if she had told him, this was all possible.

But now Kat couldn't let Pare come over for a while, in case it all came up, because it all always would come up, wouldn't it? She bit her nails, and then laughed at herself for being so basic now. Pare shouldn't visit for a while, and whose fault was that?

Well, mine, she thought, for being a liar.

So Kat returned to secrecy, which reminded her of how she became with the greenness. And just like with the greenness, she let secrets wrap around anything they could inside her, until nothing was safe to tell, or things were only safe to tell in small nuggets, but she had to avoid letting those nuggets come together, because they were like chemical substances that might react explosively or become something else when combined. She was doing his work and his work was to exhaust her.

She would tell secrets to water and stones, so no one else could hear what a crazy bitch she was. But she would stumble on the storyline, its linear form, what exactly led to this and led to that, and on the way she would discover a nugget of culpability and want to hide it away, but that meant she had to hide it all away. Everything – his sneering, his love, his intentions – would be tied in some way to that nugget of her own flaws. To relay his words and the actions would be trying to run home with a handful of hailstones.

The phenomenon came to be what she sought: one pure unadulterated moment of victimhood. Crisp and perfect. Drawn deft in quick-drying ink. Not smudgeable. Bold lines. A familiar shape, albeit a disconcerting one, a frightening one. But no gaps or overlaps or infinite lines. Wieldy. You could take scissors, snip the proof clean from the story's tentacles, and hold it up to the bathroom mirror and still see it plain. You could go out, step out and hold it up to someone – maybe they were hiding in the hall, biting their nails over why you took scissors to the easy-clean, lockable room – and behind the crisp snipped-out proof, they would not see what you've hidden in your face.

One day she thought she almost had it, this snip-outable, hold-upable victimhood. This perfect tumor would not be connected to the major arteries of who she was, her badness would not pool hot onto the floor if she cut it out. Just Stu would pool onto the floor, just he would become as weak as jelly living in a jar.

Thirteen years before the girl shot the man

'We will, sis, we will,' he says. We are in line at the Four Square. Toko and Kat.

'Will we?'

'Of course, sis.'

Toko plonks groceries onto the conveyor belt: onions, garlic, lemons, onion soup mix and reduced cream. Kat is glad to be alone with her brother. It is special. His wife, Jade, is napping on their small boat, with their son, her small nephew, Taukiri. Toko pays for the groceries, then slips his wallet in his back pocket, hauling the grocery bag up as he does. They put the groceries into the back of his truck and climb in.

'Honestly. I don't get why you are so worried we won't.'

'A feeling.'

'Well drop it.'

He turns the key in the ignition and the truck starts like an animal. He puts his hand on the gearstick, pushes his foot down on the clutch. He drives down the street. He winds down the window; his hair is the longest she has seen it.

'I don't want to go home yet,' Kat says.

'Nothing needs to go in the fridge. Want to go for a walk?'

She nods. He drives out past Jimmy Armers and to the seal colony. They walk up the path and she starts to puff. 'Oh hell,' he says. 'What's happened to the sprinter?'

He runs backwards teasing her; she puffs more and when they reach the top she sits on the wooden bench, where you can sit to look at the sea and the mountains.

'How do you know we will?' she says.

'Because it'll be awesome. It'll be mean, so why wouldn't we.'

'Life.'

'Come on, sis,' he says. 'Let's keep walking.'

They walk the cliff edges and through the high paddocks. Toko runs his hand across the top of the long brown grass. She follows him and he turns back to grin at her. The sky and sea are silver, the mountains purple. When they reach South Bay they go to the water fountains for a drink. Toko drinks first, water running off his lip and down his chin, down his neck, onto his black T-shirt. She goes next, while Toko looks out across the water and watches a boat coming in.

'Your life is so romantic eh?' Kat says. 'Like living on a boat and all.'

'Ever lived on a boat with a toddler?'

'Ha,' she says.

'We forgot coffee. Didn't Mum say she needed coffee?'

'Yes,' he says. 'I knew there was something.'

They walk back across the peninsula, up the hills, though the grass, along the cliff. His breath becomes louder. They walk along together listening to it. She strides and steps to it. The clouds have shifted across the sky. Now it is blue. A small insect hits his shoulder and he bats it away.

'I can imagine us, just us. Hitting the road. Guitars, beers.'

'Don't you worry, sis. That's us.'

They go back to the truck and climb in. Toko reaches across and opens the glovebox, fishes out some sunnies. He puts them on. Kat sees another pair. She puts them on. They drive off, back through town. There's a ten-dollar note tucked under the sun visor.

'Coffee,' she reminds him.

They park outside the Four Square. They both climb out and

go in. They both lift their sunnies and perch them on their heads. They walk to the coffee section and Kat grabs a bag of Gregg's. They walk to the counter. The woman scans the bag, Toko takes out his wallet, pays and slides it back into his back pocket. They walk back to the truck, they get into the car, they put their sunglasses back over their eyes.

Kat slides the ten-dollar note out from the sun visor. She shakes it and grins. He nods. They pull up outside the Craypot, get out of the truck, sunnies onto their heads, together they walk into the bar. They change the money to coins, and take them to the pokie room, behind the swing doors. Toko slides the coins into the machine. 'Lucky Jack, for Grandad?'

'Maxies?' Kat says.

'Of course.'

She hits the button. The pictures spin by and by. Beans, vines, a cow, a gold duck, violins. They watch the lights and listen to the tuc-tuc-tuc.

Five vines, so free games. The free games roll by, and they win nothing. One dollar left.

'Still maxies?'

'Hard.'

A row of golden ducks. Toko and Kat grab each other and hug.

'Too much, Jack,' Toko shouts.

'Yes, Jack,' Kat shouts.

Kat presses collect. They take it to the bar and the bartender gives them ten twenty-dollar notes. Toko slides one back, a jug of Canterbury, he says, and two glasses. Kat and Toko go to a leaner.

'Let's say we did,' Kat says.

'We are,' he says again, almost annoyed but good-natured. 'Can we not enjoy our windfall for a minute without you fretting.'

'Humour me.'

'A night in Christchurch, a night in Invercargill. Cross on

the ferry. We'd get off the ferry, pack only what you can carry, of course.'

'How long would we stay?'

'I dunno, whatever.'

'Toko.'

'A week. Let's stay a week.'

'Just us.'

'Just us.'

He lifts his glass. She clinks hers against it.

'We won two hundred bucks.'

'I know!'

'What should we do?'

'Aroha offered to babysit. Shall I drag Jade out?'

'Reckon she would?'

'She could be convinced.'

They drink their jug of beer and she stops badgering him about the trip she's always dreamed of taking with her big brother and sister to Rakiura. Wanting to go on the trip with her brother and sister is like a hunger for a particular food, a dish from childhood. It is her bucket-list trip. She's too young to have a bucket-list trip, but this is something she wants to do more than anything she has ever wanted to do.

Toko and Kat walk out into the day, warm from the long walk over the peninsula, the win on the pokies, a jug of beer shared, their plans.

'Yeah, I reckon we meet back here later eh. Aroha did offer to babysit sometime. I'll get Jade out the house, off the boat.'

'I'll meet you,' Kat says. 'I'll go see Pare. Stu.'

Toko rolls his eyes. 'Stu.'

'He was your friend.'

'Was.'

'He's all right.'

'Is he though?'

She shrugs. 'Not like we getting married. Just a bit of fun.'

'Stu? Fun?'

'He's not exactly road-trip material, but I dunno.'

'What are you gonna do now?'

'Walk to Pare's. You?'

'Take the groceries to Mum. Go convince my wife to come sit with me while I piss our winnings away.'

'Don't you spend it all before I get there.'

We stand on the footpath in front of the Craypot. The feeling rises up again, that we never will, never will go, just us, to Rakiura. Guitars and beers and ancestral food, and land, ocean and earth. Just us.

'Meet you here at eight,' she says.

He nods and hugs her. 'We had an afternoon,' he says.

Kat walks to Pare's. People are there. She wants to hang on to something, though she's not sure what that is, but she thinks that the people at Pare's will scare whatever it is away. The long afternoon walk and the beer has made her hungry.

She walks back to town, along the beach, and goes to Cooper's Catch. She orders a crumbed fish and half a scoop. She sits at a picnic table outside and watches people pass. She hears her order called, gets her food, buys a pottle of tartare too. She walks back through town and down to the beach. She sits alone on the stony shore and eats her food. The thing she wanted to hold on to is gone of its own accord, so she walks back to Pare's.

People are still there, eating, some drinking, a few are throwing darts. She asks first, then goes and lies down on Pare's bed. When she wakes it's already dark, and an icy feeling knifes her and she can't figure where it has come from, only it is warning her again. We won't. We won't take the road trip for ancestral food and earth and ocean, just us.

Pare bursts into the room. 'Come on, Kat. Get up. Get dressed. Here, this.' Pare throws her friend a red silk dress.

Kat holds it up.

Pare leaves the room and comes back with two drinks. Kat is still sitting on the bed. 'I was supposed to meet Toko at eight.'

'Ah, well. It's only ten. Hurry up.'

Kat is cold, but the drink is strong.

'Go on. Wear it,' says Pare. 'Fuck with that guy's head. Tell him who's boss.'

'I just want to see Toko.'

Pare brings another drink, stronger this time. They down them quick, and the icy feeling must have disappeared, because Kat puts on the dress.

They go to town, straight to the Craypot. They pull up outside.

There we'd been standing out in the late-afternoon sun, making plans and promises.

A barstool flies through the window.

She locks eyes with Jade through the broken glass, and screams.

The moment the girl shoots the man

Pale, pale green. You move to avoid its foam. You move this way and that to avoid its foam. You cannot stay put. It is always avalanching towards you. The telling moves you out of its reach; the telling is the bright green shoots, sprouting up to shelter us.

Six months after the girl shot the man

We wanted to eat together. Kat and Pare. Pare wanted to bring her cousin Hayley. Did we really want to meet Hayley? Did we really need fresh eyes on us? The thought made Kataraina feel distressed. Fresh eyes. No, thanks. But – Kataraina took some medication and soon she was able to think about how beautiful oxygen was and the white sunlight turning water to silver. How beautiful was kai? Were these things so beautiful or were the drugs so beautiful?

So beautiful, to take up the serrated knife and plough it into the tin of peeled tomatoes, drag the toothy blade – across, up, down, across – sawing a semicircle. She folded upwards a halfmoon of ragged silver to find the red wet pulp beneath the torn tin, and the bright fruit made her wonder anew how the inside of a wrist might look, despite having been happy – almost elated, like a plastic bottle bobbing – to be making Bolognese for dinner when she first took up the small tool.

She took the opened tin of tomatoes and poured it into a hot pan over the browned mince, onions, garlic. She threw in some fresh shoots of young rosemary, some thyme.

She was happy as a plastic duck. Her skull was full of air and drugs and promise.

Pare and Hayley would arrive soon. The Bolognese was good to go. She had some beers and wine and Long Whites in the fridge. Those Long Whites, they looked like mimi. Hayley liked them though, so Pare said.

She was so happy it embarrassed her. She felt yellow and sunny and rubbery. A red laughing duck's mouth painted on her face.

The mince simmered. The scent of thyme and rosemary billowed, hot into her nose.

She was so happy.

I wish I was dead, a voice inside her said.

She tasted the mince. She burnt her red laughing lip. 'Yum,' she said.

She was a plastic duck; pull her under and she'd only bob happily and forgetfully to the surface because her skull was full of air.

What's that in her heart? Joy?

Should she feel joy?

Was it right to feel so fine?

Kill yourself, the voice said, while she chopped neon-green chives.

Pare liked garlic bread. Pare and Hayley would love her homemade garlic butter with neon-green chives. It was going to be so great to see Pare and Hayley. It was going to be so good for them to see her like this, a happy hollow rubber duck.

Chopping chives, her temple throbbed and then it felt like something warm was dripping down the side of her face.

She lifted her finger to touch her temple. She brought her hand down to look at the finger. She was afraid to see, in case it was blood dripping down the side of her face. It felt like blood. It felt like the can opener that whirled by her head that day, years ago, had just now torn a hole in the thin skin at her temple. She was afraid to see the phantom blood. But she did look. She looked at her finger.

Nothing.

Not even a bead of sweat.

Still she felt it rolling, dripping, pouring. Then it stopped.

You are so fake, a voice said. *Chopping chives, lit a candle, this house smells like Neroli Dream, what a fucken joke. Hayley will see right through you, with her fresh searching eyes. No, thanks.*

The earth-red Bolognese was simmering and the sound of it was loud like a tractor engine roaring. She picked up her cellphone and went into the group chat Pare had invited Hayley to be part of. The group chat felt like eyes too.

Kat wrote: *Sorry, guys, have to cancel. Stuck on the wharepaku. Sore puku!*

Pare replied quick, but Kat didn't read it because it would be demanding, because Pare was a demanding cow these days, since … She would demand to know Kat wasn't full of shit, and Kat could reply, fucken hahahaha yeah good one you smart biatch. Instead, she turned her phone off, tipped the pan of Bolognese into the sink and rushed around shutting the curtains and locking the doors in case Pare checked in on her, nosey bitchface. She switched out the lights and went to her bedroom and she closed the door and pushed the bed hard up against the door and she climbed into her bed and pulled the duvet over her head and held the fabric tight in her fist, so tight, her legs poised to kick if she needed to.

If anyone tried. If Pare. If anyone.

She'd kick. She'd kick like she always should have. Knock anyone who tried to pry her from this bed into next fucken week.

Five sunless and showerless days and it *was* next week.

And next week Kat had a whole list of things to do. But there was not enough time in next week. And Kat was not really in next week. She was still in last week, which was when she was really still in the week Stuart Johnson threw the can opener at her, which was actually the week she was still in the week that he threw her into a cold shower, which was actually the week she was still stuck in the week – way before Stuart Johnson – of apple greenness, caterpillar greenness, seasick greenness.

Twenty-two years before the girl shot the man

The Sharks clubrooms were full, bursting with the hive noise of voices and booming laughter. We were at a table – Kat and Aunty Moira and Kat's older cousin – and Kat was fifteen.

Fifteen-year-old Kat went to a table and, on behalf of her older cousin, asked the people at the table for a lighter. A tall man, with more shoulders and hands than she'd ever seen on one man, said, 'Are you old enough to smoke?' But he didn't hesitate to reach into the pocket of his blue jeans, and as he did, he looked at her with an intensity she didn't like and didn't not like and then for some reason (his eyes) she lied.

'Yeah,' she said as he handed her the lighter. As she took it, he ran his finger along the edge of her palm, then along the outside of her pinky. It made the whole room pulse. Everyone in the room saw what he did, and it made her afraid of what they must have all thought of her. Then she looked around and saw that no one saw what he did, and she was elated, the feeling of elation moving through her like a cold refreshing river.

He said, 'I have two. It's all good.'

Later, he came to the table where she was with Aunty Moira and he asked for his lighter back.

She felt embarrassed. Didn't he say he had two? Didn't that mean he didn't care to have his lighter back? And did he really care to have his lighter back? Where was his lighter now? She'd given it to her cousin, and where was her cousin now?

She felt a bit flustered then. Her face heated. Aunty Moira was wanting to know why Kat had asked for a lighter.

'For Kaleb. He said for me to get him one.'
'He can get his own lighters.'
'He was carrying drinks.'
'He can get his own lighters. Sorry, Jared.' So Aunty Moira knew the man. 'You can have one of mine.' He put up his hand. 'No, no, it's no biggy. I have two,' he said. 'I really don't care about the lighter.'
'Okay,' Aunty Moira said. 'How's your drink?' she held up her half-full jug. He held up an empty glass. She poured red beer into it. 'This is my niece, Kataraina.'
'Nice to meet you,' the man said. 'I'm Jared.'
She remembered him running his finger along her pinky. She did not look up at him.
'So,' he said. 'Are you Hēnare's daughter? Or Joanie's?'
'Hēnare's.' Saying her father's name made her feel older.
'I do work for him, his boat sometimes.'
'Okay,' Kat said.
'He's an engineer,' Aunty Moira said, nodding at Jared.
'Okay,' Kat said.
'What are you into?' the man asked.
'Pardon?' Kat said.
'Subjects.'
'Science and English,' she said.
'I always think of science and maths fitting together, but not science and English.'
'You can't read much then,' she said, and felt rude suddenly. 'I mean you can't have a lot of time for reading.'
'Huh.' He looked down at her, a look she could not decipher.
'Huh,' he said again and finished his beer. 'Ah, John's here, excuse me.' He stood and walked towards another man.
She'd been rude, Kat thought. Aunty Moira began talking to someone else.

Kataraina looked about for him all that afternoon. Checking, checking he hadn't left Sharks. Didn't she need to make amends? And if she wasn't checking where he was, she was in the women's toilets making sure her face still looked nice for when she made amends.

It was early in the evening when she saw him grab his jacket and a woman who must have been his missus grabbed hers and they were smiling and saying bye to people, but it was too early, Kat thought, for him to leave. Then, as the door closed behind him it was like the bass in the music and the salt on the snacks and the gravy in the halved kōura and the butter on the rolls and the chill of the drinks and the punchlines of the jokes and the dancers' rhythm and the heartbeat and breath of all the people in the room went with him. Like it had all been a play on the stage, and when he left everyone stopped being the interesting people they were, they were pretending to be. It was like someone called *cut*. It was like he put it all in his pocket with that lighter she'd not given back to him and took it with him.

Aunty Moira found her, sitting at the table watching her cousins spin the stupid boring wheel making stupid boring bets about which number it would land on.

Aunty Moira said, 'What's up, bub? You ready to go home?'

Kataraina shrugged. 'Yeah. Yeah, I think so, Aunty.'

Aunty Moira sat down across from her. 'Tell me, bub, what you up to at school? Your mum told me you been working on something.'

'Yeah, an essay.'

'What's it about?'

'Some ballhead, William Hobson.'

'What he do?'

'Ballhead shit.'

'Come on, Kat.'

'I'm not really interested in him. He was just one of the people our history teacher said we could choose from.'

'Slim pickings.'

'Straight up.'

'What you going to do then?'

'Write a science essay.' Kat laughed.

'In history?'

'I'm interested in the kūkūwai.'

'All right.'

'It's been drained. I think, like, ninety per cent of it. We used those didn't we, Aunty?'

'A lot that we used is gone.'

'I'm reading about how wetlands store a sort of historical record. Like in peat, like in the water and earth. That even water holds memories. So, yeah, science in history.'

Kataraina felt he was back before she saw him. Felt the life return to the room. Suddenly back at their table, Jared said, 'Sounds deep.'

'Our Kat sure is a thinker,' Aunty Moira replied.

'I'm getting that,' he said, not looking at Kat, lifting his drink, taking a long pull of it, then smiling, knowing her eyes were on him, his face still upward, like a sun, turning Kat to a vine.

Six months after the girl shot the man

There were flies buzzing around the Bolognese in the sink. The chopped chives were now brown. The garlic butter was sour. Kat had pulled her bed away from the door so she could get in and out of the room to drink a little water, eat some dried two-minute noodles, go wharepaku, get some beer to help make it easier to take her clothes off.

'I am stuck,' Kat told the ceiling.

Fragments of her wedged – if time were a place, places – under and between the weeks and years and days and seconds and minutes stacked into and on top of each other like they were bowls. And they'd become infinite: bowls stacked atop a card table in a junk shop, and the card table was curving under the weight of the bowls of all shapes and sizes – but coloured mostly white, beige, white, white, white, white, as far as the eye could see. Stacked from Papatūānuku to Raki, absurd curved towers, unlikely to cope cradling yet another beige or white bowl – but cope they did. Over and over. Kat stopped fighting between them, because to hear those bowls crash down, towers and towers and towers of time's crockery, would be more than her already-pressed head could bear.

Between bowls there was not really space for a whole human to live.

For some tasks she'd been letting loose the ghost of her. Ghost-Kat escaped the towering bowls to do the basic things that proved she was a person. Ghost-Kat faked flesh and substance. Trained itself to hold things (and associated skills such as not falling into the earth, through floors etc); to toast sandwiches (and associated skills like making Bolognese, cooking whole roasts, peeling and chopping vegetables but not wrists etc); to hold a glass to drink water (and associated skills like drinking beer, wine and top shelf, even putting the salt on the side of her palm, licking it, dropping the tequila, pressing the lemon to her mouth but not ramming it down her throat); tidying up, sometimes cleaning even, (but not drinking bleach or window cleaner); had even mastered yahooing, bouts of laughter and some facial expressions; to reply in the group chat (and associated skills such as making/cancelling dinner plans, sending funny GIFs and memes and pressing the happy, sad, angry, hundy-per-cent emoji buttons to react to people's online lives but avoiding writing I WISH I WAS FUCKEN DEAD); to push the bed against the door; to spoon Bolognese from the sink into the bin to stop the flies buzzing around, thick and fast, more and more of them, laying white maggots.

Ghost-Kat went out into the world to do just enough. The basics. She was basic now. So basic. Her ghost did the basics, and because those basics got done no one really noticed she had been gone a while now.

But it was next week. And next week Pare was coming to see her. Pare wanted to go to a pub, take her friend to a pub for a beer. Just one jug. Just one game of pool. Just a couple of tailies in the smoking area with the *other losers hahaha*, like the good old days.

It'll be good for you, e hoa.

Ghost-Kat dressed. Her ghost put on mascara, her ghost opened the door and said awww hey girl and hugged her hoa and kissed her hoa and said sorry bout dinner last week, far out my puku wasn't good eh and her hoa looked at her hard, and Kat's ghost used her learned skills to pull colour into the irises of the eyeballs, feigning substance in the bony sockets draped in flesh framed with eyebrows she kept basically tidy.

Pare drove to the Strawberry Tree and parked right outside. 'See,' she said. 'Fuck-all people here.'

They went in. Pare said, 'You go outside, get us a table. I'll get the jug.' Pare looked beautiful, and happy to be out with her for the first time in a long time. Outside there was just one old man rolling a smoke beside his dog, a large dark beer in front of him. Kat took a seat at another table. There were fairy lights strung up above the tables. She looked up at them and took a big deep breath. This wasn't so bad. This was nice, actually. She even smelled nice. The beer would be nice and the people would not know who she was. Anyway, she was a whole new person already. Pare came back to the table with a jug and two glasses. She sat down and poured Kat a drink with triumph. She had dragged the witch from her cave.

Another person came out to the smoking area and sat alone between the two women and the old man. The man who'd just arrived had a small drink, an atrophied chest and drooping shoulders. His cheekbones were high and frightening. He looked out the side of his eye at Kat as he drank.

A woman came out and sat next to the man. She had a bar pierced into her cheekbone and she was wearing a high-collared black lace top. She was pregnant. There was a glass of orange juice in her hand. She took a sip, set it down and started to bite her nails. The man with the frightening cheekbones put his hand on her thigh just above her knee and squeezed. He whispered something, and she put her forehead on his angular shoulder.

Pare poured her and Kat another beer from the jug and lit another smoke.

The pregnant woman caught Kataraina's eye. She looked at her with malignant sympathy. The man's hand still clung to the woman's leg. She lifted her orange juice. 'Just six weeks left,' she said, touching her other hand on her belly.

Cheekbones carried on his conversation with the old man about a build. But he'd taken a sudden interest in the two women beside them, and he locked eyes with Kataraina. The man made a noise that came from somewhere behind his lungs. Realising he'd made the strange involuntary noise he covered it with a faux involuntary noise – a small cough. Kat knew he recognised her. The story of the shooting in a Clarence River farmhouse by the small girl defending the poor-poor-good-good Māori woman was told over and over, distorted over and over. Kat was defenceless that day and stayed defenceless against the way the tale morphed. It was a stalagmite, growing from a cave floor up. Looked like earth inverting, exposing its truth beneath the surface, when it was really a collection of material deposited from above.

There were many versions of the story, but in the most popular version the Kataraina Te Au character was a perfect victim. Hardworking, selfless, anything for anyone, took her nephew into her home. Homeschooled the girl too – Beth – when she was not going to school because of the trouble she kept causing.

The pregnant woman and Pare were talking about the last six weeks of pregnancy. 'Enjoy them,' Pare said at last, turning back to Kat. The bartender had come outside, and he was setting a plate in front of the old man. Bangers and mash. Cheekbones whispered something to the pregnant woman and she glanced at Kataraina.

'You hungry, babe?' Pare said, because Kat was watching the old man eat the steaming plate of bangers and mash. 'I'll order us some food eh?'

'You know I punched Stu in the face once,' Kat whispered to Pare. 'He didn't punch me back, just stared at me, shocked. If he was so awful …'

'Babe,' said Pare.

Kat watched the man spoon up the mashed spud and Pare watched Kat.

You hoiked in his sandwich once. Sometimes when things were going perfectly fine, when he was peaceful and lovely, you'd kick up a stink about something. You'd pick at some little thing to *make* him snap. Oh, this one, we gotta hear this one. He was lovely this day, even his skin was cool. The muscles in his neck were not visible. This particular day we were out of town, in some city. You knew it was a city because there was KFC but you can't remember which city. He let you drive the red Mitsubishi and he talked a little as we drove. He said, 'Could you live in a city, do you think, Kat?'

'No. I'd miss the cows.' You laughed. 'Could you?'

'Yes,' he said. 'Sometimes I imagine us going for, like, cappuccinos, or taking cold wine and a salad over to our neighbour's place for a BBQ.'

'Really? You imagine this?'

'Yeah, I used to imagine my own mum and dad walking out their door and waving to people across the street, and saying hey, come for a cuppa. Stuff like that. When I was little.'

You didn't know what to say. The way you felt for him then, so tender. You wanted to cry. You felt so helpless, and sad and then very angry. You couldn't explain the anger either. You still don't know what it was about his vulnerability that brought up this dark feeling.

'Stu, does the farm make you happy?'

He didn't reply. His face looked younger, his large hands rested on his thighs. You wanted to kiss him, and this desire seemed to breathe more life into the wild shadow in you, the anger. Finally he said, 'Sometimes I think the farm gives me ... gave my dad ...'

He paused, and you could tell he had the word he wanted to

say, just didn't think he should say it.

'Go on. You can tell me.'

'Turn here,' he said. 'Let's get some lunch.'

You turned into the KFC drive-thru.

You knew the word he wanted to say. You knew it. The word stormed about your body, prying open box after box of stored hurt.

All morning he had been encouraging your confidence driving in the city, saying turn here, slow here, stop there, oh, yip, watch that, good good good.

You'd enjoyed it. Listening to his soft direction.

When you pulled up beside the box thingy where you make your order at the drive-thru, he said: 'Right, now you can wind down your window to order.' The stored hurt rushed together, forming anger like you'd not felt before. It was as if something waiting and watchful in your belly, some line that connected puku to solar plexus, contracted. Like a hungry volatile sea creature had just snatched some blood-soaked bait.

You said, 'Are you sure, Stu? I mean are you sure I need to wind my window down? I can't just order right through the glass?'

'What?' he said. 'What?'

'You think I'm stupid?'

'You love ruining things, don't you?'

'Me?' you said. 'Me? You have ruined my whole life.'

Then you wound the window slowly saying, wowee gee whiz whowouldaeverthought.

On the road, with Wicked Wings and potato and gravy and coleslaw, you were quiet.

He was quiet like your stored hurt had been. You were quiet like a gold leaf dangling on an autumn tree.

'Sorry, Stu,' you said. 'I don't know where that came from.'

Out of the city already, driving between grassy hills and the sea, he picked up the potato and gravy and opened it.

'Shit,' he said. 'Shit that's hot.'

It was just a moment, but you felt it, an impulse he resisted, like he was trying to hold fast to a Stu going to his neighbour's house with cold wine and grated beetroot salad, and not become the Stu who wanted to know how hot the potato and gravy would feel on your scalp. Your hair, it drove him crazy. It was his boundary. *Your* head, and it seemed to taunt him. There was a road with two signs. *Beach*, one said. *Cemetery*, said the other.

'Turn.'

Maybe you turned the red Mitsubishi and parked at a river mouth. Stu grabbed his Swanndri from the backseat and you both took the KFC and followed the river to the high-tide mark. He laid his Swanndri on the sand so your bum wouldn't get wet. You ate Wicked Wings with your hands and dipped chips in the potato and gravy.

'A city might have stopped him,' Stu said. 'My dad.'

You let loose the word that'd stormed your body. 'Permission?'

Stu nodded.

'It's ugly you think my whenua would grant such a thing.'

After lunch you bagged up the rubbish and walked further up the beach. You had sex on his Swanndri in the dunes. The sky had become grey, but the afternoon remained warm. Gulls keened overhead. He seemed completely alone in the world having sex with you. He seemed to be the very last person on earth. Even you were long obliterated.

Then you both sat in the sand and threw the gulls cold chips and wing bones, as if you were calling yourself back from wherever he had put you.

'I could be someone good.'

'City-Stu!' You laughed and elbowed him. 'We could, you know.'

'What if the city—'
'Grants permission?'
'No.'
'What then?'
'Helps you leave.'
You shrugged.
'What will you do, if I'm never someone good,' he said.
You threw a bone to a large brown gull. 'I might shoot you.'
He looked at you. 'I don't want to be shot.'
'No,' you said.

'Babe. Let's get you home eh,' Pare said. 'Grab a bottle on the way.'
'Sorry,' said Kat. 'Sorry I embarrassed you. I was gone again eh. Were you talking to me? Sorry. Were people talking to me?'
Her injury, the coma. It made her honest and it made her disappear.
'You were gone again,' Pare said. Then she looked at Kat, sadly. 'Remember when you were gone all that time.'
Kat nodded.
'And I was gone all that time. And you were in that house with him, not being you. You were gone. But still, I should have tried harder to find you. I should have come for you.'
'I pushed you away. I pretended.'
'I knew you were gone, though.'
'And here we are. Found.'
'Not losing you again. And you could never embarrass me,' Pare said. 'I'm so proud of you.'
Cheekbones and his woman looked up as Pare stood, taking Kat's arm. 'What the fuck are you looking at?' Pare said, then she pointed at the man's bony hand, its grip. 'Those white knuckles are a red flag.' Then she looked at the pregnant woman, and maybe she was already a bit drunk, so she said, 'If your friends are searching, don't you hide.'

Pare stopped at her cousin Reuben's on the way for a tinny then the supermarket for red wine and frozen pizza. She put the pizzas in the oven, put on the sound system – Rod Stewart, why not? – and rolled her friend a spliff.

Kat didn't tell us the story about the picnic with Stu on the beach. She didn't say to anyone that she'd told him she might have to shoot him. Or rather, she only told Pare. With everyone else Ghost-Kat held still and quiet in the tower of bowls. This tower where all the things that had happened to her, and all the things she believed could happen to her – hot potato and gravy burning her head – and all the things he had ever threatened, but also all the potential good things – him holding her around her shoulders, cold wine in his large hand, a bowl of red salad in the crook of her elbow, scented and smiling as they strolled next door – were trapped together to fester. The people we could have been only taunted, shamed the people we were.

Three months before the girl shot the man

We were there at the house. Kat's house. Stu's house. Taukiri was in the spare room packing his bags and Ārama was watching him. Nothing could stop him going and Kat couldn't muster the energy to try. She wanted him to leave loved though. Sneak it into all his pockets, into his belly, smuggle a gladwrapped plate of it onto the passenger seat of his car maybe.

It made her sad she had to sneak love to people so Stuart wouldn't see it. A focus on anybody, any interest or curiosity in what it meant to live – not just survive, but *live* – triggered him. He respected survival, the craft and leanness of it made him feel safe. Unnecessary things like angel-shaped bars of vanilla-scented soap, faces framed and put on walls, people coming over, people staying too long, people sitting around, people making suggestions or plans – all of this taunted him. Sometimes her existence taunted him. So pointless. Stuart wrangled from her any scraps of intrigue or love she showed for an idea or person or place and using a vicious alchemy he boiled them up to an asphyxiant.

That night while her nephew was packing his bags, Kat was in the kitchen. She fried some secret things and Ārama watched her. Onions and garlic and thyme and smoked paprika and chilli. Then she fried chicken thighs and drums until the fatty skin spat itself to a crisp. She put the crisped chicken into a casserole dish and used secret white wine to pull all the secret browned bits from the bottom of the pan. She poured this liquid into the casserole pot with the onions and chicken and the non-threatening Maggi chicken chasseur flavour, and slid the whole thing into the oven.

Later she put a spoon in the thick bubbling sauce to taste the love potion. It was good. A packet job, but flash. She turned and found Ārama watching her like she was a wonderful witch, and she put the spoon in the pan and held her palm under it for drips and blew on it and put it gently into his open mouth. 'Mmmm,' he said and closed his eyes.

Taukiri said he was starving. 'Far out, Aunty,' he said when he came to the table and saw the chicken and beans with butter secretly sliding down them and the pot of mashed potatoes flecked with black pepper and a plate of white bread and more butter.

'It's real good,' Ārama said.

Stuart sat down beside her. Her nephews sat across from her. Taukiri hunched over his plate of spiked food and ate with rhythm. No knife in his hand, he used his fork to pull soft meat from the bone, scoop mashed spud over it and spear a green bean. That fork went to his mouth and his other hand took his buttered bread to mop up the gravy. As the first hand came down he took big bites of the gravy-soaked bread.

Kat stopped eating. Her own knife and fork poised, steam coming off her dinner, she forgot herself watching her nephew eat. She watched his hands and jaw move and saw happiness or peace or both because one was the other maybe, even if having thoughts like this was dangerous sitting so close to Stuart, who was eating for his hunger only. The meal was smoky, peppery, spicy, sweet and buttery. Rich and unnecessarily delicious, like she was showing off. And for who? And for what?

She ate a little then returned her attention to the happiness or peace nestled in her nephew's brow. He was humming, and somewhere in her ribcage she hummed too. She saw her brother in her nephew as he ate his dinner. She saw her father, her mother, her sister and even herself. She adored the boy, these boys, so much it reddened her marrow.

Then she felt something in the side of her face, like something dangerously surviving was watching her. Stuart's knife was hovering over a bone on his plate and he was studying what it was she found so fascinating. He smirked at the boy and at her, like he'd caught them out in a lie.

Kat realised what she'd done then. The room was saturated. Saturated in the love she had tried to sneak her nephew. You can't hide these things, even if you try to make it so dry and fine you can sprinkle it into the gravy; it seeps out.

She attempted to suck it back in and lock it up behind her ribs. She scooped at it like she was trying to tidy an ocean away using a teaspoon.

Stuart's breathing was ragged. Taukiri was still eating. Ārama, who felt everything, who had spent the day watching, powerlessly, had turned pale. Taukiri, ignorant to the fresh tension in the room, continued to pull the meat from the bone, scoop mashed spud over it and spear a green bean, to take more buttered bread and mop up the gravy. He started to bring the gravy-soaked bread to his mouth, and Kat heard Stuart grind his teeth. She looked down at her food. She needed to spook this thing out of the room, send it flying like a silent scream. Spook it under the doors and through the crack in the bedroom window.

She sat up and she laboured a frown. She laboured a sort of fucked-off breath and she told a lie to her nephew. She said, 'Oi, pick up your knife and eat properly.'

Her voice was shrill and disgusted. The shrillness was desperation, and the disgust was for herself. Taukiri could not know that though. Taukiri had only been vaguely aware of the foamy love dripping like honey from the walls and from the ceiling above his head. And he was only vaguely aware that the honey was getting boiled to black astringent crisps, blunt and heavy as butter knives, dangling like icicles above them. Taukiri looked up from his food to his aunty. His brow, which had been happy or peaceful, quivered itself stiff. She could hardly breathe as he looked at her, not quite frowning. He squinted, like she'd approached him in the street and he didn't know her face. She wanted to say, nah, jokes, neph, but any words she sent out could be turned to triangular teeth.

Taukiri put his bread at the side of his plate.

And he picked up his knife.

And he started to eat properly.

He stopped short of finishing the feed he'd been starving for. He left half a drum of chicken, four beans, too much spud and quarter of a piece of bite-marked bread.

The next day we all went outside to wave him off. Kat, Tommy, Ari, Beth, and the dog too. Stu didn't, which was good because he was not one of us. In a few months we were going to shoot him.

Taukiri got in his car, the hardness firm in his brow, and drove off with an ease that Kat was wounded by but appreciated. The dog chased the car, then went after a butterfly. Taukiri's leaving was not sad, it was a relief. Best for her, best for him. She called him an idiot under her breath – to scare off any residue that might be hovering around her like fire or dragon or blowflies – and she stomped towards the house, numb, but before she made it to the door the dog trotted up beside her and licked her hand.

'Piss off,' she said. Not even a dog should see her now.

Beth called Lupo. 'Let's go,' she said to Ārama. 'We're going to play,' she said to Tom and Kat.

Kat turned to look at her nephew. The colour had not returned to his face – the wind could have taken him – but still he went off to play.

Once, when she told Stuart Johnson she was taking the kids to the waterhole for science, she expected him to boil the prospect. Ignite the fire with a look, fuel it with words that might include: I knew taking the kid would fuck everything up. Might come to: nah, nah, nah, if I'm working here then you need to help at the sheds.

Her hypervigilance exhausted her, analysing his potential reaction to every little thing meant he didn't even have to work that hard at keeping her bound to him. He exhausted her into survival mode. Her boundaries were invisible but real, like the cows he tricked with electric fences he'd long ago turned off. Even when he didn't react to her animation of an idea the way she worried he might – like this day – she'd boil up its potential herself in anticipation. So, when she took the kids to the swimming hole, her idea about the trip was already vapour.

The dream: she was going to bring an old rongoā book on a trip to the waterhole, and search for some things they could bring home and make medicine with – probably just a simple cough medicine or soothing balm from kawakawa. She'd even thought of a waiata she could sing with them, even if she wasn't sure of the words. The karakia she was going to write down and say before they harvested plants. She had even thought she might take them to the boggy section of land and talk about the lifecycles within shallow inland waters – what lived there, what couldn't live there. She would talk about peat bogs that preserved records of time – of past climate, vegetation, even taoka put there deliberately to be kept safe, preserved – that water and earth held memories.

'Memories?' the kids would say. And perhaps at that point she would disappoint them for lack of supporting evidence or knowledge, as her own reading and fascination with such mātauraka o te whenua was siphoned away every time Stuart tried to drain the swamp – that swamp she loved.

They went to the waterhole anyway and had simple, thoughtless fun. Her silly ambitions vaporised. Something she'd done all on her own. Because when she told Stuart Johnson she was going to take the kids off for a science trip, all he'd said was, 'Re-hook up the fences as you go.'

8 January 2020, field study day five, 6.20pm–1.30am

A man set plates of golden-syrup pudding and ice cream in front of the scientists, sitting together now in the wharekai. Cairo pulled hers close and spooned a large piece into her mouth. She was still starving, even after the chop suey, saveloys, curried crayfish. The hui had gone all day, with regular stops for kai. The kōrero mostly focused on the ancestor – what to do now, how to find her story, who to find her story, the wheres and whys too. Where should she rest?

And, ko wai ia?

Who is she?

This they believed they were close to answering. A kuia stood and told the story of a speargrass harvester who had disappeared on the day a British mercenary was found murdered near a river.

It wasn't until the kuia told this story that Cairo remembered being outside in the early hours of the morning, and how she had caught the smell of fresh taramea. Ever since the woman told the story, Cairo had felt famished. A hunger she hadn't felt since she was a teenager, out with her own mother searching for their own speargrass to make perfume. The night before her mother had been reading and she'd become excited by something.

'Cairo,' she said. 'Tomorrow we are going to find taramea.'

But they didn't, and nor did they the next outing, or the next. The only thing they found was hunger. Hunger for lunch, hunger for dinner from a day in the sub-alpine air. Hunger for speargrass, hunger to understand something.

On a grassy hill, Cairo had asked her mother, 'This taramea obsession?'

Her mother had sat there, looking down at the valleys and the dark serpentine shapes of rivers finding the sea.

'I can't sing, I can't weave, I can't stand seafood. Perfume – it's pleasure. I love to think of our ancestors like this. Time on their hands for perfume.'

Cairo had her mother's book open now. 'Says here,' she said, pointing, 'speargrass was edible.'

Her mother laughed. 'Still. I want to smell it. Scents bring memories back. What if, what if I remember?'

Cairo wolfed her golden-syrup pudding down.

Eric hadn't touched his.

'Can I?' she asked him.

Eric nodded, he slid her the plate. She began eating.

'You have got to think of it like this, Eric. Other scientists would kill to be in our position, to be hearing these stories. To be spending this time here.'

Hana laughed. 'Does he *have* to think of it like that?'

'Yeah. Eric, we shouldn't be consoling you.'

'I came here to work, all this eating and talking.'

'So unproductive,' Hana said. 'Unlike your tennis matches.'

'I can't stop thinking about what we're missing, what changes are happening right now that we can't observe.'

'Yes,' Cairo said, running her finger along the empty plate, putting it in her mouth. 'It's a shame, what you're missing.'

Cairo and Hana took their plates to the kitchen. The sink was free, so they began washing up. Cairo washed and Hana packed the dishes into the plastic trays, pulled them into the sanitiser. Put the hot dishes away.

'You were up. Last night,' Hana said.

'Your snoring woke me.'

'Piss off.'

'Nah, just needed a drink.'

'Liar.'

Eric came to them with more than his own plate in his hands. 'Can you give me a cloth? I'll clean the tables.'

Someone at the back of the kitchen began singing. Cairo and Hana sang too. They all sang and sang, and when the kitchen shone clean and bright they returned to the wharenui, to the casket closed not only with a lid, but by a shroud of cotton and bright green shoots, leaves and feathers and flowers; their tīpuna's body in a swampy cloak. They sang on and on, until a woman entered the wharenui with the two children behind her. In their arms, sacking to protect them from the speargrass they carried. They walked to the coffin near the statue of the mother Mary and below the carvings of tīpuna, and they placed three fresh taramea on the foliage. And, finally, Cairo smelled taramea.

She almost cried.

She and her mother had never found the plant. Her mother never weaved or sang or carved or swung poi, and for this she had hunted taramea. Cairo had smelled it for the first time in the early hours of that morning, outside the wharenui. But that was only a ghost. Now the plant was here, and yes, it was. Yes, it was the phantom scent she and her mother had chased, hoping it would wake something in them.

She sat there in the wharenui, with the scent of taramea filling her nose, and waited to see what it would wake in her, what dormant ancestral memories might flood up.

The wharenui was filled with us and we sang and sang and sang.

Twenty-two years before the girl shot the man

We know more in hindsight. The telling intensifies the hindsight, collapses the sequence of time, like dominos, until we can see it all at once.

But still, we can't change it.

Behold him. He walks slowly to the leaner. The people gathered there adjust their bodies, slightly creating an energy that welcomes him, opens a large space for him. Some of the people gathered stand with their arms touching, narrowing, reducing their bodies to pretend they have all the room they need. He laughs loudly at something someone says only to make him laugh loudly. People do this for him. Say things to groups that are really only for him. He doesn't need to participate if he prefers not to. He just is. He's just him.

Laugh again now.

Lifts his beer with elbow out wide, tilts his upper body to the sky. Lower now, brings his arm slow, catches a woman's eye as he does, maybe. All these maybes we must consider from the hindsight we are floating in, all these maybes are a form of gravity trying to pull us down. Maybe he decides then: is she a wink-woman, a wide-smile-woman, a soft-smile-woman or a knowing-look-woman? Do whichever of these will make her think you have what she needs. If she doesn't appear to need any of these, she is not fair game. Which is also fun. Mix it up, look at her knowingly, then wink. But choose wisely; can't chase them all. Don't want people to get the wrong impression, think you're a creep.

Kat's shift is running later than usual. It got busy in the last half hour. She decides to do the bowls last – the stacks of them. The marathon is to be held the next day and it's pasta night. Alfredo, pomodoro, di pollo, risotto too, anything carb-heavy. Most go for pomodoro, carb-dense, low-fat.

Horace uses the receipts to count meals. 'One hundred and sixty tonight,' he shouts from the counter. 'Well done, Kat, bar that mishap …'

The mishap was that she'd dropped a bowl of pasta pomodoro, smack onto the main floor. All the customers spun to look at her. The red pomodoro sauce splattered as far as a four-metre radius, up a wall, onto a woman's white trousers. Only a middle-aged marathon enthusiast would wear white, she thought, then took it back. Her cousin looked mean in a pair of white jeans, but also her cousin would not have looked at her the way the woman had. Like she was useless. A waste of space.

The bowl broke into two pieces, almost right down the middle. The mistake slowed them up almost six minutes, for the time spent wiping the floor and walls; replating the meal; apologising to the person who was waiting for the meal, to the woman wearing white trousers, to Horace. To Horace again. Sorry again, Horace. He was glowering, he was furious.

'How hard is it to carry a berloody bowl?'

Sorry, Horace.

But when all the customers were gone and she heard him open the till, she knew – on a night like tonight – he would feel bad for how he had behaved. If she did something useless and he didn't have much money to count, he held on to his anger, slammed pots as they cleaned, didn't sweep to save her, didn't wipe his cooking area down. Pulled the tray out of the sanitiser so all the plates screeched, rang, nearly broke.

Tonight, Kat knows he'll be feeling sexy. He'll count the takings, count the meals, feel elated that he has managed (almost all by himself) to feed a hundred and sixty.

'Correction, Kat, a hundred and sixty-nine people.' Laughter. 'Good number.'

He turns the corner to where Kat is washing bowls. She has four towers of white bowls to wash. One by one, washing them with the brush, stacking them into the tray.

Horace stands behind her. 'I'm sorry I yelled.'

'All good, Horace. It was full on. It was a full-on night.'

'It was full on.'

Kat keeps washing bowls. Horace doesn't move. She becomes self-conscious, of how she looks from behind. Her jeans are tight-fitting, her shirt is tucked in. She washes the bowls. To wash bowls, she has to bend over slightly at the hips. She tries bending more at the knees, pulling in her butt, tilting away from Horace, who keeps standing there. 'Full on,' he says, still standing behind her. She washes bowl after bowl, and he does not move. He does not seem to even breathe. Finally, she has the tray filled and can stand straight and walk to the other side of the machine. She pulls the last tray out of the machine, slides the next in, pulls the lever, wipes her hands on her shirt, pulling it out, untucking it swiftly, pulling her shirt down. Ahh, no customers, don't have to be all tucked in.

'No customers.'

'You gonna help clean up, Horace, or what?'

'Or what,' he sneers, suddenly. 'I'm taking an hour off your pay for the bowl you broke tonight.'

She spins to look at him, a stack of bowls in her hands. 'An hour for a bowl, a single bowl, Horace?'

'Not a single bowl though, is it, Kat? Bowl tonight, plate last week, the muffin you ate yesterday for lunch without asking. Oh, that little discount you gave your brother when he was last in. It's the coffee the woman brought back because you scalded the milk, and it's the free meal I gave the woman whose pants you effing wrecked tonight.'

She feels ashamed. She stinks of restaurant work: oil, sweat, and food she did not eat. She has untucked her shirt to stop him staring at her arse and now he is listing all she's done wrong. With such ease. With the ease that this list has been all he has thought about for weeks. Her failings rather than her abilities. An energy rises into her hands and fingers; she feels the tower of bowls in her hands quiver with it.

'Sorry, Horace,' she says, then lets loose the clean, dry, white sanitised tower from her hands to shatter on the floor.

She walks over the porcelain fragments, untying her apron, dropping it too, hoisting her bag and jacket from her hook, and walking through the swing doors, through the restaurant, grabbing at chairs, toppling them. Kicks a table leg, grimaces, pushes on the glass door and steps onto the empty street, into the night, not turning back.

She returns home and walks into the house and Colleen is at the table crying. 'Mum, what's wrong?'

'Your dad sent a fax.'

'And, and what, when is he in?'

'He has to do a third trip in a row. Quick turnaround.'

'Why is he doing that, Mum. Why is he going out again?'

'Bad trip. He won't make a cent this time. Needs to go back out.'

'But a third? Really?'

Colleen taps on a pile of paper under her hands. 'These got to be paid. These bills got to be paid. He'll lose the boat altogether.'

She wipes her face. 'Look, this trip's going to be a good one. I know it. I'm sure. And then he'll get one off and he'll rest. It's going to be okay.' She waves a hand about. 'Anyway, church tomorrow.'

Kat nods.

'You will come with me, won't you? You promised your dad I wouldn't have to go alone while he's at sea.'

'I will go with you, Māmā.'

Colleen goes to her daughter and kisses her shiny face. 'Ewww, go have a shower, e kare. How was work? Horace still being a pain in the arse?'

Kat looks at the pile of bills on the table. She sees damp spots on the paper. Colleen has been directly crying onto the white paper that is charging her what she owes for living.

'Work was fine. Horace was okay.' She avoids her mum's sad eyes. 'I'll ask for an extra shift next week – to help.'

'So long as it doesn't get in the way of school. Your aunty's coming to get you. Give Kahlia some company at the clubrooms. I said she could come here but Kahlia wants to go there.'

'Cool,' Kataraina says.

'Oh, you go see your nanny, first. You go see her in the living room, so she can sleep.'

Kat goes to the living room. Nanny Liz is listening to the radio. Kenny Rogers' 'The Gambler' is playing. Nanny Liz looks at her granddaughter. She frowns.

'I'm fine, Nanny,' Kat says, and she sits on the floor in front of her and starts to shuffle cards. 'I'm fine, really. Horace was just difficult this evening. Nothing to worry about.'

Nanny Liz moves uneasily in her chair. She pats her nightdress smooth. She continues to frown. Kat shuffles the cards until some peace is restored to her grandmother's face.

'I need to go shower,' she says, and she stands and kisses her nanny on the cheek. Kat goes to the bathroom and showers. She dresses in a dark green skirt and black singlet and white denim jacket. She sneaks to Aroha's room for some mascara and eyeliner and lip balm. She sprays Impulse over herself and yells out bye, see you later, Mum, to Colleen. Bye bye, Nanny, to Nanny Liz.

Aunty Moira walks into Sharks first. Kat and Kahlia follow with their faces down but smiles, lashes, heart rates up. The coach's son is there. Kahlia likes Will. His friend Tai is with him. Kahlia wants Kataraina to like Tai but she doesn't. Kataraina feels strange. The feeling is about Horace and breaking the bowls on the floor and her mother crying over sheets of paper. Nanny's frown. It is sudden, the feeling in her. And unexpected. She is hollow and dry, especially around her mouth.

The man with the two lighters named Jared is relaxing his upper body; it cranes forward after having held it back while taking an enormous and slow drag on his bottle of beer. He looks like a tsunami might. Something you might watch from the beach until it is too late. He grabs her gaze and seems to consider something. He holds her eyes like he could see all that had happened that night: her shift starting, tying her apron, the pace increasing as more and more customers arrived, her rushing then, sweating, dropping the bowl of pasta pomodoro on the restaurant floor, cleaning it up. Horace swearing at her with ease and with as much ease staring at her behind and with as much ease listing all the ways in which she has disappointed him in the last few months.

The man looks at her like he sees the energy pull into her hands and sees her make the decision to drop the bowls and hears them shatter on the lino, holds her gaze like he saw her walk over the shards, like he saw her march out of the restaurant and arrive home to her mother sitting at a table crying over bills and because she'd go another month without seeing her husband. He looks at her as if he stops looking when she takes her shower, as if he averts his eyes and waits at her door until she is dressed in her black singlet, green skirt and white denim jacket, sprayed over with Impulse, stealing her sister's make-up. He looks at her like he has averted his eyes until she arrived here, and now she's arrived his eyes glow. He watches her sigh and hold a fragment of that sigh in her chest.

He looks at her knowingly. He winks.

He winks at the fifteen-year-old who used to have a weekend job washing dishes, stacking bowls, running around like a blue-arsed fly for a bastard named Horace.

The next day when Colleen wakes her to go to church, she does not get up.

Two years after the girl shot the man

We are under a tree. We are finally opening a non-imaginary bottle. We deserve this. We are Beth and Ari and we are Tom Aiken coming home from a long day, cracking a beer and skulling it as it seethes. After all we have seen and done, tadpoles, plasters and pretending sticks are guns are not enough, and we are sorry we thought they were, sorry we pretended they were. They aren't enough for them, so why should they be for us.

The tree is tall and usually we would want to climb it. Its branches are wonderful. But we pass the vodka back and forth between us. We stand up, and our legs are loose beneath us. The weight of their world has been lifted just slightly off our necks. Ahhh.

'Ahhh,' she says, taking another sip and wincing. 'Needed that.'

Our bellies are warm, our faces tingle.

We wander towards the water to throw the stupid bait in at the stupid mudfish.

'Down there,' Beth yells. A ferocious roar, like the booze has made her cranky. Ari sits in the grass and the damp seeps into his pants, reminding him of how just moments before we shot the man Ari wet his pants. In shame he rummages through the backpack for the ciggy. He puts it in his mouth awkwardly and searches for the lighter. We both thought it would be Beth who would take the first drag, we both thought Ari would pretend we hadn't brought it, we both thought Ari would hope Beth didn't remember, so when he took the lighter and lit the ciggy in his mouth, there was a moment before his lungs hacked out the smoke that we were in awe of him.

Twenty-two years before the girl shot the man

Let's keep telling, we say. Let's not go to the river yet.

The next time Kat saw him was at the wharf. It was raining when the boat appeared in the harbour. The rain did not bother her yet, the greenness had not come. She was standing, straddling her bike. Kaikōura's mountain range was covered in thick black cloud. The boat rumbled in. Kat dismounted the bike and leaned it against a metal container. She pulled the hood of her jacket up over her hair. She waved out. She saw a hand waving back from the wheelhouse. Once docked she could see him finishing up some work.

Hēnare disembarked. He walked to his daughter. 'Ah, tēnā koe e hine.' He hugged her. 'Sorry, I stink.'

It was a smell she loved. Oil, sweat, fish. It was her life: the smell of work on the sea.

'Yeah.'

'Fishing isn't what it used to be, my girl.'

A man was strolling towards them along the wharf. His hair was wet. His face glowed with health, as if he just did a little hard work, went home, ate a cauldron of soup and a loaf of home-baked bread, had a nap then laboured a little more.

'Hēnare,' he called out.

It was the same man who had caught her eye at the rugby clubrooms. He'd winked at her. He looked at her now, too, as she peered out from under her hood.

Hēnare patted his daughter's shoulder. 'This is my daughter Kataraina.'

She wondered if he remembered her, or she wondered if she should pretend they hadn't met, because wasn't there something secret?

'We've met.' He took her shoulder gently with his hand. Brotherly-like. It was large, covered in fuel, more wharf smell. He was young, wasn't he? But old, was he? His teeth were perfect and white, his skin smooth and tanned. He could have been twenty, but he could have been forty.

He turned back to Hēnare. 'Trouble with the winches?'

'Fair bit. Supposed to sail again in a few hours.'

'I'll take a look.'

Kat started to bike away. Hēnare went onto the boat. She biked along the wharf. Then she heard her name being called.

'Kataraina. Kataraina.'

She stopped. He was running to her. That man was running to her, smiling like a boy. 'Your back tyre. It looks like it needs some air. Come with me.'

They walked along the wharf. She felt nice with him. He had a smile you could trust. She saw it when she told him she needed a new job, because she had lost hers as a waitress.

'My boss was a dickhead,' she said.

'A dickhead?'

'Yes.'

They reached his truck. He took a handpump from the back and he pumped up her tyre. It hardly needed air. 'Huh,' he said.

We sat at the family table. Hēnare and Colleen. Toko and Aroha. Kataraina. Hēnare told his wife the big man himself had come to look at the winches. 'Didn't expect to get the big man himself.'

'Who is he?' Kat asked.

'Owns Marine Canyon Engineers,' he said. 'Employs, I don't know, maybe a hundred engineers across the country. Excellent mechanic himself but doesn't need to get his hands dirty too much these days. His dad owned the company before he did, came here from Oz, I think. Stingy as. He died five or so years ago. Passed the company on to his son, almost a bit young for it, but what a draw of the cards eh.' Hēnare's voice dropped then, like he was thinking of Toko. Like he was trying to count on one hand what he might pass on to his son.

'All hail intergenerational wealth,' Aroha said.

Hēnare laughed. 'Āe, you got that right. Whole other world eh. Come on, though. Enough about them, what about us? Tell me what's new.'

Aroha began. She was just starting her midwifery studies. Happy too. Still happy. Toko was working for a new skipper. A bigger boat. Excited too. Still excited. Kat told Hēnare she had lost her job working at Horace's café.

We ate slowly. Thoughtfully. Colleen. Toko. Aroha.

Not Hēnare. He ate faster – he had to get back to the boat. Not Kat. She ate faster – it was before the greenness and she was famished.

Toko and Kat went in the car with her dad and back to the wharf. Toko drove so he could bring Hēnare's car home this time. When they pulled up at the wharf the man was crouched on the deck of the boat.

The man with two lighters named Jared walked towards them a head taller than her father. Bones and flesh on him were being nourished before he was even born, conceived even. She didn't hate him for his luck. There was something humble about him and she admired him for it. She got out of the car to hug her father goodbye. The man stepped away.

'You shouldn't have trouble, Hēnare,' he said. 'Have a safe trip. Bye, Kataraina.'

'Call me Kat,' she said, in a surge of courage.

'Nah,' he said and walked away.

She and Toko stood and waved Hēnare off. The boat cut through the dark green water, towards the open ocean. Once the boat was too small to see, Toko climbed into his father's car. 'Kat,' he said. 'Get in.'

The rain began to fall, and Kat imagined Jared's skin with rain on it.

One year before the girl shot the man

They hadn't had a fight for a while. Maybe the dark batter of their love had almost been whisked smooth of lumps. They almost fought tonight, though. It could have come to something quite vicious, something with its own momentum. She felt the pull. She felt the force inside her that sometimes made her say something, like just, Fuck. Up. About. It. Already.

Tonight, she stopped herself from *saying something*. She stopped herself from saying something because she anticipated his reply, which would include bringing up that time Tom Aiken made her fingers lift like spider's legs when he thought Stu was not watching. He brought this up because it helped create the momentum that sent her spiralling. She stopped herself from saying something. And it was good. She felt good. Sometimes it was good to stop yourself from saying something. And when she went to her bed and switched off the light and nestled into the tearless silence, no clouds of cruelty bobbing above the bed that she'd put fresh sheets on, she was happy to be there with the saying-something stuck in her windpipe. Even if her breath was shallow for the saying-something trapped there in her windpipe, she was proud of herself, content even in the rasping peace that disturbed her sleep. He snored. Snored and snored. And when morning came and she woke, the saying-something was no longer in her windpipe. She didn't know where it was now.

Maybe in the clouds, she hoped.

Maybe gone forever, she hoped.

Maybe she could always be so good.

13 January 2020, field study day ten, 3–4pm

She trudges north, with her eyes on a lone lush tarata. Under her right arm she holds a camping card table – inherited from her grandfather. In her left hand she has a large plastic toolbox – also inherited from her grandfather – which she has refurbished to create a portable lab. Inside she keeps a graduated cylinder, a pounamu toki, a beaker, a microscope, droppers, pH-testing kits, scissors, a craft knife and tweezers. She also stores some items that serve a more divine purpose: a piece of ruby rock, a notebook of pressings, kākā beak, pōhutukawa, kānuka, kōwhai, tikumu.

She reaches the lemonwood tree. Cloud hides the sun and mountain tops. There is no wind and no sound of the sea. Even the birds must be resting. Beside the lemonwood she opens her card table. Her grandfather painted the periodic table onto it. She has had this table since she was twelve years old. She rolls out a harakeke mat across it to hide the table. It is not a rejection but a layering. The periodic table is still there, of course. For the sake of accuracy, she also sets out a wooden board to place her tools. She checks it with a box-beam level. She adjusts the mat and board, until she has a flat surface to work. Eric often told her off, told her to axe the harakeke, it was putting her out of whack. She argued that it was a ritual, and she always found the flat, and it never hurt anyone to take some time preparing, to engage with their work space.

With her mobile lab set up, she takes a beaker and walks to the edge of the dark lagoon. She plunges the beaker in. A ray of sunlight breaks through the cloud, a lone bird squawks in the grasses. At the card table she pours the water into the graduated cylinder. She eyes the meniscus to ensure she has exactly four hundred millilitres of swamp water. The graduated cylinder has a one-litre capacity. She sets the measured water aside, walks to the lagoon to collect more. She takes a clean beaker for this. She scoops the water close to a layer of duckweed and *Alisma lanceolatum* – the aquatic plant with hermaphrodite flowers. She walks the water back to the table. With a dropper she drops beads onto a slide and gently pushes it under the microscope. She examines the water – and she is not surprised to find it is rich in globe algae. There are water bears. She watches several of the micro-animals ride the *Volvox*. She watches some of the *Volvox* put out new colonies. It looks like the globes are birthing smaller globes. She studies the claws of the water bears, the teeth – it never fails to impress her, this tiny life. These details form a meditation. *'Do you remember that wild stretch of land with the lone tree guarding the point from the sharp-tongued sea?'* she says, reciting what she can of a poem by Hone Tūwhare, while watching an ancient world in a single drop of kūkūwai. The stores of information. Stores and stores.

She watches the water bears until her eye stings.

She checks the water in the graduated cylinder. The meniscus reads the same. Four hundred millilitres exactly. She takes her ruby rock, rolls it in her palm to think. To think magically.

The question so far has been about tributaries.

But, she thinks.

But, what if?

The moment the girl shoots the man

You were either dead or in the dream inside the coma. In the dream, inside the coma, we were all together again.

The dream inside the coma was vast. It was forested and carved with rivers, with tributaries to the kūkūwai and adorned with mountains, and it had weather, snow, blizzards, hail, wind, soundless summery Sundays. It had waiata. It had strum, it had beat, it had salt, and smoke and wetness and dryness and warmth in its many suns' rays, and cold in its many moons' beams. It had ice, which we touched with our tongues. It had weka fat infused with mokimoki, lemonwood, kōpuru, and the furred, fragrant pātōtara flowers, which we massaged over our puku and breasts and thighs. It had karakia and tangi. Demons, witches, dragons.

In the dream inside the coma we were royalty and we filled the hollow bones of our enemies with taramea resin and wore those bones around our necks.

It had a house, and we had a box of matches and we burned the house down. It had a car that we zoomed about in, with the window down and the music up, and a cone to smoke and some Woodies to drink, because driving under the influence was not a problem in a place where we could influence the sea to rise up and wash everything away. We did this and did it again and again. Each time the dream inside the coma became too frightening, too unusual, we lifted the sea from its bed and annihilated the world inside the dream, inside the coma.

It had bowls. White bowls. Towers of them. And after years of preserving their status in towers, not rocking the boats, not poking the bears, not looking the gift horses in their mouths, not throwing stones in the glasshouses, even if the people who told you not to throw stones wheelbarrowed all your stones there and dumped them inside the glasshouses, then put you in there too and locked the doors of the glasshouses so you could think infinitely long and hard about those stones.

They say, through the glass, 'How about all those stones?'

Ha?

'I mean, don't they look fun?'

And after years and years of not throwing stones in the dream inside the coma we smashed the white bowls. And then everything went silent like the ringing silence only heard after many things are smashed.

In the dream inside the coma, there was a table that we sat at and watched our nephew eat his chicken chasseur with a fork in one hand and bread in another, how he would spear the chicken, spear a bean, stick it all in his mouth and mop gravy up with his soft Tip-Top bread and pop the gravy-smothered bread in his mouth. We watched him do that for many years in the dream inside the coma.

You heard a noise, a metallic, stormy noise.

You looked out the window and saw a pair of inky-gold eyes.

A dark creature moved along the grass like it was a sea.

Taukiri looked up and said thank you for the kai, Aunty Kat, and you said, call me Hākui. It was a word you had learned, a kuia had told you about it, and the kuia said it meant mother, but sometimes it meant aunty, because it was from a place where the lines between aunty and mother bled into each other, became each other, needed each other, and when you learned it, you realised how wrong we'd always, always been obeying those deft foreign kupu. But he didn't call you that. It was too unnatural now; it felt too late.

If only we'd known, back when … but in the dream inside the coma he wrote you a song and in it, he called you Hākui. It was sublime being called Hākui. And that is art, you do these things, you use the words stolen from you, and you feel so much closer to yourself without wondering who you're trying to be.

Hākui, he said in the song, ōku hākui.

Our love, which flooded out from you and to your nephew like the rich gravy inside the kōura and in the dream inside the coma and the man decided that he couldn't be fucked with the way your nephew was using his bread and lovely face to soak up all your love, diverting it from him to *him*, and in the dream inside the coma he started to asphyxiate you, so we took the gun out of the safe place you kept it, which was your mouth, and we shot him.

A hundred and twenty-eight years before the girl shot the man

We are still telling, we are still listening. Our imagination and our remembering are a wild thing here, near this kūkūwai. This evening we listen to a man with deep-set eyes and a whale tooth strung around his neck. He is here at the telling to reveal what he has learned, that a woman was returning from a pilgrimage to the mauka Kairuru with her people. They had gone to harvest taramea.

The woman's name was Tikumu. Her mother named her after the mountain daisy that thrived on Kairuru. She named her after something from this land, this mourning land. Because she was a descendant of love found in the brutal war that killed many of her ancestors. Through her veins ran the bloodlines of friend and enemy.

Tikumu harvested the speargrass with her sister and brother for their grandfather, who made hei-taramea to trade. It was near dusk. Tikumu had a sore on her leg where a taramea blade had gouged her. She was hungry for the tītī they would eat at the village, but she told her sister they should go on ahead without her. She needed to wash her leg in the river first. Her sister would have refused to let her go alone, but she was unusually tired and they were close to home. They could already feel the safety of home. Returning to her tāne and pēpi.

She was at the river, rinsing the dried blood from her calf muscle and cleaning the cut, when a man approached her and offered her some peaches from a can.

He stood on the riverbank, and she felt vulnerable low down in the water. No one around. His strange hat and pale grey eyes.

He held up a tin and a tool. 'Peaches, my lady?' he laughed.

Though she was famished she said, 'Kāore.'

'That's your word for no,' he said. 'And what about no, thank you? What are your words for that, then?'

She frowned at him. She had her own food. Tītī awaited. That was what her grandfather had promised them on return from Kairuru.

The man with the deep-set eyes and whale tooth strung around his neck says, 'If my grandfather promises tītī, I get my arse straight home in case I miss out, but those must have been times of abundance. She did not need his food.'

The man with the peaches did not like that she didn't need any food from him. 'Watch,' he said, and he took the thing with its crescent-moon blade and began cutting through the tin. Inside were peaches in syrup. The fruit did not appeal to Tikumu. She was not impressed by his utensil. At home she also had utensils, including the stone blade she had with her now, in her basket.

She looked at the basket. Up on the bank beside the man.

Slowly she made her way up, out of the river.

He set the fruit and the utensil on the grass.

He stepped towards her.

'Aren't you grateful?' he said.

We believe she moved towards her basket. With her back to him she felt a chill on her spine. She saw her error. She needed no excuse. She side-stepped as he lunged. He lunged to the right, but his can opener was in the grass to the left. She sprinted for it, and she grabbed it, and in the second he was upon her she thrust upwards. She stabbed into his sternum and into his heart and his pale eyes fluttered, his pink cheeks twitched, and before he hit the ground he was dead.

She, then, the mountain daisy.

At the riverside, his bladed can opener in her hand and his food on the ground. A witch at the riverside, unsure what to do. She *looked* like a thief. A violent thief. Killing in the name of peaches.

There were prisons now especially for people who did what she'd just done. And what had he done? Nothing. Her intuition told her that he planned to rape or maybe even kill her. He planned to rape maybe even kill her for one of two reasons. First was her being vulnerable and silly if she'd accepted his food, if she'd been impressed by his utensil, and she needed to learn the hard way not to be so naïve while at the river alone. His second reason would have been on the grounds of her ingratitude, her disdain, having not accepted his food or been unimpressed by his utensil.

For a while she sat beside his body, she said a karakia for his soul. She said a karakia for hers. She nuzzled into Papatūānuku and prayed for the tears of Rakinui. But for this man Rakinui had no reason to cry. She did not want to wash in the river; she did not want his blood in the river. So she decided to follow it, through the marshes, through the swamp, across the estuary, until she reached the sea.

She felt split from her world, our world – this very world – her deep and complex world; she was in the shallows of another world now, and it was frightening. She felt exposed, a fish writhing on cold rocks. She needed to deal with this herself, involve no one else. Protect her universe from what happened while she very briefly was tugged to his. She wanted to ask someone what she should do with the utensil.

The woman pressed her ear to the ground. She asked a question, but she heard no reply, just the sound of a horse's hooves thud, thud, thudding, and she knew she had no choice but to make a choice. She closed her eyes. She saw then, in her mind, another man wielding a very similar utensil, perhaps the same one even, she could not be sure. She saw him raise it. He was wearing clothes that were not familiar to her. He was in a room foreign to her, with things that were foreign to her. Water was coming right out of a silver mouth. Red-hot coils. Small doors stuck to walls, polished bright white. She was looking through a portal, a veil, but when she touched this veil it was hard and cold. A kurī was howling, and this blue-eyed man booted the kurī in its guts.

Ah, we know this man.

The blue-eyed man in the room was yelling at a woman.

She was someone to her.

The woman with the utensil felt tears come to her eyes. She needed to protect this woman, tangi for her. The woman in the house with the man wielding the can opener was afraid, but it was a specific fear. It was unlike fear she understood. It was not fear of the single event she was experiencing; it was layered. It was a more consuming fear that came from below, above, beside, before, after and during the event. It was a fear that had been crafted, shaved, gouged.

E kare! The woman called through the hard, cold veil. *E kare! Don't be frightened.*

She saw her own nose on the woman, saw her own hair spilling down her own neck and over her own shoulders. But she saw that the woman had lost a connection to something essential to her.

And suddenly!

The woman in the house with the man wielding a can opener looked right at the woman beside the river who had just murdered a man with a can opener. She looked right into her eyes. But she blinked then, like she did not want anyone seeing her. 'Not even a dog should see me now,' this woman said, but not out loud. She was whakamā. And the man threw the can opener and it flew towards the woman beside the river, puncturing this bizarre veil between them to shards. Broken, like it was broken for good. Like he destroyed something so powerful, so vast, so immense, a whole world had been razed.

The sound of a horse again.

And the woman decided.

Take the can opener. Bury it.

Keep it from him, this man, this man somewhere ahead, somehow reaching her, from wherever he was.

She took it, and ran towards the swamp, away from the sound of horses and the men's voices, and the house with the silver mouths and red coils. This house that was not yet built, but would be, right here; her descendant not yet born would live in this house. She ran to the swamp like it was an entry point back to the depth of her own world. She went towards it.

The man with the deep-set eyes and whale tooth strung around his neck might be crying, but we are by candlelight. Taukiri goes to him and rubs his back. 'Tēnā koe Matua.'

Kat looks at her nephew, comforting the man, who was telling a story that has been living like a universe in her puku, and just now the day has broken there for the first time in aeons.

Our wild imagination, memories, the passing on of pūrākau. Is this not how legend is crafted? Is this not how we raise us up?

Twenty-four years before the girl shot the man

She is at Nanny Liz's and Nanny Liz's cheek is swollen. Kataraina is almost thirteen – she doesn't spend as much time at Nanny Liz and Grandad Jack's lately because she has so much sport and so many friends, and so many boys think she is pretty. She walks in town wearing denim shorts, but a hoodie, always a hoodie in case her brother or cousins see her and shame her out.

It has been a long time since there was a mark on Nanny Liz, because Grandad Jack has 'softened in his old age'. Don't they say that? They just soften up. Her aunties were talking about men in the kitchen the other night, drinking wine, and Colleen said, they're always lovely and soft, and Aunty Moira laughed, get the fuck out if you're always *lovely and soft*.

Nahahahahahaha.

Now there is a mark on Nanny Liz's cheek. Kataraina wonders if it's her fault for not being around so much anymore.

They are sitting out the front cutting apples in the sun. There are some old pots where they used to grow swan plants over there, reminding her of a world they'd once busied themselves with. Kat was watching Nanny Liz. It was not always fun to be near Nanny Liz, but it was always darkly magical. Nanny Liz peeled, cut and carved the apples into simple shapes: moons, stars, leaves, curves like rivers or waves, diamonds. She looked over at her little granddaughter. She held up a star. 'You remember this job, e hine?'

Kat nodded. She pulled her hand out from under her thigh and put it out. Nanny Liz's hand shook as she handed her a star cut from apple. Kat wondered how she used the knife at all. Then she returned to cutting, carving and the shaking stopped. Like magic.

'What's your favourite animal, Kataraina?'

'Dolphin.'

'I'll practise,' said Nanny Liz.

Kat lifted the star. She held it up and closed her eyes.

'That's it,' Nanny Liz said.

Aunty Joanie took the shapes and put them into a plastic bag, with lemon juice. When the bag was full, Kataraina said goodbye to her nanny. She followed Aunty Joanie to the car with the bread bag filled with shapes and they drove away. She took the shapes to a place, a house. 'Who lives here, Aunty?'

'Women. Mums and sometimes their babies.'

'No men? No dads?'

'No.'

'They've come here. Like Nanny Liz did once.'

'They'll have apple sponge tonight.'

'Āe.'

Kataraina doesn't leave her next visit too long. Again, they are sitting on the porch, where they can see the old pots for the swan plants. Nanny Liz lifts the blanket tucked around her feet. 'Look,' she says. 'Look what I did to my feet.'

They are scarred, leathery feet. Blackened in places. Rough as bark. They're crusted like dried earth. They do not look sore now, but they look like they have once been immensely sore. They have been wounded. At first her walk was aimless, she says to her granddaughter. She was just walking away in the still of night from a now-sleeping Grandad Jack. She hoped she was making her way towards water, but often she was unsure. She walked until she came to a wall of harakeke. No fence. No paddock. Suddenly swamp. She put her bleeding feet into the cold weedy water, and hoped a fistless monster would come and swallow her alive.

Aunty Joanie comes out and growls: 'Nanny, you can't talk to your moko like that. You'll upset her. You'll give her bad dreams and worried thoughts.'

Kataraina doesn't say she's too old now for bad dreams and worried thoughts; she lets Aunty Joanie misunderstand her.

Nanny Liz blinks. 'I'm sorry.' She stares at Kataraina. She blinks again. 'I thought you were someone else.'

The moment the girl shoots the man

We stand before this wild noise and its bright green shafts of wild quiet, and space comes into your spine. Lifting it. Bubbles of wild noise and wild quiet rush into your spine, readjusting it, first in your lumbar. The bubbles of wild noise and wild quiet lubricate, put cushion back between the columns inched too close together like toes pressed tight against frightened feet.
 Bowls stacked.
 The wildness is a song and it enters your spine of white bowls stacked too high on a card table in a junk shop. You feel an exquisite light popping and crackling. The bubbling moves up your spine slowly, finally reaching your neck. You have always been frightened by little noises and little silences and little sensations in your body. Stuart Johnson slowly chewing, his eyes darting, his mind searching for a reason to kick off.
 Neither thing threatened you more than the way this hologram of fear played out onto the inside of your skull bones and behind your eyelids, made your spinal bones and its discs and columns seek comfort in each other. And as they sought comfort in each other, pulled to each other, they strangled the nerves and receptors that passed information from the puku to the brain. Now the puku is holding all this information, all these messages, and some of them have been discarded to your kidney, where they've fossilised.
 As you stand there, your bare feet on Papatūānuku, standing before the swamp listening to the wild noise holding the wild silence, one nerve pulses to life, finding space and air and light

between the parting columns. Stuck, trapped right at the nerve's root, there is some sound from long ago that has been released from your puku but never reached your brain. This sound rises up the spine, no longer stacked like white bowls not leaving enough space for a person to live, and rises and rises and then on, reaching the place of the alchemy, where sounds from the past are transmuted to meaning, and you hear, finally: 'E kare.'

Twenty-two years before the girl shot the man

The man named Jared is running his finger up the edge of her palm to her pinky again. Everyone must see him do it again and she feels afraid, though she doesn't know why. When she realises not a single person has seen him do this enormous thing, she feels relief and her fear transmuting to relief is refreshing.

The world is always brand new when a new thing is proved possible.

Private things only known by one or two, perhaps three people, is how magic happens, and not that baby magic, not that 'let's make potions out of leaves and swamp-water magic', not that 'let's keep lizards as pets and boil bones on a campfire', not that 'let's sellotape toilet rolls together to look at stars magic'. No, not that magic.

This night Aunty Moira has brought the girls back to the clubrooms – to help serve up the kai. They can be the ladies in the kitchen. The team captains will thank the ladies in the kitchen. Jared is here and his wife is not with him. Kat is wearing a tank top and white jeans, torn at the knees. Before she left the house her brother, her beloved brother, why did she not listen, said, 'You look thirty. Put a hoodie on.'

Kat did put a hoodie on, then took it off as quick as she could.

She grabbed the man's eyes with hers this time, grabbed them. And she couldn't believe what she was doing but she didn't let them go. Her own boldness made her feel alive, like smashing bowls did.

Even he seemed surprised by her. He didn't blink.

The world is always brand new.

And then she spun away from him, quick, wrenching her beautiful face (and it *was* tonight, she knows) towards another person.

A tall person with a quiet laugh. Will. Young Will. The coach's son. She is fifteen going on twenty-three and Will is seventeen going on fourteen. She can feel the man watching her laugh with Will.

She laughs too easily, she thinks, and feels foolish.

Somehow, suddenly, he's at her table. 'Moira!' he says. 'How are you?'

'Jared!' Aunty Moira says. 'I'm bloody good. You remember my niece Kat? This is my daughter's boyfriend, Will. My daughter's just in the kitchen, helping. Will and Kat were about to go back out and bring in the hāngī. Albie's just carving.'

'Love Albie's hāngī,' the man says.

Another man falls against their table, stumbling, and he looks right down Kat's top then at her jeans, which are ripped across the knees. He is sweating and his hair is grubby. He says, with his face right against hers, 'Spend some time on your knees, don't cha?'

Kat looks to her aunty, but her aunty is just at that second turned, yelling over her shoulder, directing Elaine where to put the buttered bread rolls. Kat looks to Will, whose expression is vacant, he is fourteen after all, what should he do but hope he can stop himself from picturing Kat on her knees. That's all he's got strength for. He keeps his mouth shut.

The grubby-haired man is still so close. She has no bowls in her hand to smash on his sandalled feet. She looks at Jared. He steps forward and pushes the grubby-haired man just slightly, just slightly away from Kataraina. So slight, not a scene. Reassuring.

The engineer says, 'Fucken cock,' quietly to the grubby-haired man. Not a scene. He seems almost bored. She could die.

Her head is spinning. How did she get so much beer?

'Oh, right,' he says, 'Your aunty isn't looking now, Kataraina. Quick.'

Hahaha!

Behold the man.

Now she is walking the concrete steps of a deserted grandstand, behind the Sharks clubrooms, in front of an empty field, moonlight making the grass glow a pale green like dying caterpillars. That is the colour of the grass below the grandstand as the man says, 'Kataraina, Kataraina.'

How did this happen? she thinks, drunken and poisoned in the wasteland of what he has proved possible.

14 January 2020, field study, day eleven, 5.30–6am

Cairo walks to the lemonwood tree. The night is lifting. It is cool outside and birds are the only noises she can hear, besides her footsteps. She goes to the table she trusted alone for a night. The graduated cylinder and its plastic lid. Covered by a ritual of growth, mosses and leaves. A feather, in case the magic needed privacy. She expects magic, wants it. She can feel the anticipation as she walks beneath a dark morning sky. The world. Possibility, always. Evidence of a revolution in a graduated cylinder. Will it have increased in volume by millilitres, or will it be its own new kūkūwai? Will her table be gone and all evidence of it; will it be swallowed to form a new peat dome?

She dreamed last night that when she returned to find the graduated cylinder all she found was a brand-new kahikatea tree, which reached all the way to the stars. A roost of kāhu, hundreds strong. She comes closer to the tree, and her heart sinks when she sees it there just as she left it. Her heart sinks to see no river has shattered the glass. But still there is hope, she thinks. Still, any measurable increase in volume will be enough for her.

In front of the table now, she does not want to eye the meniscus. Her heart already knows she will not find the proof of magic she wanted. The answer to their question is as plain as the question. No one remembers a time the swamp wasn't here anymore, except for her, and us.

The moment the girl shoots the man

Called now, e kare. Walking now, to the swamp. It's young. Bursting. It is one part healing to one part strengthening. There is a deserted grandstand, you stop walking to the swamp, and make your way to that anti-monument instead. No one is in the grandstand. No one. Not you and not him. It is before it ever happened. No one is there. Just a cool wind. Just te marama never turning her face from us in shame.

You climb the concrete steps, sit down on a bench splotched with gull shit. Water rushes across the field towards the grandstand like a tsunami. Something large moves with the water. Something with inky-gold eyes and an eelgrass pelt.

Funny, though. You should be frightened but you're consumed by a thought. A question, really. A secret question that had barely bothered you before he died, but since he was shot has tormented you. On and off. And you have been on and off angry at everyone for shooting him because you feared you'd never figure it out. The question, once a dog barking somewhere distant, is now shrill. Even here, where you have more to worry about: the tsunami moving towards you, drowning in it, being eaten by whatever that is with bright golden eyes. But still, you are worried you will never ever find the answer, never remember.

'Remember what?' she asks, twisting past, sheets of water sluicing off her weedy hide.

You don't mind that the taniwha has read your thoughts, and you answer her question easily. 'Why he threw the can opener in the first place.'

'Why do you need to know?'
'So, I can hate him better.'
'Will that help?'
'You know, don't you? Why he threw it, but you won't tell because it will make me feel—'
'Feel?'
'Complicit.'
'Ahahahahahaha!' The monster's laughter – a roar – reaches through time, finding you in the womb, causing you to be born with a worry. 'He's dead. We shot him. How much more complicit could you be?'
'Ouch. That hurt.'
'Cry me a river.'
'Your English is excellent for a monster.'
'Yes, our English is excellent for monsters.'
'Low blow. I don't like how your teeth are set in rings.'
'Your skin looks dry. That's ironic, given the circumstances. Anyway, you are right.'
'About?'
'I do know why he threw the can opener.'
'And?'
'And?'
'Tell me.'
'Youse were having a laugh. It was interesting.'
'Yes. Ah, I remember laughing.'
'Then?'
'Then we weren't laughing. We took it too far. City-Stu. I did a bit. Impersonated him. Did I?'
'You're the one telling the story.'
The taniwha glides by again. She has been circling the grandstand, her weedy hide glints in the moonlight, her inky-gold eyes are open wide to the stars.

'You have work to do,' she says, swimming faster now, sending the water into a spin. 'So, go now.'

'Go where?'

The grandstand shifts, as if there has been a shallow earthquake. 'Anywhere but here.'

You race down the concrete steps, to the edge of the dark water.

'Will I die?' you ask.

'Yes,' the monster says. 'You always will.'

One day before the girl shoots the man

We are camping beside a river. The children are in the tent with the dog. She is in the tent with Tommy.

'You don't deserve this, Kat,' he says.

She turns her back to him, her eye throbs. Maybe she wants to turn around and stab Tommy right in his chest just so she can be alone. But she doesn't want to be alone.

'Kat …?' he says again. 'You know that, right?'

She sits up. 'What would it take?'

'What would what take?'

'To deserve it?'

He doesn't answer.

'You don't actually know me. Maybe he knows me.'

She thinks about Stuart at home in bed now, alone. She is glad to be away from him – she is very glad to be away from him – but she can't help seeing his face that day when she opened her eyes beside the swamp, his face flooded with relief.

She thinks then of the time, years later, when he said, 'I should have let you die in that swamp.'

Sharing a tent with another man now makes her very angry. He reaches to touch her arm and she shakes it off violently.

'If you knew anything you wouldn't say I don't deserve it.'

'You don't!' He opens his mouth to continue, to list the reasons he would never hurt her. But she slaps his face so hard her palm pulses.

'What about now?'

He's stunned. 'You're upset.'

'I'm often fucken upset, and Stu's often fucken upset. Everyone's upset. Tell me, Tom, what about now?'

'You don't deserve it.'

'But you'll take that slap, won't you? You'll nurse that sting. You'll excuse it. I honestly can't be fucked hearing what you think I do or do not deserve. You didn't deserve a slap in the face either, but go on, moralise to me.'

'Sorry,' he says. 'I'll let you be.'

'Pfft, *deserve*.' She hates the word. It means nothing, not here, not in this place with clock-in cards and clock-out cards. She knows people getting what they don't deserve, never getting what they do deserve.

How did the world become so devoid of magic?

Tom's breathing was shallow. She could tell his eyes were wide open. She could hear Beth and Ārama whispering to each other. What would they make of this life? Why should Ārama have to live without his mother or father, his uncle, his brother? Did anyone deserve to suffer and if they didn't suffer did anyone deserve the peace that could only be found in wisdom?

She knew what it meant to want to see him cry, want to cause him to ache, want to see him disarmed by his own capacity to ache. It was a long time before this day, this night in the tent by the river, that she'd realised she was never going to snip the proof free of the story; she was never going to find the moment of perfect victimhood, the golden ticket to leave. And she had given in.

He'd accused her long enough.

To be honest she wasn't even sure anymore which had come first: her having sex with Tom Aiken, or Stuart's malignant suspicion she was.

'I love you, Kataraina Te Au,' Tom said.

'And you *deserve* better,' she said, and climbed out of her sleeping bag, took off her T-shirt, took off her knickers, leaned and kissed his neck; and because of her leaning, the flesh around her eye found an aching heartbeat, making her feel sorry for herself, making her need this lonely sex in this lonely dark with this precious lonely man.

A hundred and twenty-eight years before the girl shot the man

In the crafting of the legend, we took the can opener. We took the can opener and ran. The woman, our tīpuna. Back to the foot of the Kairuru.

When dark came and the bush began to crackle and groan with the weight of night, she sheltered under a rock ledge. She held tight to the can opener. When she heard noises she sat up quick and gripped the can opener. Held it up, prepared to stick a belly or eyes, or a foot.

In the morning, she woke and felt hungry. She went into the bush. She found a rotten log and carved into it with the can opener. Inside were huhu. She ate three of the fat grubs and went to the river to wash her face and hands. She decided to follow the river and make her way out to the coast. The bush was thick. She cut vines away with the can opener but this made her pace tedious. As she travelled, the river stretched wider and opened deeper. The banks grew tall and rocky.

She climbed down and used a ledge between the bush and the water to conquer some distance. The ledge gave her half an hour of easier journey before it tapered away, threading into the bank. The thick ribbon of water moved swiftly here, so she climbed back up into the bush, which was getting thicker. She heard noise then, men shouting.

She burrowed into a dark thick tangle of vine and lay on the ground. She clawed at the dirt and rotted leaves on the bush floor and covered herself. She felt a biting and she almost screamed out but the sound of the men's voices, urgent and sure, made her hold her tongue between her teeth.

She pulled up her hand and an enormous wētā was latched on to it. Her skin crawled to a boil. She used the can opener to flick it off. The men's voices got louder until they began moving off up the river. She stayed under the vines and leaves until she had not heard them for longer than it had taken her to walk the ledge by the river. Then she crawled through the vines, pulling her body along until she reached an opening.

She raced across the clearing to hide among some horoeka. The sword-like leaves hung thick and she recognised the largest tree, helping her situate herself. She moved between them, not losing sight of the river, until the bush pulled back into itself, trying to hold her out. She wanted to crawl into the dense bush and make a place to shelter for the night, but she needed to put more distance between her and the hunting party. She went to the riverbank and peered down. The bank was very steep, but large rocks cut across the river and she could use them to reach the other side where the bush was more open.

She used the can opener to cut a vine free from a tangle of vines. She took it with her hands and slid herself, shuffled herself, over the bank and slowly lowered her body down. It was then she felt a person watching her and she froze.

She was dangling between the trees and the bank.

If she clambered back up she would need to navigate the bush; if she went to the river she would be in the open and she'd have to escape to the other side quick. She decided to climb down, get across the river, stab the person with the can opener if she had to. She had not looked to see who was watching her yet, just knew the person was there. She'd always held this skill, to feel things, know things. She'd always held this skill, to push the story out from the shores of the present to the ocean of infinite time.

She made it to the edge of the riverbed. She stumbled on the rocks, fell forward landing on her chest and hands, cracking her chin and cutting it open. She looked to see who it was that might be set to pounce on her. It was a woman. She had long hair pulled high onto her head. She was wearing taoka: pounamu, feathers, bone, and she had a kete, and the snout of a kanakana hung from it.

The women knew each other, but perhaps not well, or so we believe.

Tikumu went to speak. The other woman held up her hand, strained. She could hear the men. They listened.

The woman with the kete dug her hands into it and pulled out a large piece of pounamu shaped like a disc; she slid it into Tikumu's hand. She dug into the kete again and pulled out two blue eggs, a piece of dried shark. Realising something, she packed everything back into the kete and passed it full to Tikumu.

'He kimihia,' she said, to send her off. She promised she would find Tikumu.

She threw stones far into the bush. Men shouted. The hunting party's noises moved towards the rain of stone. Tikumu crossed the river.

Clutching the kete filled with two blue eggs, dried shark, a can opener, a pounamu tool shaped like a disc and one large kanakana she tore into the bush. With the new treasures she ran from Kairuru, the mountain where she harvested taramea, where her name came from, where her placenta was buried, and headed for the dark shelter of our kūkūwai.

Nine years before the girl shot the man

Aroha called Kat. 'Come walking?'

We often wanted to walk together, out under the sky, to shores and banks, up hills, mountains even. Yet we weren't the people printed on the tramping brochures, promoting our land. No Kathmandu shirts, no neon headbands, no Nordic walking sticks. We wore sneakers and three-stripe Warehouse leggings and baggy T-shirts with Bob Marley emblazoned on them. Barefoot with league stubbies. We weren't on the brochures, but we were the great outdoors. We were the very whenua.

Aroha called Kat. 'Come walking?'

Taukiri was home from school because he had punched a kid in the arm the day before. Aroha wanted to take him to the saltmarsh. That was before, when he lived there with Aroha, the aunty he called māmā. His father's twin sister.

'I'm picking you up,' Aroha said, and hung up the phone before her sister could say no.

It was a Wednesday morning and Kat was hungover. Yesterday their brother would have had a birthday, maybe even a party. Aroha had had a birthday, but no party. Without Toko, without her precious twin, it seemed pointless. Aroha felt bad. She should try, for Taukiri at least – or that's what she said to Kat on the phone.

'It's not right. That we don't talk about him to Tauk, that we don't make one day all about his pāpā. It's not right that I don't muster some energy for him on his father's birthday.'

Kat had sat silent on the phone. Her head spinning.

She celebrated his birthday. Every year since Toko was killed, when his birthday rolled around, Stuart Johnson came home with a crate and hugged her. He usually called Colleen and Hēnare too. Nanny Liz came with them once, but she became agitated in Stuart Johnson's house. Several times Colleen and Hēnare came for dinner, usually roast. Usually, Kat and Colleen would argue. The valley between them scooped deeper and wider with the words they said. It often started because someone would mention Tauk's māmā. Usually, it was Stuart who would mention Jade, like last night when he said, 'Kat thinks she might know where Jade is.'

Her name always startled Colleen. Each year she seemed surprised Stuart would bring her up at all; each year she seemed surprised her daughter would still be looking for her. Colleen would reach for her handbag, take out the pounamu beads.

Kataraina would huff and roll her eyes, and drink. 'God forbid, god forbid we mention her bloody name.'

'I could go my whole life ...'

'Good, good, leave it then.'

'But I won't. Why are you still looking?'

'Because we need her.'

'Ha!'

'Why are you so hateful?'

'Have some compassion.'

'Me?'

'You antagonise me.'

'How so?'

'Jade this, Jade that.'

'I didn't ... I mean, for fuck's sake ...'

Kat was trying to remember how Jade's name had been brought up. She was already a bit drunk by then. Stuart stayed quiet,

Hēnare looked at him.

Hēnare said, 'She didn't bring her up, love.'

'No, but you did, you do, all the time. She's the last thing we need,' Colleen said.

'Taukiri calls Aroha "Mum",' Kat replied.

'And? There's no shame in it, she's his mum, now. There's no shame.'

'I know, it's fine. But, there's still Jade.'

'You know what? I don't care – you keep on searching. Search your heart out, Kataraina, but she's gone. She doesn't care. She's gone.'

'I don't believe that's true.'

The next morning Stuart kissed Kataraina and said, 'I'm proud of you for standing up to your mother.'

'No more dinners,' Kat said.

'If that's what you want.' Snip, snip.

When Aroha called, Kat was still in bed. Stuart had even brought her Panadol, a glass of water and a cup of coffee. He was often gentle with her after she had been engaged in conflict with other people. Supportive. He validated her feelings. In bed that night after Hēnare and Colleen had gone, she'd said, 'How can she not care?'

And he'd said, 'It's cruel.'

Kataraina had cried, and he'd patted her back. Together they sat and contemplated this cruelty, Colleen's callousness. It was a cruelty they could navigate their way towards and away from. And together they scrutinised this cruelty.

It was the safest cruelty they could investigate together, so that's what they did. They poked and prodded and dissected it. They judged it. And although Kataraina cried, it was a beautiful relief, this space between them and cruelty, crying over cruelty that could be held at arm's length was almost luxurious. Over there, Colleen's face was stony and her thoughts un-Christian, and over here they were sitting on a bed hushing and wishing. Over here, they were comforting each other.

He was holding space like Hēnare would, like Toko would, like a good man does.

Maybe Jade was never coming back, Stuart Johnson must have thought. Jade was never coming back, Stuart Johnson must have thought. Such a perfect person for Kataraina to love, he might have thought. A disappointment, a ghost, a good-for-nothing … Such a perfect person for his woman – his woman who seemed hellbent on loving people – to love.

'It's okay, baby,' he said. 'No more dinners eh, no more dinners with your mum for a while.'

But that was last night. Today was a new day. Stuart came back into the bedroom after Kat put down the phone. Kat lifted her hand to her forehead and shook it.

'Who was that?' he said.

'Aroha. She wants to take Taukiri walking.'

'He should be at school.'

'He's in trouble.'

'So, she's rewarding him by taking him out?'

'Don't start.'

'Hey, hey, hey,' he said. 'I'm the one who has to sit around and listen to you whinge about all the ways your family can't get their shit together.'

'Hang on,' she said. 'Just hold up.'

'Nah, it's true. It's true, all the time. Taukiri's in trouble for this, Aroha's struggling with that, you and your bloody mother. I mean, give me a break.'

'I told her no, all right. I told her I'm not up to it.'

'Yeah, 'cause if you are up for a walk you know I got three cows bloody over at Aiken's again. I could use a hand here.'

'You thought I should rest today—'

'That's when you weren't well. But if you are well—'

'I'll tell her.'

There was the sound of the car. Aroha was already here. Stuart marched out. Kat could hear Aroha say hello to him, and him growling a hello back.

'Oh,' he said. 'Happy birthday for yesterday.'

'Thanks, Stu,' Aroha said. 'How's Kat?'

'Under the weather, hungover. Had another fight with your mum last night.'

Suddenly there was Taukiri at her bedroom door. The nine-year-old grinned at her. 'I'm in trouble again, Aunty.'

Kat patted her bed. 'Come here.'

He sat down. 'Mum's taking me to the saltmarsh.'

'You know …' she stopped herself, then let herself go. 'You know … you can call her *aunty* again if you want. Being an aunty is a beautiful thing. We are all so lucky to be your aunties.'

Taukiri stared at Kataraina. He cocked his head. He looked at the empty beer bottle on her nightstand. 'I punched a kid in the face,' he said.

'Taukiri! Aroha said it was in the arm.'

'It was in the face.'

'Why would you do that?'

'He pissed me off. Mum said I'm like you. You're just like your Aunty Kat, she said.'

'I've never punched anyone in the face.'

'But you want to,' he said. 'Do you?'

Kataraina climbed out of bed and chucked on a hoodie.

Taukiri looked at her shorts. 'Are those my dad's Warriors shorts?'

'Yip,' she said, brushing her long dark hair then. 'Your māmā gave them to me. Your māmā Jade gave them to me.' She put the brush down, pulled her hair into a low ponytail and pulled on a pair of Stuart's work socks. 'I'm going to find her, neph. I miss her and I love her, and I want her back home with us.'

Taukiri balled his fists.

There was Stuart in the doorway then. 'Kat,' he said.

'Come on, neph,' she said. 'We got some cows to find before we go to the saltmarsh. We got some mahi to do first, boy. You don't go round punching kids then go on little excursions with your soft-arse aunty … māmā. Aunty Māmā! Now that's what you should call her. Feels too late for hākui eh. But come on, *Aunty Māmā* is gold. You help me round up these cows and then we can go to the saltmarsh. Go get Aunty Māmā, go tell her, tell her I said so.'

She walked past Stuart, brushing him, still standing in the doorway. 'First things first,' she said. 'Cows.'

The outdoors. The three of us walked across the paddocks until we found the section of fence the cows kept breaking through. It was close to the boggy land, once a swamp, but now it was just boggy land.

Kat saw Tom Aiken pulling tools off his four-wheeler.

She waved out. Aroha waved too. Taukiri ran over to him. 'Tom, Tommy!' he said.

'Buddy,' he said. 'No school today?'

'I punched a kid.'

Tom frowned at him. 'Not good, buddy,' he said. 'Here,' he handed him a toolbox. 'Take this.'

Kat said to Tom, 'You don't need to fix this again.'

'Well, it's our fence, I guess. No matter how bloody well I fix it up, it falls apart. I dunno eh. Maybe it's haunted.'

'A haunted fence?' Taukiri said, leaning slightly towards the fence, frowning. 'Haunted?'

Aroha said, 'Kat nearly died here.'

We fell quiet, in the paddock, at the fenceline between Tom Aiken's and Stuart Johnson's, close to boggy land that had once been the centre of an expansive wetland. Maybe a hundred years ago eels swam right where we stood. Weeds grew. Perhaps there was once a tree here, a tall kahikatea, and maybe sometimes a kāhu sat in it and peered across the swamp, looking for silver eyes close to the surface of the black water.

Tom said, 'Let's just fix the fence once more eh. One more time. Good skill for our boy to learn.'

There were dark clouds clinging to the ranges. A wind swept over the paddocks and pushed against us standing at the broken fence. Kat saw the cows Stuart had sent her out to round up. Tom's dog, Lupo, was useless. But we got the cows over on Johnson's farm before we started with the fence.

Tommy and Kat knew the wire would be sagging down like stretched guitar strings within a month. There'd be no reason for them to lose their purpose, to become pliable as a silver chain necklace. It was the chaos here. You didn't know what you were looking at, you didn't know what you were doing.

Taukiri said, hammering the dirt rather than the nail Tommy told him to hit, 'How did you almost die here, Aunty?'

Two years after the girl shot the man

We go out, searching for them. The children. By torchlight we see movement near the water, and the sound of crying. We hear us crying.

It is Jade, finally, who finds the movement in herself – this woman who likes to lounge, and rest, all because of a memory of returning from sea and not feeling the ground beneath her feet properly – and runs. Taukiri, too. Mother and son towards the children, again and again, just like in the old story: the mother and son arriving to the house to help us shoot him.

Kat finds herself stilled, as if by starlight. She listens to them crying. Beth and Ārama.

Have they ever cried so loudly and if they haven't why has that not worried us? Why have we been so comforted by plasters, guns imagined from sticks, luminous toetoe in the air above their heads. Tadpoles, *tadpoles!*

Kat watches as Taukiri and Jade reach the drunk children. Their bellies hurting and heads swimming.

At home, at the house we share near the swamp, we wash them like they're babies – vomit from their chins and necks – and we put them in clean cotton, and we comb their wet hair. When they fall asleep on the couches we do not move; not even Kat is caught up in her incessant need to walk away from us and busy her hands. We sit near them as they sleep, pale and unwell with not just vodka-spiked water and a single cigarette but our insistence on pretending too. And that night we begin telling. It enters their sleep, and we talk all night. We ask, what should we do, then, if pretending is clearly not working?

    Clearly, we say.

    What then?

    Are they not too young to hear?

    Clearly, we laugh.

    Still, let the telling crack this open, let it tell us who we are, beginning here, with Kataraina.

Twenty-two years before the girl shot the man

She didn't know what she was looking at, across there, through the trees, away from Jared and his truck and his bored voice, saying dangerous things. It was discombobulating to listen to someone who seemed bored with their own destructiveness. It made her nauseous.

'Why apple juice?' Kat said and opened the door quickly to vomit the sweet juice onto the grass. She climbed out of the car. Aroha's bellbottoms swept up some of the vomit. She picked up a stick and smacked it against his window. Close by a farmhouse light was on.

She used the skin of car light to launch herself into a web of vines off the road.

He called out, 'I will take you home. I'm sorry, Kataraina.' But he still sounded bored.

A car came closer. She was drawn to something, but she wasn't sure what it was. What it was she was looking at.

He called to her, but she ran through the bush, and came up out on farmland. Johnson's land. What was she looking at? A lake? A puddle?

The sea?

The moon?

A woman?

It was a tree, bending and leaning across a ditch like it was praying. She walked closer, and the ground became boggy, and Aroha's bellbottoms were soaked and muddy and started to drag her down. She could hear light watery noises, like dripping or whispers in caves. It took her some time to get to the tree that she'd mistaken for a woman. It was a broadleaf, and it was not leaning over a ditch but a small swamp. She could see it all now. There were large glossy leaves winding over the broadleaf and around it like a cloak. The branches were thick and flat and heavy and inviting. The darkness and the dampness were refreshing, and weighty in a comforting way. She took big breaths of heavy rich oxygen, right into her belly. She looked up and saw the moon.

No one knew where she was, and suddenly she felt fresh and alive. Like her brain had been rinsed clean of scum. Of a sticky scum, of the anaemic greenness. Here, this small swamp, green but a better shade, was so dense it was almost black. She took in breath after breath of cold, damp, rich oxygen, until her heart was sitting supple and fine in her chest.

She climbed onto the branch. Now she was right up, it was easier to see what it was she was looking at. It was clear and plain and fine. From afar it could have been any one of the things she'd thought it was: river, puddle, lake, cloud. Upon it now, up close, there was no confusion. She took off her shoes and threw them onto the grass, and she sat down on a branch. She started to hum waiata. She didn't want to spook away the peaceful feeling that had settled on her, so she didn't use kupu, she just hummed.

She thought she saw a star fall out of the sky. She wished for the night to stay forever. It was so lovely to not feel accused by the sun. She kept humming, looking down into the dark water. She saw her face, her sister's bone heru in her hair. She didn't feel ashamed. She felt sorry, a bit silly, but not ashamed. Then there was a flash in the water, a movement or bulge like when wind fills a sheet and falls away. What was it that had pushed up against the surface?

She saw something golden and blacker than the water. It blinked. She screamed – not loudly though, nor sharp enough – but she wished she hadn't made a noise. Somewhere a dog barked.

Kat stood up on the branch. She wasn't afraid. She just wanted to see. She just wanted to see the eye again. It had looked right at her. Golden and peaceful. Knowing.

She searched the water. She decided to go further up the branch. Out of the corner of her eye, she thought she saw another star fall out of the sky and right into the swamp. She spun and Aroha's heavy bellbottoms caught around a knot on the branch. She went to lift her leg, and she slipped, knocking her head against the tree trunk as she tumbled. She was dazed when she hit the cold water, but she was not afraid. The water was perfect, cold and heavy like a damp cloth on a hot head.

The water was perfect.

No need to splash, no need to fight. The inky-gold eye was looking at her then. She touched its skin, covered in eelgrass. The thing pushed her to the edge and it made a strange noise, a deep and tormented but beautiful noise. There was no need to splash, no need to fight.

How Stuart Johnson, the farmer's son, found Kataraina Te Au is a rusted hook in our bodies.

She remembers first feeling the grass beneath her, then the sound of his four-wheeler, his gumboots, then him, then his mouth, then his yelling, then him saying her name, then him shouting, 'Come on, come on.'

But the story as he told it, as it was printed in the *Kaikōura Star* (with his photograph), as it came to be accepted, even in a sort of defeated way by Kataraina, was that he heard her scream, the strangest most desperate scream he'd ever heard. 'Metallic, I dunno, like stormy?' the young man called Stuart Johnson told the paper, which would come to be the most poetic and true thing he would ever say in his life.

'Yeah, like metallic, like stormy. But a scream, no doubt in my mind. It was her scream.' And he leapt out of his bedroom window, onto his dad's four-wheeler and found her face down in the water, blood spilling from a gash in her temple.

He pulled her out of the water, and he gave her mouth-to-mouth, and she coughed, and when she opened her eyes she said, *golden eyes*, and this he forgave, because she was so dazed. But when she finally opened her mouth a second time – warm and dry and back at his house, his father's house, waiting for Colleen and Hēnare to arrive – he expected she was about to say what he was dying to hear, she looked at him, her mouth open, and she patted her head, and she said, *my sister's heru!*

'You must be so grateful,' people said to us. Colleen would cry and pull the pounamu rosary beads through her fingers, beads the colour of the weedy swamp.

'So grateful,' Colleen would say. 'I can never repay him. I won't ever forget. I won't ever stop counting our blessings. Never.'

Six weeks before the girl shot the man

We are at the river. We float in the cold water, facing each other. Ārama and Beth. Django and Monsieur Candie. Django and Broomhilda. Django and King Schultz. Pretending. It is good for us to pretend. And we are sitting, too, on the bank watching. Tommy and Kat. A chilly bin between us. There is the house in the distance. It is Christmas Day.

Kat and Tommy want to have sex together, perhaps (we think to ourselves) in his truck or shed, but we are pretending we don't want to have sex with each other because that is what we do now. Pretend. Even without the sex, it is still lovely to talk about the fish we nearly caught, the book we couldn't finish, the new song we almost learned, the leek-and-potato soup recipe we might try, all the other things we don't do. And the best we can ever manage is say, 'All right, piss off already, would ya?'

None of this is pretending. The only thing that is pretending is the not having sex.

This day we are sitting together, drinking beer and watching little Beth and little Ari play. Kat says, 'Beth is going to grow up to be a problem. Things she says, jeez.'

'And one day you'll get a call from Ari asking you to come bail him out of jail because he's peacefully protested the theft of more land. He'll call you.'

'And I'll call you for a loan.'

'You won't need my money.'

'Ha.'

Tommy squeezes her leg. That's not pretending. The only thing that's pretending is his not kissing her. Her not kissing him.

We smile without teeth. That's pretending. The muscle on her leg tenses and he takes his hand away. This is also pretending.

The birds above them stitch the sky, joining this moment with another.

Stitch, stitch.

Kat is taking the kids to the waterhole up at the waterfall. It's a hot day and she has on her rugby shorts and a white T-shirt. Ārama has plucked a piece of grass and stuck it in his mouth. He's happy. His happy spins away from him in cartwheels. Beth wants to manu off the rock, and then he crashes out of the bushes and says, 'Boo!'

'Wanker!'

'Hahahaha.' We laugh perfect laughter all the way to the water.

Stitch, stitch.

Thirteen years before the girl shot the man

We are on the *Felicity*. Kat, Aroha and a pregnant Jade.

'You need to find our tikanga. For your work, Aroha,' Jade says. And later, in a separate conversation, 'You look pale. You don't look well.'

'It's the pressure,' Aroha says. 'If something happens, you know, it's not something happened to a mother and baby, it's something happened to a mother and baby being cared for by a Māori midwife wasting her time on bullshit. Rituals or whatever they wanna call it.'

We should eat. Kat should eat.

'Eating's cheating,' Kat says.

Kat talks about her latest love, her newest distraction from a greenness only she knows about. She's searching for an adjective to describe this person.

Jade offers one. 'Brazen?'

'Yes! It's delicious.'

In Jade's belly, Taukiri kicks.

And we all worry.

Stitch, stitch.

Three months before the girl shot the man

Us boys. Taukiri and Ārama. We drive to her house.

Aunty Kat comes over to Tauk's car when he leaves and folds her arms. He turns the song down before Snoop says the N word. 'Go easy,' she says.

She and Ārama walk towards the house, glowing bright in the sun. 'He's an idiot,' she says, and hates who she has become.

Stitch, stitch.

The moment the girl shoots the man

We are not there when you step into the swamp, Kataraina. This you must do alone.

The grandstand is already gone, and the monster too. You walk further into the water, you wade in, right in, not afraid of what lurks. Not afraid of the cold hard animal slipping its way around your ankles. You stride through the swamp until it is cold on your hips and you keep going.

You stand on things that feel like bones, like spines. Like teeth and wings and large eggs and tails. You bite your bottom lip, close your eyes and stride forward, further into the water until the ground turns to silt and gives way beneath you, and you slip under, but then you scramble upward and must swim, so you swim.

You think of how people say if a shark is near, you shouldn't thrash. The shark senses fear and the shark thinks fear is yummy. You try not to thrash but you are afraid and even if you don't thrash, probably the monsters in this water can already taste the sweetness of your fear.

You reach a fallen tree and scramble onto the trunk and breathe deeply. You tell yourself you should not be afraid because you are either dead or in the dream inside the coma, and both are places you should not bother being afraid. It is pointless, hopeless to be afraid in such pointless, hopeless places.

Then there is a sound of water being cut. Small waves forming under a slow-moving pressure. A boat pulls in, weaving through the flax and slowing before you. You recognise this boat. Your father's first boat. In the belly of this boat is a secret.

You, Swamp-Kat, stand on the tree and understand what you must do. You must tear open the hull of the boat, peel back the floorboards and let the light in there.

Twenty-two years before the girl shot the man

Jared calls her Kataraina. She says, call me Kat and he says, nah.

And like wow, like what a dick thing to say, how obnoxious. It's my name, it's my choice. I like being called Kat, she thinks. I know my name is beautiful, but to be straight up I like being called Kat. I know that people should learn to say my name properly and roll the *r*, sound the *a* softly, like *aahh,* but still, leave me the fuck alone and call me Kat. I like Kat.

Swamp-Kat has climbed aboard her father's boat and she has walked down to the small mess, and fifteen-year-old Kat is in the mess and she is making her pāpā lunch today because Colleen has the flu. Kat is making her pāpā chicken soup here on the boat for three reasons. First: I'll get out of the house, Ma, make it there so Dad doesn't catch it off you. Second: I can clean up the mess, too, because it's got yuck. Those men in there cooking let it get yuck. Third: Jared is coming to take a look at the engine.

Swamp-Kat stands in the doorway of the mess. Mess-Kat is fifteen years old and slices leeks as good as Colleen slices leeks. There is a small pile of peeled potatoes beside her. The mess is filled with the sweet smell of sautéing onion and garlic.

Mess-Kat is thinking: Wow, I mean, rude! I like being called Kat. I don't like being called Kataraina. Who does he think he is with his big boots and his stupid slow strides. She hears a noise up in the wheelhouse.

Jared's here. She picks up the oil can and looks at her face in its reflection. She washes her hands. Tucks her T-shirt into her jeans, untucks it.

Tucks it.

I said call me Kat, she says to the leek, shaking the leek. I said call me Kat, she says to the pot, slamming the pot. I said call me Kat, she says to the chicken carcass, sticking her hand up its arse, pulling out the gizzards.

There is a stomping and then there is her pāpā. 'Spoiling me eh. Make sure you take plenty home for your mum and nanny. Just got off the phone with her and she sounds awful. You finish here and get home to her, kare.'

Her pāpā moves from the mess door and towards the engine room. Jared steps through the door; he's hunched so he can fit inside the boat. 'Lunch smells good, Kataraina.' He taps the doorway with his hand, a hand with flesh enough for two people's hands. She opens her mouth and she almost closes it, then she tells him straight, 'I said call me Kat.'

'All right then, *Kat*. Anything you want.'

He follows Hēnare.

Swamp-Kat watches Mess-Kat make the soup then clean the kitchen. This guy eh, anything you want. Ha. This guy. So full of himself. Wonder where he lives eh, like I just can't help but wonder. His bed must be huge. His bed must be enormous. This guy eh. Such a fucking blowhard.

Swamp-Kat sits in the small booth seat behind Mess-Kat. Swamp-Kat whispers, 'Kat.' Mess-Kat does not react; she washes a chopping board. Swamp-Kat whispers, 'Kat, don't.' Swamp-Kat puts her wet head in her hands and says, 'Kat, stop it.'

Mess-Kat does not react in any way, not a flinch, not a jump, not a startled look on her face for even a fleeting second. But Swamp-Kat knows she can hear her because she remembers hearing her, she remembers making this soup and having these thoughts, and she remembers hearing herself say to herself, 'Kat, don't. Kat, stop it.' And she remembers hearing herself say to herself, 'Stop what?'

The mess is clean and bright. Mess-Kat turns down the pot of soup to simmer. Then she turns it off and sits for a while to let it cool, and ladles some into an ice-cream container to take home for Ma and Nanny Liz. She goes to the stairs and suddenly there beside her is Jared. This close, this near, in this tiny space, he seems both smaller and larger. He's smaller because this close, this near she can see smaller things about him: his eyelashes, a soft line between his brows, a small tattoo – a name, *Lana* – on his wrist. He seems larger because he stares down at her.

'You first, Kat,' he says, and lifts his chin to the narrow staircase. Then his hand is suddenly on her lower back, and then it is gone before she has registered it was there. Like maybe it wasn't even? And though she spins to look at him and tell him off, he's just sort of smiling, and he's just sort of strangely comforting to look at, and she feels warm where his hand either was or wasn't. She steps onto the stairs, and she walks up them, and he waits at the bottom. Not a sound behind her until she is all the way up.

Swamp-Kat is standing beside him now at the bottom of the stairs, and she is older and she is drenched. Her hair is wet and it is knotted up with swamp weed. She says, 'Jared, don't,' and even as she wonders if he hears her, she knows he doesn't. Her heart as greedy as his, only hears what it wants.

Swamp-Kat goes back into the mess and sits. She stays sitting there a long time. Unsure what to do, unsure why she's here. It doesn't matter though. She is either dead or in the dream inside the coma, so whatever. She should just stay here, let them turn the machines off. Let them. Switch them off, you cunts, she yells. Still her heart makes the graph spike.

Then her dad is in the mess.

He looks tired. He has engine oil on his arms and face. He puts the pot back on the hob and heats it until the soup bubbles.

Swamp-Kat watches him. He takes a big bowlful of steaming soup. He sits at the table. Swamp-Kat says the karakia mō te kai with him. Even alone, he makes the food noa to eat.

He starts eating and Swamp-Kat tries to take his hand. She says, 'Pāpā.'

He stops. She sees he can hear her. From wherever it is she is, either the dream inside the coma or death, he can hear her.

She limits her words: 'Pāpā. Kataraina. Jared. Stop.'

He has a look on his face like you do when something heavy dawns on you, but you need to figure out why it has just now dawned on you and why it is so heavy. What is it that has just taken up so much space in your gut?

Realising he has heard her, she says again: 'Kataraina. Jared. Stop. Him.'

He shakes his head, but the look remains in his eyes. He eats, but he knows. He knows now, and now Swamp-Kat knows why he starts growling at Mess-Kat for coming to the boat all the bloody time when we are trying to sort this bloody engine. Kat, haven't you got better things to be doing, for god's sake, *child*, and when he says *child* he looks at her and he looks at Jared with a curl in his lip.

None of this is any use, because in desperation he shamed her, and shame only serves the shameless.

And Kataraina is a *woman*, not a *child*, cleaning your mess, making you soup, and making a man – an enormous man, with some grey hair in his beard – want to put his hand on her lower back, call her by her full name, watch her climb stairs.

When Hēnare leaves, Swamp-Kat fucks the kitchen up, throws pots and pans around, and pours the soup into the sink. She ransacks the cutlery drawer. Finds a knife, slices her wrist, which doesn't bleed, slumps to the floor, screams: 'Turn off the fucken machine already.'

Swamp-Kat is woken by a noise. Mess-Kat is back in the mess. It is dark. He is with her. Swamp-Kat doesn't really need to be here to see this because she already knows what's happened and what's going to happen. Mess-Kat and Jared have run into each other at a bar in town. A bar, yes a bar. This is the first time they are sneaking into a bar, but it's an easy one. She could put her hair in pigtails and suck a lollipop and wear her school blazer and the bartender would pour her a drink. She sees Jared there.

This is how they came to be here, on her father's boat, alone, in the early hours of the morning.

He came to her – she was leaning against the jukebox – and he said, about the other night. And she said, don't worry, and she grabbed his arm, twisted it, that enormous arm, to show the tattoo. I won't tell your wife, Lana, is it?

He pulled his arm away.

'No, Lana is not my wife. Lana *was* my daughter.'

Kat stammered, lost strength in her calves, 'I'm sorry. I …'

He turned away from her.

She attempted to recover, by having fun, and fun is best served in tiny glasses that make you shudder and look like a party animal.

She went with her fake ID and her beautiful smile to buy her second drink in a bar.

When she'd bought her first one the bartender had looked her over. Now, he was pensive. Jared was just down the bar and if Kat didn't know any better, she would think he was watching it unfold, knowing how it was about to unfold. She flashed her fake ID.

'Couple of shots,' she said.

'Can't serve you,' he said. 'It's been brought to my attention that you are underage.' He glanced at Jared and Jared was leaning and watching, leaning and watching.

'You've already served me tonight.' She shook her ID at him.

'I know, but …' He looked down the bar towards Jared, who had turned away now. 'It's been brought to my attention. I shouldn't have.'

'Oh, come on.'

'Your ID is fake,' the bartender said. 'So piss off.'

She could feel Jared watching again and she looked but he was not watching at all. He was talking to a woman. A pretty woman, a woman who wasn't being kicked out of Carsen's Tavern, where no one has been kicked out for being underage, ever.

'You gotta leave, Kat. Take your friends with you.'

Kat didn't go to her friends though. She needed fresh air. Kat went out front to the street alone.

And there he was leaning against his car. He was always going to be outside leaning against his car. 'Leaving?' he said.

'Yeah, this place sucks.'

'Get kicked out?' He smirked.

She ignored him and walked towards a taxi parked in the next block.

'Kat,' he called.

'What?'

'Look, can I say … about the other night. In the grandstand.'

'What?'

'I can't stop thinking about it, you. You, I mean.'

She looked down at her feet. The little bit of skin she could see between her jeans and her sneakers was caterpillar green. She couldn't bear to be alone with the illness overwhelming her. The greenness. She felt cold and nauseous. So green.

'We should go somewhere to talk,' he said. 'What happened between us …'

She saw the grandstand and it was devoid of people.

She was never there. He had never cum in her mouth while saying her name over and over while she couldn't say a thing. And now she couldn't be alone with this.

He opened the door to his truck. 'Just a drive,' he said.

They drove to the wharf. She could see her father's boat, bobbing, just there. Just bobbing. It was a place she felt strong in, sovereign in, wasn't it? You cannot own the sea. They could be equal on the sea, at least?

In the car she shivered. He did not turn on the heat. He pretended not to see her shivering. He did not offer his jacket. He pretended. He pretended not to know what he was doing. She shivered and shivered. He wound his window down to smoke a cigarette. She shivered.

'I might have a jacket on Dad's boat,' she said, feeling ill.

'Ah, oh there's your dad's boat,' he said, still pretending not to know what he was doing. 'Let's go get it. And maybe a hot drink.'

And that was how they came to be here, on her father's boat, alone, in the early hours of the morning.

In the mess, Swamp-Kat's asleep on the floor in a puddle of weeds, a kanakana writhes near her, its snout dark and frightening. She wakes with a start when Mess-Kat comes in.

Mess-Kat fills the kettle.

The man pulls a hip flask out his jacket pocket. 'A hot drink?' He laughs. She does too. She can't be alone with the greenness. He is keeping her company in the greenness. Even if he made the greenness, he is still the best person to comfort her in it, because he understands.

He saw the caterpillar. He was there.

Swamp-Kat despises him now as she haunts this boat. Swamp-Kat can see all the truth Mess-Kat can't. Mess-Kat is buzzed. To

Mess-Kat he is something else. Grouchy, almost. Shy, almost. Very serious, but laughs easily, loudly. Able to fix engines and drink anywhere he wants whenever he wants with whoever he wants. He loves secrets, and she loves secrets.

Swamp-Kat's beside the almost sixteen-year-old Kat and across from thirty-two-year-old Jared.

Don't, Kat, Swamp-Kat says, but sambuca has soaked the air between them, so there's no way her voice can get through. Don't, Kat, she says again, but it's pointless.

Don't ask him, Kat. Mess-Kat chugs on the hip flask. Don't ask him, Kat, don't ask, Swamp-Kat whispers. Don't ask. And Swamp-Kat knows Mess-Kat hears, because she remembers chiding herself, don't ask.

But she asks. 'Tell me about Lana?'

He sighs. But he knew she'd ask. He sighs. But he knew.

And he tells her about the death of his daughter, dead on a road, and though he doesn't describe the gore, Kat imagines Jared's child's brains on the tarseal. A man in the driver's seat, saying no, no, no. His pain injects energy and creates new momentum. It utterly breaks his heart, and he needs to tell it, he must. And it breaks her heart and she needs to heal it, she must.

He has never talked to anyone about this before, he says so.

She doesn't very much want to take off her jeans, but there is something crystallised behind his eyes. He stands so tall and he looks down at her like he is resisting so many urges. She is the cause of so many urges. She is the cause. It's all her fault. Doesn't want to take off her knickers, but under him, below him, his shoulders blocking out the light, she can't see the greenness. If he steps away from her all the greenness will climb into her throat.

She knows it is going to hurt, but not as much as the greenness hurts her, since that night in the grandstand. She wants to be away from the greenness. If she could just get him to stay with her forever and ever he will block out the greenness, he will push it away for her without causing a scene. He will push things away from her forever as if he were bored. He doesn't have a condom, and why doesn't she?

'You must be on the pill?' he says, like he is asking for ID and the memory of being kicked out of the bar smarts her skin.

She is alone in her room now. Is she alone in her room? Her lovely clean room. Is it? And the ceiling spins, and does she vomit a bellyful of writhing caterpillars onto the floor? She does. Aroha is there. Is Aroha there? And Nanny Liz is thumping on the walls and growling. Kat hears something break, maybe a glass or nanny's lamp. You made her wait up, Kat whispers to herself, you did that. And the caterpillars climb into her bed, and onto her skin.

Swamp-Kat assures herself, because the two of them now have this ugly regular sex in the engine room, against the engine, which is so munted you might as well just throw it overboard. Swamp-Kat whispers to Mess-Kat. None of this is your fault, nothing that comes from this is your fault, e hine, you are not to blame for what happens next, e kare, and after and forever, you hear me, this is not your fault. But she knows this is all in one ear and out the other. Mess-Kat won't hear that, because the shamer is a beast, and it doesn't eat apples and eggs and creamed corn or pain. It slurps up hope and the people you might have been. Gorges on her brilliance.

Thirty years before the girl shot the man

We were in the lounge, the curtains closed. Kataraina and Nanny Liz. Nanny Liz had been crying.
'Why do we cry tears?' Kat asked her.
Nanny thought for a while. She looked at her mokopuna a while, the tears still wet on her face, and it seemed to Kataraina she was trying to access a memory, some dormant mātauraka, but the answer remained just out of her grasp.
The child asked again, 'Why, Nanny?'
'To make our people come to us, to signal our distress, to ask for comfort.'
The girl went to her and snuggled against the woman's side and put her hand on her puku.
'I'm here, Nanny,' Kataraina said, but she was not appeased. 'Have you ever cried alone when no one could see?'
Nanny nodded. Kataraina let silence ask the pātai.
'Every question answered,' said Nanny, 'creates at least another three questions.'
Kataraina nodded. 'Maybe our eyes are like the milk bottle filled with water at the urupā, Nanny. Maybe they're the water we tie to the gate.'

Twenty-two years before the girl shot the man

We are in the kitchen. Toko, Kataraina and Hēnare. Hēnare must take another mortgage on the house. Toko stalks the room.

'It's going to be fine, son. It is. Your mother has applied for a job at the supermarket.'

'Jared gonna let you pay the bill off?'

His name in the room. His name just there in the room. They'll see! Then they don't see. His name can be in a room with her. The world is always brand new.

'He's sorting a deal for us. We've been good customers.'

'He's always at that engine.'

Hēnare doesn't answer.

'Pāpā?'

'It's going to be okay. Maybe Nanny would like some tea?'

Kat gets up and makes Nanny a cup of tea; she takes it to her. She sits on the floor in front of Nanny, shuffles cards, plays patience. Nanny Liz lets the tea go cold, stares at her granddaughter. She hardly blinks.

'No,' Nanny says. 'No.'

Kat doesn't look up at her, she doesn't know what all the talk about Jared and the engine, and his fixing, and her dad owing him money is doing to her but it is doing something to her. She deals the cards to herself and doesn't look up. She whispers Jared's name, but with Nanny it doesn't feel the same. With Nanny she feels unsafe with his name in the room.

Nanny's tea sits and sits.

Kat goes to the clubrooms to help Aunty Moira with the food. Jared looks at her in a way that tells lies. The look says he's never done what he's done. And then he leaves with his missus, and the salt is out of the spuds, the butter is off the bread, the rhythm is leeched out of the people on the dance floor, because the beat is out of the music and the chill is sapped from the beer and it's so fucking boring, any room, any town, any world that he is not in.

We were at the beach party.

Jade, Toko and Kataraina this time. Kataraina was sitting on a sand dune away from the party, thinking how boring it was when Jared wasn't there. Toko was playing his guitar – a sound she usually loved. The music drifted over to her, and she tried to cry over it.

But it was boring.

She thought about how boring the sea looked. The whole world was a muted, watery colour now.

There was a woman, padding over, a hooter in her hand. And she sat beside Kataraina. They sat together silently, the woman smoking the hooter and not introducing herself.

'My brother is playing the guitar.'

'Ah, your brother.'

'Yeah.'

'My Jade got the hots for him. She's over there dancing for him. Maybe we will stay and live here forever.'

'It's boring.'

The woman offered her the hooter. 'This might help.'

Kataraina took it and sucked back the sweet smoke. It tasted green and she didn't mind.

'My name is Savannah. People call me Sav.'

'My name is Kataraina. People call me Kat. Why are you here?'

'A boy.'

'A *boy?*' How old was this person, this Savannah, beside her?

'A man child.' Savannah laughed. 'I'm not a good person.'

'Who then? I know everyone in this town.'

'Tom Aiken.'

'*Tommy?*' Kat choked on smoke, laughing.

'That boy. Doesn't need to be *the man*. Where I come from everyone trying to be the man.'

Stoned, Kataraina began to tell this woman she did not know everything about the engine and Jared and the sex and the wife and Lana, and it was good to feel the cushion filling again, because of the way Savannah listened to her story. Nodding, smoking, and after long periods listening she would blow this sweet smoke into the sky, and each time she did, she blew colour back into the world. In one go, she blew the moon and stars back into the sky, a shimmer back onto the sea, mauri back into Kataraina's own cheeks.

Eventually Sav said, 'Your brother doesn't know about all this?'

'No,' Kataraina said.

'Tell me something else about you,' Savannah said. 'Tell me it. I see it, tell me. I don't want to hear another word about this fucken fool. Tell me, I see it.' Kataraina shook her head and Savannah swiftly slapped her calf. 'Don't fuck with me, girl. You tell me something that's got nothing to do with that fucken fool or I'll give you a hiding.'

'I wrote an essay.'

'Yeah?'

'Yeah, I entered it into a contest.'

'And, what's it about?'
'Terra nullius.'
'What does that mean?'
'Land belonging to no one.'
'Ah,' Savannah said.
'Ironic, isn't it, how it was true? But if you said it greedily it was a lie.'
'Far, that's spinny. Do you like writing?'
'Sometimes.'
Savannah stood and took off her dress. Kataraina looked away. Savannah ran towards the sea, cackling. 'No one owns this beach, e hine, come get wet.'
Kat took off her jeans and T-shirt and went down to the salt water where Savannah had become a sea creature.
'Tell me more about your essay,' Savannah asked.
Kataraina picked at the toikupu in the essay because it was night time and they were in their undies and bras in the soft water. She picked at the toikupu like taking the flesh from a fish and leaving the spine. She told Savannah that in her essay a man named William arrives on a shoreline and sees fit to explain terra nullius to a woman he has found, a woman who belongs to the land. She is Hinenuiterepō, a swamp maiden, and though her land is hard to walk on and has taken her thousands of years to understand, she belongs to it and its water and its trees and its tiny creatures.
In her essay Kataraina did what she wanted.
'In my essay this ballhead William Hobson says to the woman, the goddess, "This land is terra nullius. It does not belong to anyone." And she laughs and laughs, because it's stupid, the man is stupid, standing there stating the obvious to her. She ignores him. She digs in the sand for tuatua, and she fills her kete. He watches her dig for food, and attempts to negate her humanity, dipping his pen in ink and writing TERRA NULLIUS, but then she grows large.

So large. While he recedes to the size of the paper he's scratching lies on, she opens her mouth and the kāhu spill from it, the weedy water spills from it, and he is swept up, and turns to a black paper fish, and the kāhu dive at him.

'They dive and dive at him, until he finds the bottom of the swamp and sucks against it. He morphs. Diamond-shaped and mud-coloured. This is the middle of my essay: a man becoming a flounder, and by the end, he is a rounded diamond of wet bones. He is picked clean – the wind blows him dry – and he is buried in the land that does not belong to anyone. Not one single lone aching man.'

'I didn't know an essay was like that,' Savannah said, and she cupped the water and washed her own wet face. 'Always thought they were, like, all dates and facts and boring shit.'

'Mine has facts too. But it also has this. It's mine.'

'Too much,' Sav said. 'Too much, bub.'

And it was only then that Kat saw the wrinkles around Sav's eyes and a grey streak in her hair in the starlight.

Kat began to cry in the sea. Her tears landed softly in the water. Sav kept swimming. She said, 'It's going to be okay. It's all going to be kei te pai, e hine.'

And Kat wanted to know for sure what she was crying about, because it didn't seem like it was over him. The tears had sprung up when she'd begun to talk about her essay, and the history of it, the impetus of it, the whakapapa of it. Here she was in the sea with a woman, and she'd come here to feel sad, and make herself more lonely so she could feel more sorry for herself, and here she was, in the water that held a vast number of scientific facts and secrets – mātauraka – and every question answered about te moana created ten thousand more, and it was the body upon which her ancestors had travelled, finding their way by stars, and it was connected to te marama, and it provided kai, and inspiration, and a place to come to, to feel either bigger or smaller, whichever it was you needed, and people who didn't understand the need for both were troublesome. That's what Nanny Liz said – she used taiao to manage her size in the world. They'd be on a beach and she'd say, 'What should you look at when you need to feel brave and large?'

'The sea, Nanny.'

'Āe and what should you look at when you need to be humbled?'

'The sea, Nanny.'

And she would do the same if what they could see was mountains, and she did the same under a night sky, so thick with stars it seemed as furred as a caterpillar.

Caterpillars were a thing they all studied together. Grandad Jack brought home swan plants and put them in the garden with the pile of busted wheels and the rusted broken-down car, and the pumpkin patch and the corn stalks and the bins marked STOLEN FROM TALLEY'S, which were filled with black sand from the time Grandad Jack went to the West Coast searching for gold.

Caterpillars were a thing they watched together, these three people, in their new ancient world. They watched the caterpillars and they studied the cocoons and they wondered how nice a cocoon might be, but also how messy it might get. Once Kat arrived at their house, and she saw one of the plants on its side against the garage. There was dirt on the garage wall, spilling down it, and Kataraina knew Grandad Jack had thrown the swan plant against the garage in anger. And Kataraina knew this was not something he would do to their plant and their caterpillars if she were there.

She saw Grandad Jack was putting a bag into the truck, and Hēnare was still parked out on the road, watching, sensing something. 'Dad,' Hēnare yelled out, 'is Kat still with you and Mum today? That's what she reckoned. But she can come home eh?'

Grandad Jack looked at the little girl looking at the ruined swan plant. He hid his bag.

'No,' he said, 'she's with us today.'

'Oh,' Hēnare said. 'Kei te pai.'

Kataraina understood. She'd arrived in time to stop him leaving, and because she'd arrived in time, Nanny would have a sort of lovely day.

And in the sea, the sea she'd thought boring when she'd first arrived to be sad and alone on the beach, she looked over at Savannah, who might have seen the tears shining on Kataraina's face, because she dived into the water and swam to her and stood in front of her, she stood in front of her, and she kissed each eye, and she said, 'Wash your face now, e hine.'

Kataraina washed her wet face with the sea, and then she lifted her face to the sky furry with stars, and she laughed.

'Those tears weren't for that fool, I see that. And that's good,' Savannah said, then she looked at Kataraina again. 'Enchanting, kare.'

'*Enchanting*,' Kat scoffed, and splashed the woman.

'Enchanting as.'

An octopus shifted out of its hiding place between the rocks, as if to see us. Kat with Sav in the water. Down the beach, at the fire, Toko strumming his guitar, and singing 'Just One Look'. Jade dancing near him, shy and stoned. So much science. A spark lifted on the wind and landed in the rockpools. Across the dunes a dog barked. People's bodies held up their sheets.

Her sister's heru was in her sister's hair. Her grandmother was sitting in her chair at her son's house wearing her very old red Angora jersey, a new pair of the same black velvet leggings. Waiting, always waiting, for Kataraina to come home. The bony boy was a man by that fire. The scar crimson on his torso, for when Sav would come for him he would discard all boyishness for her. The engineer was driving around in his truck, grease on his hands, his eyes surveying the places an almost sixteen-year-old girl might haunt, like she was a ghost now, like he'd made her his ghost now, but he would not find her anywhere he would think to look. Tonight, the small miracle was that she had moved beyond where he would think to look. A farmer's son lay awake, Stuart Johnson, listening to his father berate his mother. After something smashed there was an icy, whipping quiet. All this science. Our children were not born. Their fathersmotherssistersbrothers were not dead.

Somewhere, a gun was in a box. Her tears fell into the sea. The octopus retreated into its hiding place between the rocks, leaving a cloud of ink, not because it felt threatened, but because the moment asked for ink.

They came out of the water, Kataraina and Savannah, and again Kat saw something. The way her wet skin shone, how she sprung up the beach, her broad, straight back, her hunger for life.

She said to Kataraina, 'You want to come back to the party.'

'Nah,' Kataraina said. 'I'll go home.'

'Promise?'

'Yes.'

A hundred and twenty-eight years before the girl shot the man

We watch her, the wahine from the ancient world, led into the past by the man with the deep-set eyes and whale tooth around his neck. His kōrero. His telling.

He says people from the new world hunt her, to put her behind their bars, their steel.

She is in the saltmarsh, digging for tuatua. Listen to her sing. The can opener, though interesting, and occasionally useful, is insignificant to her survival. She has the skills and knowledge and intuition to keep herself safe, for now, and when she senses it is safe to return to her people, her tāne, her pēpi, she will.

She has Marama. Marama is significant to her survival. Marama is why it is possible for Tikumu to sing in the saltmarsh, despite her mamae, her longing to return home. But the men are still asking questions about the dead man who was doing real work. Quantifiable, measurable important work. The man she killed was working for the Crown, and his job was in blocks, acres, pounds. His work had a deadline assigned to it, and a deadline is a deadline and the word deadline is part of the new language, and the new measure of worth, and the new and fresh wave of destruction.

The men are watching her tāne, Marama tells her. They watch him to see if he sneaks away from the pā with eggs in his pockets, or fish in his basket, or a warm cloak in his arms. They watch her pēpi, her precious daughter. They watch her! Don't watch her! This is why Marama sings across the fire, never catching his eyes, never saying it straight, but smiling as she sings. Telling him what his wahine ate for her dinner. Another warm sleep beneath the branches, and stars, she sings. Another morning she's woken, and another morning she's walked to the saltmarsh, come back to the swamp, boiled her water on a fire, sharpened her fishing spear, eaten kanakana.

Sometimes Marama can find Tikumu by the fragrance of taramea. Today Tikumu has collected enough tuatua for Marama to take back to their families. Marama tells Tikumu how the people are, how all her people are, she tells them about a fight those grumpy kaumātua had, over a kererū. 'E tāku kererū!' one man said.

'Kāore, e tāku kererū!'

And one man called the bird by a name, and the bird laughed then swooped down from its branch, making the tree heave, and it darted towards the other man and made him fall backwards.

Marama described how Tikumu's kuia was laughing and laughing, and it was good to see her laughing. She has been so sad without you, Marama says, but I sing. I sing across the māra kai to her, I sing across our tamariki to her, I make sure there are other noises, I make sure I hide the truth in toikupu, I make sure I don't look in anyone's eyes, but I sing about you, kare. I sing about you and I hide you in poetry, in lyrics, I hide you, kare, and I comfort your people, and their prayers are so strong for you now, kare, they will sustain you, kare. The nights will be warmer than they should for a while longer; the rain will come only in the day; the kanakana will climb out of the water and lay themselves at your feet; and the birds will put eggs in the ground around you. A kuia sees a taniwha – inky-gold eyes, a pelt of eelgrass – and this taniwha sees you. Normally you should be afraid. She is not a lovely beast – you have heard stories about her, how she used to eat our people, our lost, wandering people – but she sees danger, she sees an endless fight ahead, and she believes one day your mokopuna will need to engage in this fight. The taniwha sees this, how your mokopuna will pull silver from their mouths to keep you alive, to keep the beast safe.

She is a selfish monster, Marama says. If she didn't need you, she'd eat you, swallow you whole in your sleep, and ignore your wet gurgling screams from deep in her belly.

Tikumu thinks of her people praying for her. She thinks of the taniwha watching her, practising restraint, not eating her for a greater survival. She respects this. She thinks of the kanakana climbing out of the water and laying themselves at her feet, the birds putting eggs in the ground around her, the nights staying warmer for her.

On her way back to her resting place, her waiting place, she looks at the bright green shoots coming up out of the whenua, and she feels so sure her heart surges. Leave out food for the monster. An egg for you, water beast, and an egg for me.

Eat the shoots, these bright green shoots.

Let's swallow this magic.

The moment the girl shoots the man

Swamp-Kat will cry for days and days in the engine room until the roimata become so salty they draw thick chalk lines down her cheeks. In the last few hours of crying something happens. The engine has been lifted from the room. Perhaps it is the salt, so dense now, helping it float up. The engine cracks through the boat's hull and heaves into the black murk of the swamp, up towards oxygen. It thrusts to a dramatic bob beneath pink scaly light and the noise of winged escape. The swamp sucks at the engine like it is no different, no larger, no stranger than any one of the numerous things the swamp has allowed passage through its complex system as the whenua's kidney. The dark swamp pulls the engine into a soft part and folds around it. The fresh silence after someone has wailed falls and the dark watery organ begins the process of eradicating the man's metal.

Swamp-Kat swims to the car now, which must have arrived in the swamp while she was tearing up the engine. Swamp-Kat swims to the car methodically, no longer confused, gets in the car and sits beside City-Kat. She closes her eyes and rests. City-Kat will wait while Swamp-Kat cries.

One day after the girl shot the man

And we do too, we cry too, thinking of her there, behind the walls of her skull, her eyelids holding back an ocean, her body holding up the sheets, her heart making the graph spike, her mother at her bedside, her rosary beads, Bible and can of beer in her handbag.

She prays to other things, too, which is hard for her because of the sermons, and the thin pages and pages and pages, and her devotion to that sickly goodness she was prodded towards, even attained, only to find that this goodness did not empower her. It sucked at her, drained her, reduced her, and this reduction became tarry. Colleen doesn't know all her gods, so she starts easy, sending out her prayers to rivers and seas and mountains and trees and birds and bones. And when an image of a white man in the sky intrudes, she finds again her pūkana. She squeezes her daughter's hand, goes to the sink, turns on the tap and splashes herself with water. She keeps the Virgin Mary though. Hine ngākau. Whaea o te ao. The glorious mysteries.

Is Colleen done with all that lacks imagination? With all the poor interpretations of the Old and New testaments, how encouraged she has been to oppress her family's magic, mauri, mana, lest it get out of hand, lest it shame someone and become a target for shamers, lest it make her mourn her own magic. Nah, nah, nah. No more fear. She's done, she's back. She disappeared when they all needed her, she let her mokopuna go to her daughter. But she's back. She went away to lick her wounds, and even if she didn't want to, she went to find Jade. She went to get Jade, like her husband had. Because she was her daughter's sister too. She was. And even if she came to Jade's door on the island of Rakiura, and growled still, even if she couldn't just admit she was there to get her, she was.

Twenty-one years before the girl shot the man

Shall we tell how he was this gorgeous day? Shall we tell what Kataraina saw about him?

Kat biked to Stuart Johnson's father's farm, curiosity pulling her along the hot road. A year had passed since she was in the grandstand with the engineer, a caterpillar's foamy green guts on the bare skin of her thigh. The curiosity to see the swamp again propelled her forward. She stowed her bike in a dried ditch and snuck under a fence far from his two-storeyed home, but close enough to see it. In the field she looked at the house, wooden, painted white, peeling. A farmer's house, and she thought it looked lonely but she fought off a feeling of loneliness for him, because the Johnsons offended her.

Kat walked through the field until she reached the rātā and kahikatea trees. She stepped into the bush and walked under scraps of light, soft-edged like torn paper. She exited bush and found gorse and attempted to find an entry. The wall of green thorns pushed her back, until she was forced to return to the bush and choose another place to exit. She walked its length, crawling through vine, then escaping from a thick bulge of rātā, ponga and vine, only to find more gorse. She walked along the green-thorn wall, which pushed her away from the bush and nudged her out into the field, into the open. The land became boggy under foot and then she realised the gorse and paddock had tricked her and she was now in the open. Then she heard the roar of a four-wheeler.

She hit the deck, hiding in the long grass. She stayed still until her heart stopped beating against the earth. She bobbed up.

There he was. Standing. On his grandfather's, his father's, *his* land, looking at her. On his land, he said, 'Stand up, Kat. I saw you.'

She stood up.

'Why you being such a dick?' he said. 'You know I'd let you walk around here?'

She shrugged. 'Let me, yeah. I didn't want to ask.'

'That's honest.'

'I didn't want you to *let me*,' she said.

'And why you here?'

'The swamp.'

'Really?' he said.

She nodded.

'Come on then.' He waved her to him. 'I'll ride you there.'

Getting a ride seemed as bad, or worse, than him *letting* her walk in the paddock, near the mountain, near the sea, but she followed him to his four-wheeler. He patted the seat behind him. She climbed on.

He drove slow; Kat had expected otherwise. He pointed things out to her. An old deer hunter's quarters, a cave, over there, the other farmer's land, 'Your friend, right?' Tommy Aiken's place.

The terrain rose a little, then fell a little more. Then there was a row of trees, floating. Willow trees lined a riverbank, willow that didn't believe they were willow, thought they were running water.

'There it is, that swamp.'

She saw a machine in the grass, bleeding rust.

'Every one of them chokes,' he said.

'Has your dad ever thought to give up, leave it be?'

'He would. Maybe I could convince him,' he said, and then looked at her like she had asked to wear his jacket outside a pub on a cold night; like she should find her manners and soften her face. Ask nicely.

'Can we go closer?' she said.

'Of course. We have before.'

She avoided his eyes.

He led her through the long grass. The ground became boggy and she pulled off her boots and socks, hiffed them up near the four-wheeler, rolled her jeans to her knees.

He bent down. He took off his gumboots, rolled up his jeans too. His feet, ankles and calves were white like the damp-sheeted sky. His toenails were cut close to the flesh. He hiffed his boots. One clipped the side mirror of his four-wheeler and smashed it. He laughed at the damage. Bull in a china shop. 'Whoops,' he said.

He held his hand to her. She avoided looking at it and started to walk. She felt his sense of rejection. She looked at him and saw it rise through and stiffen his shoulders and jaw.

'Nothing much different to the last time you were here. Only this time you are safer. With someone. With me.'

It was another shovel in her, another attempt to dig it out of her. She was a mountain; somewhere in her was a peat buried so long it had become black and shiny and precious. It could fuel him, this fossilised gratitude.

At the swamp's edge she climbed onto a fat broadleaf tree, clambered along its long low branch that was like a giant's finger and sat down. She let her legs hang off the tree's ledge. She whispered something to the swamp.

The farmer's son looked at her. 'Did you *thank* it? After what happened here, did you thank it?'

She nodded.

He seemed to grapple with this and conclude something about her – a conclusion that would stay with him and become something ugly in the years ahead – and he said, laughing, 'Sucker for punishment, aren't ya?'

He stepped onto the branch and attempted to crawl along it,

but he was too large and untrusting. He slipped. He clung like a tomcat slipping from a fence. She giggled, and across the swamp the sound of her happiness echoed. He said, 'Help me!' And she said, 'I can't. You're too heavy. We'll both fall.'

'Try,' he said.

She shuffled across the branch and said, 'There's a branch behind you, get your foot. Flick your foot back.'

He tried, but his body was rigid.

'Try again.'

He did.

'Try again.'

He did and this time he caught the branch behind him with the front of his toes.

'Well done,' she said.

He smiled up. She smiled down. 'Okay, take my hand but don't pull on me. I'm going to move your hand.'

She felt him charge under her touch. And though she felt no charge for him, his charge for her was energising all the same.

She guided his hand to a strong young branch that he could pull himself up with. He grasped it. With the front of his foot on the branch behind him and hand on the branch she'd found for him, he hauled himself back onto the giant's finger.

'It would have been sad if you'd fallen in and died,' she said. 'I can't drive a four-wheeler.'

'That's dramatic. I would have just got wet.'

'Hmmm,' she said.

'Hmmm?' he asked.

'This swamp sure is hōhā that you Johnsons keep going at her.'

They sat quietly on the branch together, searching for its smallest movements. The air did not agitate and stiffen under the boredom she anticipated would seep from him, because there was no boredom. He was looking at the swamp too. He was pointing at a dragonfly. He was nudging her to see a spider on the water.

He fished out a Fruju wrapper with his toe, balled it, put it in his pocket.

'Should we leave it alone then? Should I convince my dad?' The darkness of the swamp was heavy in a lovely way. 'Well?' he said.

'Leave it. You remember the saltmarsh? Playing there?'

'Yeah,' he said.

'This swamp is kind of tied to the marshes. Or it used to be. The marshes and the swamp met at a point near the river, just barely met when there was enough water. The sea misses this swamp, and if you don't give it back, the sea might just take it back.'

'Deep,' he said.

'You reckon he'll leave it?'

'Yeah. He doesn't need it,' he said, with conviction.

It was a first contract between them, and his eyes couldn't help but search her face, survey its boundary. And even though she'd been surveyed before, she believed that this time the outcome would be different. He was a fresh chance, a new opportunity to prove her boundaries, strengthen her limits.

Then!

'Oh my god!' She pointed to a place where the swamp was deeper and darker and she saw it, bone. 'Is that ... Aroha's heru?'

'Are you sure?'

'No.'

And he looked at her face startled and flushed and bright. He unbuttoned his jeans and took them off, then his shirt. Standing on the broadleaf branch, a young pale strong Stuart Johnson looked down at Kataraina Te Au. 'How much does she hate me, this water then?'

'Not at all. She likes you – loves you – actually, she's all goods with you, she'd never hurt you.' Kataraina laughed up at him.

'Promise?'

'Promise.'

Stu climbed into the water, and he went to the deeper darker spot where Kat was pointing, and he dived under once, twice, and finally came up, weeds in his hair, mud on his face and a yellowed bone heru in his hand.

'Thank you,' she said, reaching towards him, the heru. And he stood before her, the swamp lapping at his waist and she saw it then, the reason he seemed to hate himself: he wanted to be beautiful too.

The moment the girl shoots the man

Swamp-Kat is sitting in the backseat of a car. Here to face a thing that might have never happened, here to face the thoughts he might have never acted upon. He has been lovely. And she is angry, because he is capable of being lovely, and he denies them it.

City-Stu in the driver's seat.

City-Kat in the passenger's seat.

Which is wrong, it's not the way it was. The dream inside the coma is losing its structure, its honesty.

They are in the car, which now bobs in the swamp. They are covered in moss and weeds, and at their feet a kanakana writhes. Its open mouth, a jawless sucker ringed with small teeth. A large kāhu swoops down in front of them and takes a rabbit from the water. City-Kat and City-Stu sit in the car together.

'Switch places with me,' she says.

'Sure,' he replies. They clumsily switch, Kat climbs over and Stu slides across.

Righting the inaccuracy from within is deceitful, dangerous. She feels it. The animals in the swamp multiply and grow. The water's surface boils with movement.

He looks out the window. He cannot see the swamp. That is to say he sees what he sees. He sees only his land, stretching on for forever.

'Gotta get this land under control, gotta hump and hollow it, gotta get it making some money.' A black swan floats to his window and stays there, side-eyeing him. But he does not see it.

'Stu, you promised you'd leave it be.'

And it pours out of him. He says, oh shit did I sorry think I'm going to have to renege on that for just this bit it's a hazard honestly lost five calves in there now I mean you of all people know up the river further up there's a smaller section of wetland what do you even do here why do you even care surely you are done with it now surely surely you are tired of caring about this surely I give you haha better things to worry about.

He leans across and kisses her face. He probably always knew that there would come a time when he could go ahead and drain the swamp anyway.

Suddenly the hot potato and gravy is in his hands.

'What do you want to do with that, Stu?'

'Do I want to burn you with it?'

'I think so.'

His hand is shaking. 'I won't,' he says. 'Don't worry. I won't.'

The black swan's neck has morphed. The swan's head is a gun now, pointed at him. He starts crying. 'I won't.' But his hands and arms are shaking.

City-Kat says, looking at the fight he's having with himself to not burn her, 'I might shoot you.'

He looks at the black swan. Its head a gun.

'I don't want to be shot.'

'No,' City-Kat says.

Twenty years before the girl shot the man

We are at the pool. Kat. Pare. Tommy. It has been two years since the man with the two lighters took Kat into the grandstand, had sex with her on her father's boat, then came to the clubrooms and looked at her with a wipe, as if she was a dead insect cleaned from the cold glass of his eyes.

The greenness is gone, though. She pretends it's gone for good. Here is sunlight. Chlorine. The bright blue lining of the pool. Our skin shines; it is all young. Our skin is all still here to touch each other.

Kat is tough. Whatever. Her time with Jared had its moments that made her feel extraordinary. It was strange, though, and a bit gross in hindsight, but people are always sniffing her out to absorb their mamae. In his case, the pain of losing his daughter. She remembers the tattoo – *Lana* – on his wrist.

But today, the world is always brand new.

Pare is up on the fence pushing the smoke out over the top so the pool attendant doesn't growl at her again.

The bony boy says, 'I should tell your aunty you are smoking.'

Pare says, 'Fuck off, egg. You won't.'

'Might.'

'You won't, though, 'cause I'll give you a hiding.'

'Let me have a puff,' he says.

She passes it to him. Tommy is older than them, but still so boyish; he looks strange smoking.

'I hate you,' he says to Pare, puffing smoke.

'Hate you more, boy.'

He steps on the pool edge and flips into the water. Light bounces off his white elbows, knees, Adam's apple.

'Tommy!' Pare shouts.

Tommy bursts out the water. 'What?'

'Don't do that.'

'Do what?' He climbs out, water dripping off him like liquid diamonds. He sets up again. 'Do this?' He grins and flips.

She grabs her heart like a madam might. 'For fuck's sake.'

He bursts from the water again, laughing like a god.

'I'm gonna be a stuntman one day,' he says to Kat, flopping down on his *Baywatch* towel beside her. She remembers Savannah on the beach. That woman who could have been nineteen or forty – who could guess? – and she was into him! A feeling strikes her heart. He is like her, old and young. She has only seen boy Tommy, and suddenly she sees what Savannah must have seen.

'Are you?'

'Yeah,' he says. 'I'm going to be in movies doing flips and car chases and leaping from building to building – you know those massive ones they have in America – yeah, that stuff. I'll do all that for those pussy actors.'

'Sounds fun,' Kat replies lazily.

'I'm learning piano,' he says.

'Cool.'

'You don't mean it.'

She told him Pablo Escobar played the piano, though she doubted he did.

'Did he?'

'Yes.'

'Who's Pablo Escobar?'

Boy.

'Some guy. Some guy you might need to be the stunt double of one day when someone makes a movie about him.'

Tommy goes to the pool, leaping up like a child, but as he flips backward into the water she sees an outline of something strong in his body, an abdominal muscle, chest muscles.

Man.

He's having gull fun in the stars at dawn. He's beautiful, she thinks, though she has no idea where this thought, or feeling, comes from.

Pare comes to Kat. 'Don't encourage him,' she says, but she uses the back of her mouth so her madam words sound hori.

'I don't, I just don't *not* encourage him. Anyway, he's good. He knows his body. Let him go nuts.'

'I hope summer lasts forever,' Pare says.

Kat closes her eyes. She rolls over. 'Sunscreen please,' she says.

Pare rubs sunscreen in the bare place on Kat's back, and shoulders. 'He's a pain in the arse.'

Kat whispers, 'You like him?'

'Fuck no.'

Kataraina feels relieved, and that's strange to feel relieved her best friend doesn't like him. Does Kat like him now?

Tommy and Toko are playing rugby in the pool. They cheat by running along the edge with the ball. Toko is a man, really, and now Kat sees Tommy might be too.

'They'll get growled at for running soon,' Pare says. 'Someone might slip, crack their head open.'

Kat and Pare pretend to fall asleep under the sun. It makes them feel beautiful.

Tommy comes back to sit with Pare and Kat. He starts to sing a song, quietly, like a whisper, like the words don't belong here and he is doing something dangerous.

Pare says, 'Where'd you learn that?'

He shrugs, but his lips fall about asymmetrically, in that innocent way kids' mouths do. Left bottom lip lops down, right top lip curls up. Kat sees something inorganic in the way he moves his face though. Like he knows it's a kid face he's pulling.

'It's a really beautiful song,' Pare says.

Tommy beams.

'Don't get a fat head.'

'You're a fucken fat head.'

They get on their bikes.

Tommy hauls his sun-pinkened scrawn up onto Kat's handlebars. Toko takes off ahead.

'Should have got my brother to double you.'

'Don't want your brother to double me.'

Tommy leans back and lets his head fall against her shoulder. She sees the scar from where the stick went into him, a few years ago now. It's small and silver. She can smell his hair. It smells like apples and chlorine. It's a sudden strange urge, the urge to kiss his neck. He might be older than her, but he's always seemed a year or two younger. He's not though now, is he?

Instead of kissing his neck, she says, 'Come over to ours? See Toko, stay for tea?'

His boyish voice is shaky. He can't hide how happy he is to spend more time with her. He's too young at heart to know you must pretend; he's too young at heart to know eagerness corrodes romantic love. Doesn't know yet that you have to lie. 'Bike me home? For a shirt.'

Whatever, Kat thinks.

Then she realises, it's not immaturity at all. It's him, he's happy to be him.

He smiles at her and even if she has learned that eagerness has no place in love, she stores this image of him, this lovely trusting expression on his face. She doesn't know why she stores it, but something inside her tells her that one day they will be like children again, and she will not mind his eager smile out in the wide, wide open. There is no man like this, who smiles eagerly, cannot be bored, is ravenous for fun in the sun. There is no other man like this who doesn't need to be the man.

But before she's even got them home, the feeling is gone. She couldn't possibly deserve it after the things she's done in grandstands and on boats. She keeps pretending the greenness is gone. But here it is.

An hour before the girl shot the man

We are in the house. We stand there and we watch. Kat and Tommy. We hear the gunshot. She winces, but she lets herself believe the children and the dog and this world are safe even though – on paper – the man who has shot a gun out there on the land, with the siphoned swamp and the poisoned river, owns the world within this fenceline, to the river, to the highway, to the hill.

'Tommy?'

'Yeah, Kat.' Not touching her face.

'Nothing.'

There is the sound of the truck then, sudden, urgent and loaded. The truck skids to a stop outside and the door is opened and the door is slammed so hard the house shakes, and the house continues to shake because he's charging through it.

Fuck fuck fuck.

It's okay. It's okay. Tommy goes down the hall, going to sort him, sort him for good.

'Ahh, Aiken,' Stu says, and he boots him in the nuts, bringing Tommy to the ground.

Kataraina braces herself. This is everything she's wanted, again and again and again.

Proof.

Proof he is a monster.

A mongrel.

He's going to beat her and this time it will be the last. It's going to be bad this time, and she doesn't care what she does or doesn't deserve. A black eye is one thing, but this is going to be something else. Going to be all she needs to know – to prove – she's not crazy.

She is frozen then, and when he appears in the doorway – swaying on his fuckwit feet, looking a decade older than he did yesterday, before she took the boy and the girl to the river to catch eels under the small piece of moon and to go to the tent with the man to sleep with him just like she had that one time years ago, and then, once more, a decade later – she recognises herself. She sees her own desire in him.

Her reflection.

Her own badness reflected back at her.

This is everything he's wanted again and again and again.

Proof.

Proof she's a lying slut.

He wants to catch her this time and it will be the last. It's going to be bad, it's going to destroy him, but finally, what he'll see in that bedroom will be all he's needed to know – to prove – he's not crazy.

He sees her frozen; he sees the shoelace string of her singlet is off her shoulder; he sees her bag, her knickers sitting on top. She's wearing shorts. Her legs look shaved and moisturised. And though he hasn't caught them in the act, he's caught them in the act of something. Finally, he thinks. She sees it in his eyes. The relief. He isn't crazy.

She sees it.

Then he slings her into the wall.

The moment the girl shoots the man, the dog can't bark. Somewhere, far off, maybe in a parallel universe, it starts to rain. A taniwha with inky-gold eyes and an eelgrass pelt has woken from an ugly mourning that has lasted a century. She has been woken by the bones in her throat. She has stormed the land all day, seeking a portal, and found the sleeping girl with blood in her hair, blood from a cut from when she hit her head on a rock, from when the man pushed her but not before he shot her dog.

The taniwha wakes from a century-long mourning to more violence. She is seeking a portal, and she climbs in the girl's mouth and takes the girl, dazed and pale and bleeding, towards the house.

Kat was sitting on the roof of the house and the time was dawn, a dark purple and silver dawn and she was every age she had ever been and ever would be. The water was coming up, and she stood on the roof and watched it rise around the edges of the house. She could hear heinous noises coming from inside the house. She could hear ugliness.

She had been happy eating blackberries and creamed corn but now all she could hear was her own mamae and the sound of water rising. The dawn light began swirling around her, the dark purple and silver, turning to pink in a distant vortex above the earth. Then the sounds began layering onto themselves: her crying, his shouting, Ārama sobbing, Lupo howling, her screaming, her swearing, his screaming, his swearing, and there was a gaping hole of noise that Toko's music once filled ... She covered her ears, but it was no use. The sound and the no sound were coming from inside her skull.

She hugged her knees – they were every age she'd ever been and every age she'd ever be. She rocked. She cried, 'Auē, te mamae.' More sounds came from before and she was reeled back to hear them ...

Grandad Jack was saying things, awful things, glass was breaking, doors slamming, and a fist thumped and thumped and thumped on a table. Jared groaned and groaned and groaned. But it was the sound of Grandad Jack saying things and saying things. It was words she had forgotten she had heard. It was like she was caught on a hook and being reeled through a river of noise, reeled back to the original splitting of herself, the moment she was made vulnerable to men forever after.

It was Grandad Jack who wielded the original mere; it was him. And she remembered it now, as she stood on the roof in the dream inside the coma and looked up into the vortex and listened to the sounds, and she could see herself, in a room below, lying on the floor. And then she remembered something she'd snipped, a memory cut out of her own story. Grandad Jack calling Nanny Liz ugly. In the memory, Nanny Liz was wearing her velvet tights and red Angora sweater. In all Kat's memories, Nanny Liz was wearing those clothes. This was how a memory could lie and tell the truth at once.

Ugly. The word roared in her ears, echoed. She looked on the swamp, and there reflected by a dawn moon still clinging to the sky was an event, happening and happening and happening.

There she was, sitting on Nanny Liz and Grandad Jack's old green couch, a wad of New World coupons in her mitts, the door to the kitchen slightly ajar, her knees dirty, the tops of her fingernails dark crescents of earth. Outside maybe a butterfly was ready to bust from its cocoon because it was so sunny, but inside it was dark, because Grandad Jack was being mean. Little Kataraina heard him call her nanny ugly, ugly in the outfit Kataraina would draw when she drew pictures of her nanny. If she was at school, and she was drawing her family, there was Nanny Liz in black and red.

Nanny Liz walked into the lounge and sat beside her granddaughter, her face dry as paper, cool as a cloud. Like nothing had happened. Kataraina touched Nanny Liz's velvet leggings, the red wool; she touched them softly. Nanny Liz ignored the gesture.

'Come on then, Jack,' she called. 'Just get over yourself. What are we going to do with her today? Come on, Jack. Let's just have a day.'

He stepped into the lounge, his eyes dull as ash. Like nothing had happened. 'Planting?' she asked. And he looked at his moko and nodded.

And that was all it took to split; this was the pounamu mere.

Witnessing
the
pretending
that
nothing had
happened.
Seeing
how much
better
a day could be
if you just
turned your eyes to ash.

Kataraina saw the old green couch floating on the water. She saw herself sitting on it. Swamp-Kat leapt from the roof of Stuart Johnson's house and swam to the couch where Kataraina was. She climbed onto the artefact.

The water was rising. Over there it lifted the house. The windows broke, under pressure, creating more noise. She looked up to the vortex, and she said the words she'd heard before, heard the words she'd heard before. She took her own small hand, the one with crescents of dark earth at the tips, and Swamp-Kat said to herself, 'E kare.'

'E kare,' she called. She called again and again, and Kataraina, at every age, in every season, at every time of every day she'd ever lived, and ever would live, felt the words, felt the call, and even if nothing could be changed because it was in the past, everything changed.

It was this call that brought up the water, it was this water which made the rinsing possible.

It was this.

E kare.

And up came the bright green shoots.

Up came the water, swallowing the house, and the moment the girl shot the man Kataraina didn't even hear the gunshot. The house was swallowed, and Kataraina swam through the cool swamp water, with the words *e kare* ringing through her own nervous system, so she was not afraid.

The world is always brand new.

She swam towards a large hospital bed, floating on the moonlit swamp water. She saw her mother sitting there, floating on a chair at the hospital bedside, pulling pounamu beads through her hand. Hail Mary, full of grace. And she said the first glorious mystery. The resurrection mystery. And she began to cry when she recited, 'Why do you seek the living among the dead?'

Kat climbed up her mother's leg, she climbed up her torso, along her arm. She climbed into the hospital bed, the swamp water dripping from her tiny body. Weeds in her hair, a gentle kanakana loosened itself from her ankle and swam away, kāhu after kāhu after kāhu lifted from the roost that ran along her spine.

Her mother said, 'As it was in the beginning, is now, and ever shall be, world without end.'

Stop, Swamp-Kat whispers. She only heard the sound, *e kare*.

Come on, sis.

E kare.

She lay there and let the sound run through and through her, filling even the space where Toko's music once was. And Swamp-Kat grew, until she was big enough to hold up the sheets, until she was bright enough to open her eyes, until she felt safe enough to reach out and find her mother's hand.

A hundred and twenty-eight years before the girl shot the man

Our ancestor once lived close to the house where the man was shot. She was at the river when a man approached her and offered her some peaches from a can, then attacked her. Offer food, attack. As if he were luring some small beast into some savage steel trap. Instead of entering his trap, she drove his own industrial tool into his own chest. Afraid for herself and her family, she escaped along the coast, eventually finding her way to a swamp.

One day, months later, missing her people, she walked around the swamp. The can opener with her. She was ready to bury it. She was ready to let it go. It was time to go home. She heard noises. People working, people cutting and chopping and calling out to each other. She saw a white woman standing under a tree, wearing a dress and a hat and gloves, her hand on her forehead.

Our ancestor ducked into the trees and watched. They were busy, the people, chopping and clearing and hauling. She wondered if they were building a sort of pā. Taking her time to find a place to bury the weapon so she could return home, she became interested in the building and returned most days to see what they'd made that was new. She saw a sort of wharenui forming.

One day she returned and found it was done, but the people had all gone. There was just the white woman left behind, and one man. Just the white woman all alone with the white man. The building, which looked like a strange wharenui, was large, and she could not understand where all the people had gone who had been working on it. It was very strange, ridiculous. Tikumu laughed at how silly it seemed. She knew soon she would return to her people. She would not like to have such a big house, so far away from her people. So alone. So isolated, like she had been so many months now.

She was thinking this when the man stumbled out from the house, and he stumbled towards the woman who was sitting under a tree. He grabbed her by her arm. She cried out. He dragged her to her feet and then towards the house.

Tikumu wanted to stop the man. She wanted to help the woman, but she was distrustful of them both. She was distrustful of their choice to be out here, alone, without their people who had come and helped them build this grand whare. She gripped the utensil. The one she had used to kill another man. She would not do that again. Not for anyone. But she crossed the grass, carefully and slowly, and went to the house.

Inside the house she found a small wharekai. She could hear sorrow – it was such a sorrowful place. Standing there in it she felt miserable for the woman, but there was nothing she could do. The utensil in her hand was from this world, and she had used it to protect herself from a man from this world. It felt desperate, and feeble, but she said a karakia, she whispered a karakia to the silver thing from their world, and she saw a hole in the wall, and she slipped the thing into the hole, hearing it clunk onto a wooden ledge inside. When she turned around, there in the doorway was the white woman.

For a pause the white woman looked at Tikumu. Her eyes were swollen and her skin was blotchy and pink. Tikumu saw the woman was getting ready to scream, but instead she looked at the hole in the wall. Tikumu backed out of the wharekai. She went out to the open grassy whenua, and she ran off into the bushes, leaving the silver can opener in the wall. Leaving the woman with the scream in her mouth. Doubtful she'd helped at all, but happy to be rid of the thing. Happy it was back with the sort of people it belonged to. Sorry but happy to be free of the thing. Leaving it there with these people.

Mr and Mrs RA Johnson had three sons. When they were two, four and five, Mrs RA Johnson filled a wooden crate with things from her new kitchen. Tinned corn, apples and blackberries. She saw the woman who lived on the other side of the swamp seemed fine without these things, did not need these things, but Stuart Johnson's great-grandmother was a wretched woman, and before she went she wanted to do one good thing. She took a long walk to a place in the swamp where she knew the woman was hiding from her husband and her husband's gang, and under a kahikatea tree near the dark swamp she left the wooden crate of tinned corn, apples and blackberries. Then she filled her pockets with rocks and made her way into the dark water.

Mr RA Johnson had three sons, and when they were two, four and five, his wife walked into the swamp, the swamp he stared at and thought was such a terrible waste. Three days after his wife disappeared – Stuart Johnson's great-grandmother disappeared – he rode his horse to the township and he went to a bar, and he said to the barman, 'I heard a Lawrence Aiken drinks here?'
The barman said, 'Yes.'
'Heard he knows a thing or two about taking care of swamps.'
'He's a machine, Lawrence Aiken. Turns water and mud and weeds to green, green pasture. Like magic.'
'I'll need a bloody miracle to get rid of this one,' Allan Johnson said, and he'd finished three pints before Lawrence Aiken finally walked in the door, mud on his knees, sweat in his hair, ready for a beer, a day of working his magic – draining wetland, to pave a path to a brighter future – behind him.

Three months before the girl shot the man

We are together. Two Te Au sisters at Kataraina's kitchen table. Aroha has come from Cheviot. We both have mugs of tea. There is a packet of Gingernuts on the table between us.

'Go on. Come with me,' Aroha says.

'Yeah, right-oh,' says Kat. 'Good one.'

'Why not? We're going on the boat, we're going to go get her. You've wanted this more than anyone.'

We will, sis, we will.

Will we?

'Have I?' says Kat.

'More than anyone else that knows they want it.'

'I can't. Anyway, why are we being so weird and secretive.'

'No one wants to poke the bear,' says Aroha. 'No one wants Mum worked up.'

'Best I stay here then. If I go too, Stuart will start shit. Best I stay behind.'

'I guess I was just thinking how mean it would be for the three of us to be together again.'

'We will be,' says Kat, 'when you have her back here. Then we will be. I'll get us something ready for when you bring her home. I'll make food. Who will stay behind and prepare food when you can't tell Mum? Who will have it all ready for her?'

'True,' Aroha says. 'True, sis. Will you do something special?'

'It'll be massive.'

'Will you manage?'

Kataraina wishes she could get Pare round to help her, but

things are strained between them. She sees too much, so Kat has pushed her away. Even if things are good between Kat and Stu, Pare feels things and she bristles easily. Kat will be fine on her own. She will start today, with shopping for some stuff that can be frozen. She frowns, realising something.

'I could leave you some money,' Aroha says. 'In case Stuart's an egg about it all.'

'Ha ha. In case? That's a guarantee.'

Aroha goes into her wallet and pulls out her Eftpos card. 'We have another one. You use this for the food. Don't even think twice. Whatever you need.'

Kat takes the card, her head down, whakamā. She swallows it away so it doesn't foam. 'Thanks.'

'No, sis. Thank you. It's a big job. Maybe ask Aunty Moira to help. She'll keep it secret.'

'You reckon?'

'I reckon. I dunno, but probs.'

Kat starts to imagine what she could do for Jade's welcome party. She can feel the energy rising in her. There's so much she can do. Tommy has a digger. They could even lay a hāngī.

'Could I do a hāngī without Dad's help, you reckon?'

'With whose though?'

'Stuart's,' she says, doubtfully. 'Tommy's,' she says, sure.

'You could, I reckon. With Aunty Moira too. Taukiri's coming with us. I dunno, who else, Kaleb? Aunty Joanie ...'

'Me and Tommy could do it just us two.'

Kat is picturing her and Tommy digging the hole together. Sweating, laughing, swearing, drinking, music on. Stuart enters the daydream and buries her and Tommy in the hole with pig and cabbage and spuds they were yet to clean.

'Let's talk when I get back eh. Let's do that.'

Something overcomes Kataraina. A desire. To hold herself up, tell the truth, without snipping herself clean. Without finding a caricature of herself first, a caricature of her goodness. Imagine it! Not needing to unravel herself from the mamae. But not today.

'Kei te pai. When you are back.'

Aroha stares at her. Tears fill her eyes. 'We want to believe you're okay. You want us to, too.'

'It's not your fault.'

'Let's go into town. Let's go buy us something.'

Aroha watches Kataraina weigh up her options, the consequences.

Kataraina knows her face has paled.

'I have some fencing to help with,' she says at last.

And Kataraina can see Aroha is trying to calculate another equation. She knows better than to push her sister, doesn't she? She doesn't want to be the cause of anything, any trouble.

'What if I help you with the fencing,' says Aroha, 'then we go for some food and buy us something? Why don't we have a day today before I head off tomorrow to bring us back our Jade.'

'You know Jade probably has made a life. You might not be able to just say we are ready to accept you now.'

'I won't expect her to come. I know she will have made a life where she is. But we can't leave this door closed.'

'Who closed it?' said Kat.

'Did I? For Mum?'

Kataraina shook her head, but said, 'Maybe.'

'A day together?'

'Sure. Let's go out and do that fencing.'

Kat and Aroha drove the dirt road to the paddock. Kat thought about whether or not doing the fencing without Stu was the right choice. Aroha said, 'He'll be stoked when he sees we went ahead and did it without him.'

Kat nodded, her hands firm on the steering wheel. 'Yes. He'll be stoked.'

Aroha laughed. 'Won't he?'

Kat nodded. 'Won't he.'

He did need her help, she knew. She was strong and able. But he would not appreciate her going ahead and doing the job without him, and that was because more than he needed her help, he needed opportunities to harness her day to his. Though he needed her help, the cream he liked to skim off the top was something very precious to him: her waiting. Waiting in the kitchen for him. Her sitting there wondering. Each morning he would tell her a job he needed help with, and she'd ask, 'What time you reckon?' And he'd shrug. 'Depends.'

The real beauty of never giving her a proper job on the farm, the real beauty of never giving her consistent and predictable expectations of her role, was that her main role became her waiting for him. And grateful. She was not tethered to six mornings a week milking. (Aren't you happy you're not milking every morning?) No, her tether was to him, not the jobs, but him. Kat came to these conclusions as she drove to the paddock where she and Stu were to tighten a fence, some time that day, together. And she started thinking about the way he had tethered her to him after Aroha said, 'He'll be stoked when he sees we went ahead and did it without him.' Because Kat knew that was so far from the truth she should have laughed.

Waiting for him was her role on the farm, she realised as they pulled up into the paddock. Waiting for him was an energy, and this energy was expelled into the house they shared, and he consumed it. Her waiting debilitated her, made it difficult to concentrate on things that would not be comfortably interrupted by his arrival, his tooting the horn, his yelling, 'Come on, Kat, I don't have all day. Got to get that job done now. Fucken hurry up.'

Hanging out washing was safe. A load could be left, half of it hung, half of it sitting in a damp pile in the plastic basket. Washing dishes was safe. Half a load could be left, half of it dripping suds into the rack, half of it attracting flies. Reading was safe, though it was a thing she didn't want to be caught doing, like writing, or walking to drop something back to or borrow something from Tom Aiken.

Cakes had sunk; cheese had soured; showers abandoned, conditioner still in her hair; conversations with her family cut short at the sound of his horn. She thought of the chooks' wings she clipped to stop them flying off and laying their eggs in the long grass by the river for the weka to eat, and all these jobs she'd never finished were little feathers in her, being clipped, clipped, clipped.

Kat walked across the paddock towards the sagging fence and said, 'Won't he be stoked.'

Aroha heard her. 'Have I caused a problem, suggesting this? I don't understand – but, sis, tell me.'

Kat sat in the grass. 'I'm so tired, sis.'

Aroha sat beside her. 'I didn't realise. I mean, I see you're tired – I didn't realise it was from the farm. From these jobs. I wouldn't have said to do the fence. I thought that would make it easier for us to get out for a bit later.'

'It's not the jobs. Maybe it's the lack of, I dunno ... I can't be pleased.' She tried to laugh. 'I'm so tired of navigating. I'm so tired of waiting for it.' She laughed again.

Aroha did not laugh with her. 'Stu?'

'I don't want to talk about him. When you get back eh. Just, yeah, no way will he love that I've come out to do this job without him. Without his saying so.'

'I'm sorry.'

'Not your fault, sis. Hey, tell me about Ārama. Tell me what's up with him lately.'

'He just wants to be everything Taukiri is. Taukiri is giving him a guitar for Christmas. And he'll teach him. Can't wait to see his face.'

'Far out, I forgot Christmas was so close.'

'Sure is. Imagine. This year, Jade might be with us. I want to make things right.'

'She might be.' Kat looked at the fence, the sagging wire. 'Maybe things will be better.'

'We can try.'

'I just miss him so much.'

'Me too, Kat. I miss him every day. His laugh, his songs.'

'The fun! I think things might have turned out so different if he was still here.'

'Our lives would be so different. We'd all be so different.'

'People don't tell you that eh. You mourn the unknown when you lose someone the way we lost Toko.'

'Nothing could make up for it,' Aroha said.

'Nothing ever.'

We sat in silence in the grass. Aroha and Kataraina. Both of us imagining the worlds that died when he died. The suns that stopped turning, the buildings that crashed to the ground, the birds that fell from the sky, the children, photos, car rides, bike rides, Ferris wheel rides, roller-coaster rides, train rides, plane rides, knee sits, bed sits, fire sits, hand holding, giggle holding, songs written, songs sung, the songs, songs that went out like matches. The words, words. The sis, sis. The oi, oi. The Kat, Kat! Look, look. The yeah, nah, nah, nah, bro. The yeah, nah, nah, nah, sis. The hell no, hell no. The get in the car, get in the car. The heyyy babyyy, heyyy babyyy. The world he'd left half done when he was killed, which had fallen to waste, rotted, and there was only the echo, now, of her scream flying through a broken window, pale green bile flooding free from the bar where her brother lay dead.

Kat heard the four-wheeler. It was not Stuart. It was Tommy. Toko's Tommy.

Her Tommy, their Tommy, our Tommy. Us.

'Aroha!' he said and climbed off the bike and he hugged her like he always hugged her, like he was hugging his lost bro. He didn't hug Kat like that. No, he hugged her like he was just hugging her, just her.

'What are youse up to?'

'Well,' Kat said, 'Aroha is here for a night at Mum and Dad's before she makes a big secret trip tomorrow. And she thought fencing would be fun.'

'Ahhh, right. Yas want a hand?'

'Fuck it,' Kat said. 'Yeah, I'm too far in my head. Let's just get it done. Let's just get it done.'

'Am I missing something?' Tommy asked.

'Not from this angle,' Kat said grinning, almost impulsively – and eagerly – admiring him.

Tommy stared back and his shock rose to his face and made a bright boyish smile, which reminded her of an image she had stored away of him, on a road, her on a bike, his hair wet from the pool. And was this the first time she'd flirted with him out in the wide, wide open?

Aroha laughed. Kat laughed too.

'Come on,' Kat said. 'Let's just get it done.'

The sky is a different blue, and the grass is quite a different green with this tiny bit of truth out of her mouth, buzzing around, turning lovely, turning to liquid. She smiles and thinks she would not be surprised if something magic happened, something like her sprouting wings or the mountains standing up like they'd just been giants asleep under green and purple bedspreads all this time. If a river became a woman who stood up on the rocks, dripping in pounamu, and started to dance under the sky, she would only laugh and not die of fright. Something small she feels is out in the world. *Not from this angle.* And it's an extraordinary feeling to have said something she really feels out in the wide open. It is an extraordinary feeling to have been silly and flirted, to have played with the boy, Tommy, and the man, Tom Aiken. To have shared something huge but small with her sister in a way, a strange way.

Āe, the sky is quite a different blue, the green is quite an astounding green. It is as if this truth takes them to that world left half done, though not to the bar, where Toko is dead, but this field, this paddock, but not exactly this field, not exactly this paddock as she knows it. It's as if those words she said, *not from this angle,* were words from the world they exited when the metal came fast and heavy down into her brother's face.

It's as if Stuart can't come here, to this place where a single, simple, sublime line of her truth also exists. It's done something unstoppable. How did she not know such a small thing could feel so lovely, so magic? She could fix and fix and fix this fence, here, she thinks, a hum around her and around her sister now, and him, it's making him sing, as he watches her swing the hammer, as he watches and watches her swing and swing the hammer, making him sing and sing and sing.

A hundred and twenty-eight years before the girl shot the man

Our ancestor once lived close to the house where the man was shot. She was at the river when a man approached her and offered her some peaches from a can, then attacked her. Offer food, then attack. As if he were luring some small beast into a savage steel trap. Instead of entering his trap, she drove his own industrial tool into his own chest. Afraid for herself and her family, she escaped along the coast, eventually finding her way to a swamp. Then ahhh, a crate, ahhhh, food: tinned corn, apples and blackberries. And once she had finished the food, she started to tell a story, carving it into the crate. Carving, carving the proof.

The sound of hooves wakes her. There is an eel at her feet and an egg near her shoulder, so breakfast will not be a concern today. The sound of the hooves is wet and muddy, slurping and rude. Close. The rider sees her sit upright, so does the taniwha. The crate marks her days and nights, it is patterned with love and hate, loneliness. It is carved with a night sky and a bright dawn. It is marked with her people. It has been carved so thoroughly it looks larger than itself. You could crawl inside and sleep, you could crawl inside and hide, you could crawl inside, light a fire, look at its roof and know everything there is to know, yet wonder; so vast has this woman made a plain wooden crate. She sees the snout on her: two metal eyes of the shotgun.

The taniwha lunges too late, after the crack, after the birds have been frightened into the dark morning sky. The taniwha chooses her, keeps her from him. Swallows her body whole, tastes her blood, the metal, the astringent smoky powder. The horse bolts with James Harrison on its cold sweaty back, eyes rolled up into its own brain as if seeking shelter (the horse will never be the same, the man will never tell). When he's gone the taniwha sets her back down on the grass, near her crate, writhes around her, noses the egg to her, noses the eel to her, noses her, nudges her, but when she does not open her eyes the beast claims her, and her tiny wooden cave sinks below the water's surface, buries itself in the mud, and begins stewing there, crying tarry tears, dark as meconium, begins an ugly mourning that will last more than a century.

Eleven months after the girl shot the man

Come and stay with us, we said. Kat and Pare asking Jade. Come up, from the island. We have his ashes. So Jade made the trip north, as if we were all in a vortex of coming and going from the island to Kaikōura. Around and round, until.

Stuart Johnson's ashes were still in the red Mitsubishi. When his family didn't show up to collect them from the funeral home the funeral director had called her. She'd left them there another three months before she called the stern woman back, a copy of the *Press* open in front of her. She introduced herself, reminded the woman of the man's ashes in the storage cupboard. 'Are they still there?'

'Yes,' the woman said.

And Kat drove there propelled by the same energy she'd used to make the call.

She picked the ashes up and put them in the boot.

Left them there.

We were in the kitchen. Stuart Johnson's ashes still in the boot of the red Mitsubishi, which was parked on the street. Pare was chopping onions, Kat was chopping mushrooms, Jade was washing spinach. Pare had her eighties soft-rock playlist on. She poured another drink for Kat and herself. 'Sure you don't want one?' she asked Jade.

Jade shook her head and stacked another bunch of washed spinach in the colander. 'Another job?' she said, looking around.

'Spuds, shall we have some mashed spuds?'

'Gotta have mash with chops.'

'Mash, yuck. See that car out there?' Kat said. 'His ashes are in the boot now.' Kat put down the knife, one small mushroom split like a heart beside it. She fished in a tote bag, pulled out the *Press* and put it on the table, took a great big chug of her drink. 'No one seen today's paper?'

Pare shook her head, Jade nodded.

Kat opened the newspaper and slid it in front of Pare.

The headline: '*I deserved it.*' *Abused woman speaks out on Clarence River killing.*

But we were not part of this telling.

Pare finished reading the full-page article, fleshy with facts from court and police stories written in the weeks following and right after the girl shot the man, fleshy with facts about Toko, Jade, Aroha – much beautiful, beautiful death. She said, 'How do you feel about this?'

'It's not true. Despite all the facts, it's not true.'

'You scrub up nice.' Pare laughed.

'Fuck you,' Kat said.

'It's not you, it's not Toko, it's not your mother or father. It's none of us. It's so—'

'Snipped.'

Kat poured another rum now, threw it back without Coke. She wiped her lips. 'His ashes are in the boot of that car, right now.'

'A taniwha was there, Kat – it's true. I saw it in the girl's eyes. Inky-gold eyes. I was like honey, honey, honey, for fuck's sake. I can hear myself, looking at those scales in her eyes and stammering, my hands shaking, my feet glued to the floor.'

'I know the taniwha was there. I know. We stood in front of each other, and I whispered into the taniwha's ear, *Shoot him.*'

Chips, chops, buttery spinach and creamy mushrooms. Another spliff, and a song is on for us again. Kat. Pare. And Jade.

'Yes! Turn it up!'

'Give me that newspaper ... Pass that lighter, yeah the safety ... Got any deodorant? No! *Ssspray on*, egg. Sorry, kare, but whatsss I'm gonna do with roll-on, give it a lick of sssummer dreams. Hahaha! There we go, yes. Right ssstand back. Ahhhhh. Tongue of fire, dragon'sss tongue. Hahaha. Dragon-fire breath eating up that half-arsed attempt at the truth. White cunt. Fucken yeah, I'm talking to you, Lois Lane! Put Whitney Houston on. I wanna dance with somebody. Yeah! Wow! Wooo yeah!'

The newspaper is ashy scales now.

And where the embers still glow, the ashy scales are a burnt inky-gold. Kat's drinking right out of the bottle, dancing on the wet grass in front of the house. Jade's smoking, Pare's dancing too. Pare's hot neighbour and his hot mates are coming over.

'See!'

They've got beers and they're wearing stubbies.

'We heard there's a party!'

Kat says, 'Tell them to fuck off.'

But she says it so loud, no one needs to tell Pare's hot neighbour and his hot mates and a couple of their hot girlfriends to fuck off.

They turn around and one says, 'Ungrateful bitches.'

Kat stumbles towards them, 'Whatjuu say, whatjuu say? Juu say *ungrateful*. What I gotta be grateful for from you, ya fucken ... bitch.'

'Bitch?' The guy with the mullet laughs. 'First time I've been called a bitch.'

She lifts her bottle, and she throws it, and it hits the large hairy-shouldered mild-mannered-looking one in the back. A young woman beside him says, 'Settle down, psycho.'

Jade, sober, tries to haul Kat inside now, but Kat weaves away from her and runs to her car. Her keys are in the ignition. Jade and Pare stand dazed, then run, too, to stop her.

Kat slams the door and snaps the lock. Both women stand in front of the car. Kat puts the car in reverse and backs away from them, smoke burning off the tyres. Jade and Pare are running towards her in the headlights. They turn inky, and gold, and Kat laughs, reaches a corner, spins the car around and starts making her way out to the empty farmhouse, with its windows broken, like teeth falling out.

The house is covered in graffiti: SLUT. KILLER. BURN IN HELL STUART JOHNSON. LAND BACK. WHITE PIG. WHORE. There's a swastika. Kat moves towards the house and stands in front of the words: KARMA IS A BITCH, which could be directed at either one of them.

Jade's car screeches up behind her. Pare gets out and starts making a pointed stumble towards Kat. Pare is crying. She looks angry. Her fists are pumping the air. 'You can't scare us like that.'

Kat doesn't move. She's frozen to the spot and Pare is a chaotic, staggering, beautiful mess. She reaches Kat and she puts both arms around her, and Kat holds her back, and they fall onto their knees in the dry dirt, the house and its graffiti lit up in the headlights behind them. Pare rocks her. Kat puts her head onto Pare's knees. Pare runs a finger along her friend's neck, down her shoulder, down her arm. She touches her head. 'Can I?'

Kat nods. Pare looks. Kat feels her touching it. A very small scar on her tapu head. Not even a scar, more of a discolouration.

'I wanna tear that house of his down,' Pare says.

An image flashes back to Kataraina. The corner, the signs. *Beach*, one said. *Cemetery*, the other said.

Maybe we turned the red Mitsubishi and we parked at a river mouth.

Or maybe we never went there at all.

Her memory is a swamp now, after all. Effervescent and brimming with life, busy, busy, busy. Timid in places, treacherous in others. Of course they went to the river mouth, and of course they went into the sand dunes together and he put down his Swanndri. Yes, they talked. About City-Stu.

But was it that day?

No.

Now Pare is only looking at the discolouration on her scalp. It helps Kat remember.

'We could start with the car.'

'The car?'

'Where he burned my head.'

We're driving.

It's been a long rainless summer, and the land is dry. The women – Kat, Jade, Pare – roll over the paddocks in the red Mitsubishi. It is ours now. We have inherited the car now. Pare puts on 'Dragons and Demons'. And she yells the lyrics out the window about how everyone has secrets, things they won't tell or sell. She blows smoke out the window.

We are dragons and demons and sluts and maggots and we cook a mean mutton chop and we roll a mean joint and write a mean essay and make a mean cuppa and can lend a mean ear and will let our patience be tested for love. It's all for love. We are mean Māori, mean. We're too much.

This proximity to death makes Kat feel holy.

The whenua is an ancient seabed beneath them; the red car rolls over it like a ship on a sea, glowing in the moonlight. The headlights touch the kūkūwai first, black as a tarn, desperate as a sick dog.

'We made it.'

Jade gets as close as possible and stops the car. The sudden silence is sobering.

We step out the car; a light rain has begun. It refreshes our eyes and skin, such magic.

'Taken the handbrake off?'

'Āe.'

Behold the women.

We stand at the back of the red Mitsubishi, his ashes trapped in the boot. First we look at each other, wide eyes confessing doubt, and then Pare's wide eyes become a pūkana. One of us says, 'On the count of three.'

We push, down and across, like we are pushing a big mound of dough into a knead. We heave, we're sweating, and when we finally get the car into the water only the tyres are submerged. There's no hungry swallowing. No release.

Tom Aiken had heard the noises in the night: the car, the cackling and the swearing and crying. Early the next morning he walked down to see what mess last night's teenagers had left. He saw Kat's inherited car, partly submerged in the swamp. He panicked and strode into the water, calling her name. When he found the Mitsubishi empty, he laughed.

He laughed and laughed, and at the table, alone in the house, he drank coffee after coffee, smoked smoke after smoke, until he could taste his own thick breath. He stared out at the farm and delirious with nicotine and caffeine he stood in front of the bathroom mirror brushing his teeth, staring at his own eyes that were cracking open like blue eggshells.

He walked back down to the swamp, and there she was.

'You keep coming back,' he said.

She didn't look up at him. She strode into the water and leaned into the open front window, grabbed the keys and went around to the boot. She unlocked it, lifted the lid and stood there, staring like she was facing a mistake.

'Didn't kill anyone last night, did you, Kat?'

'Thought about it,' she said.

She leaned in and pulled out the urn. Her face was dry and pale. She opened the urn and upended the ashes, right there into the black water. 'There you go, you bastard, fight it now.'

She walked up onto the grass and sat down.

'It's gonna rain something wicked tonight, Kat.'

'We need it.'

He sat down beside her. 'This water came up while you were in hospital.'

She nodded. 'Plateaued a bit now, huh.'

'Yeah.' He glanced at her. 'Even magic needs a helping hand. Even magic is just a bunch of seeds that could use a little something from us.'

'I'd kill for a feed and a coffee.'

Tom Aiken stood up and put out his hand. She slouched. He bent down and grabbed her under her armpits, lifted her up and hugged her.

'Come on then,' he said. 'Come have a kai. Come have a sit.'

Later she went to have a shower, and he threw her a T-shirt and shorts to wear, clothes she'd last worn beside a moonlit river writhing with eels. He'd kept them. 'Rain's coming,' he said.

She stayed under the hot water of the shower until her legs got tired.

We ate bacon and eggs, balanced on our laps while watching *The Fresh Prince of Bel-Air* reruns. Kat and Tom. Just Kat and Tom.

Kat fell asleep. Tom put a blanket over her. A square of sunlight fell on her shoulders, neck and face, and black hair.

She woke from a dream about her brother. Toko was there, watching her sleep. Tommy was hunched in the armchair near her, his head in his hands.

'You all good, Tommy?'

'We could go hundies you know, Kat. I mean we could really let this thing go.'

'How do you mean?'

'More water,' he said. 'Move a river back.'

19 January 2020, field study day sixteen

We are in the wharekai. We have moved here from the wharenui. The telling moves from room to room with us.

Cairo has her notes in front of her at the table. The room is full of people. Everyone has come today to begin the fight to grant the swamp personhood. A mihi is given to Te Urewera and its people, who made history fighting to grant legal personality to the mountainous Tūhoe land in the north. Here now, we discuss the same for Te Kūkūwai o Tikumu. No longer Johnson's Swamp but our ancestor's.

Eric, Jordy and June sit opposite Cairo. She can't look them in the eye, not even Hana, beside her. It's like in their research – they storyboarded it, but then traversed some other place. Cairo feels like she's woken from days on psychedelics, trying to repurpose what was found in the wasteland of collective derangement.

The man with the deep-set eyes and whale tooth strung around his neck arrives, his eyes gleaming, his mouth relaxed, but ready as if with a joke. Everyone has come for the ancestor – that's what keeps us here – that's what changed everything.

The man stands to kōrero further. Cairo thinks of how they came here because a swamp regenerated miraculously, as if overnight. The man with the deep-set eyes and whale tooth strung around his neck has told and told the story of our ancestor. Outside, by candlelight, in the wharenui, beside the statue of the Virgin Mary. In the wharekai. When we walked close to the kūkūwai.

Today, though, we are here to begin the real mahi. To name the swamp after our ancestor – and seek the swamp personhood. Like a river and land in the north, we seek this.

Are we pretending? Like Cairo is?

She knows she is favoured because she sees the dual timeline where the parallel trajectories have finally merged. But are *they* pretending! The swamp has always been here? The swamp has always been here. It was never drained? No, it only waited for us.

The man invites a woman to speak, now. She stands, nervously.

She begins, introducing herself as Kataraina Te Au. Her voice is soft, worried, hopeful. She acknowledges the scientists, thanks them for their work. She looks at Cairo, who remembers her taking her hand, leading her to their tipuna. She remembers wondering about the scar she thought she saw at her temple.

'Now,' Kataraina Te Au says. 'Our work has changed. Engari, there will come a time when it is right to understand her better – the kūkūwai – that's what I've always wanted. But for now, we must let her be. If we seek personhood, we treat her so from this day, until …' She shrugs and smiles. 'We do not interrogate, or prod. We do not ask questions, we do not force an explanation from her. We are her bright green shoots. We protect now and the answers we want will wait.'

Cairo is afraid to look at Eric, she is afraid he is going to argue soon, ask if all his work here has been a waste of time. Then she thinks, so what? His problem. If he stands to argue, this time he's on his own. So she looks, and what she finds is the face of a younger Eric, just here, just fortunate to be here.

Kataraina Te Au continues. 'A taoka has been returned, and if we leave the gates open to everyone to pick it apart, we've learned nothing.'

The man with the deep-set eyes and whale tooth strung around his neck winks at Cairo, welcoming her into the space, the swamp, where all possibilities have come to roost.

Three days before the girl shot the man

If our stories are vines, are we the sun coaxing them up out of their whenua, or are we their whenua?

No. We are the rinsing. We crave the rinsing and we are the rinsing.

Ko wai tātou?

Ko wai tātou.

Kataraina Te Au was walking a dry stony patch of land. A way people could drive to the creek. Stuart Johnson had tried to level it out the previous year and get grass on it. Tom Aiken had come over and said, 'What the hell, mate? That's public access for people to get to the creek.'

Stuart Johnson had said, 'I don't need people going up to the creek. What I need is the creek to stop feeding into that paddock and making it boggy. What I need is that creek to fuck off.'

'Leave the bloody road and leave the bloody creek,' Tom Aiken said.

'Why you so mad, Tommy?' Stuart Johnson asked, sneering.

Walking, Kataraina could hear Lupo barking, and she could hear Ārama and Beth playing in the bush by the creek behind Aiken's house. A bird stitched the sky above her.

Suddenly lethargic, she sat on the wet grass. There was cow shit all around her. She could see the old broadleaf tree where she and Stu once sat. The place she'd once almost drowned. It was black and mucky there now, not enough water to drown a mouse. It was hardly pleasant to be sitting there, surrounded by cow shit, but sitting there relieved her of the crushing weight that had come upon her then. And sitting there like that, she imagined the swamp, or maybe she saw it, a hundred years or more ago. The vision was sudden and vivid and came up around her. The water was black and red and thick as ink, and where the sun shone it turned to gold.

Jobs to do really, but she was here to sit and be strange and achieve nothing. She faced the blue sky. She was only here today to welcome back these bright green shoots, to face the dark movement, an inky-gold eye, a large serpentine body covered in eelgrass. Red water rising up.

When she got home Stuart Johnson said, 'I saw you sitting in the grass. You looked very worried. You looked … torn.' He was angry. 'What's tearing you up,' he said, stepping towards her.

And she knew. She knew what was tearing her up, and it wasn't Johnson's place, that way, or Aiken's place, that way. It was a new ancient world inside her, trying to escape her ribcage and fold over the whenua with her, spread out from her, and remember its way up towards the sun.

Many years after the girl shot the man

We are walking together, walking over the hills. It's one of those special days, where we are all together, we who are not ghosts. At the river we will take off our clothes, down to our undies, shorts, bras, go into the cold quick awa, let it rush over our face, these faces, and through our hair.

Nanny Liz waits in the house above the kūkūwai, waits for us to return, growing older and older. We pull up watercress from the clean, fresh waterways to cook for her, and so, she says, she might live forever.

When you shoot a man something inside you wants to be repulsed by who you are. You feel you can't ever manufacture – through deeds or words or service or prayer – goodness again. And soon you understand that is tika, to be far, far beyond standing on the line, dressed in white aprons, at the goodness factory.

We walk. Then, just before we find the plateau, Kat, Kataraina, Aunty Kat, bends over and laughs louder. Ārama a young man now, with long muscled arms and legs, a thick, dense torso, his thick hair knotted atop his head, and a soft musical voice that says, 'Come on then. Kōrero mai.'

She keeps laughing, tears are rolling down her face. It spreads and Jade is pawing at her arm gasping. Taukiri's chest is rising, ready for a goodie, some dickhead done some dickhead thing. Tom Aiken grins wide, in love with all the sounds she makes. Colleen says, 'Oh, come on then, girl, come on then.' Hēnare is silently praying he won't forget this moment.

'Faarr, come on then,' Ārama yells.

'Auē,' Kat sputters. 'Auē.' She laughs.

'I remember why he threw the can opener,' she says, and she laughs on and on and on, roaring up at the sky. 'Ahhh, what an egg,' she says, grabbing her belly. And we all laugh with her, in awe of her, and none of us asks her to tell. No one needs to draw a line around her joy now, and she doesn't tell. She just laughs it out, and that old pātai, that gnawing question about why he threw the can opener and whether or not it was in fact her fault, dries up. She laughs on.

'I remember. What a halfwit. What a waste of his good ballhead fortune.' Kataraina spins, gesturing to us, and the world around. 'All this.'

A crevice opens, widens, and her laughter is like cool water, and her cool-water laughter finds this new channel and rushes through it, like a dam has suddenly collapsed, and the cool-water laughter rushes through the channel, right back through time, rinsing us clean.

Further reading

Resources I am grateful to have found to read and learn from include: Rob Tipa's *Treasures of Tāne – plants of Ngāi Tahu* (Huia Publishers, 2018), Gordon Stephenson's *Wetlands: discovering New Zealand's shy places* (Government Printing Office, 1986) and Rachel Buchanan's stunning *Te Motunui Epa* (Bridget Williams Books, 2022).

Smaller resources include articles such as: 'How Hokonui Rūnanga are working to restore kanakana numbers' by Louisa Steyl (*Stuff*, 21 May 2022). And I very much enjoyed listening to Nicola Toki speaking about parahia, and reading further to learn there were records of the plant until 1959. It once grew in weedy abundance in our kūmara crops but was considered extinct by 2012. Three years later, botanist Shannel Courtney found the plant near a tributary of the Waiau Toa / Clarence River.

I'd like to acknowledge the work Spencer Kahu has done regenerating wetland on his whānau's Kaikōura farm. There are some cool articles to read about you, Spence. Coming for a cuppa and a hīkoi, one day.

Ngā mihi

I would like to thank all the people who read *Auē* – each of you opened up my life. I got to meet so many writers and readers. Readers are so precious and if you have now reached *Kataraina*'s acknowledgements, kia ora anō. A special thank you to readers like Chloe Fergusson-Tibble, who seek to amplify our voices.

Dear Mary and Paul at Mākaro Press. I am forever grateful to you both. Mary, all your work you do to help me make the writing sing, tell the story. And you and Ian have opened your home and hearts to my whānau – treasured memories for life. Paul, a well-typeset book is a piece of art. How you manage it with an author who is cutting and rewriting things right up to the last minute is a wonder. Thank you.

Kataraina was partly written in Dunedin, where I was honoured to be granted Otago University's Robert Burns Fellowship. This fellowship was life-changing. I am forever grateful to have had the opportunity. Kia ora to those of you in the English department I crossed paths with. My deepest gratitude – for just how rich the time I spent in Dunedin was – is with Talia Marshall. Thank you to you and your boy.

To Tusiata Avia, thank you for the FaceTimes while we did virtual writing hangs. Thank you for your mahi, kare, and your words supporting this book. To Jenna Todd, whānau, thank you for your kupu too!

To my friends: kā Samuels, Forsyth, Nikora, Bird/Crackett whānau – wouldn't have wanted to try get through the last few years without yas. Love yas. Grateful for the circles, kai and songs.

Big mihi to my bro Tokohau Samuels for reading this book and your aroha for Kataraina.

Dad, may your love of the sea and its taoka be seen. Thank you for taking us to Māori Beach and Ringaringa Beach. Tāua and Pōua's favourites. I love you.

Mum, your support for my writing always remains unaffected by outside influence. Thank you for always being there. I love you.

My bro and sissies. No matter what, my writing is informed by us. Kodes, you are a pou, with a bloody sound compass. Nic, you are a bad bitch, with stories and stories that make me laugh and cry. Tam, thank you for helping raise me. Shout out to the greatest sister-in-law ever, Renée, may you always have all the books and coffee you ever need. Love yas.

Love to all my cousins, aunties and uncles. We understand things about each other no one else can. Kellie, you have been an incredible support the past few years. We are so lucky to have you. To my nieces and nephews, the poem is for youse – and us, who try to be there eh. We can all scowl. Love yas.

Ma- and Pa-in-law, Sharon and John Manawatu. I feel lucky that you're both proud of my mahi. It means a lot. Kia ora Maurice Manawatu for answering my questions and helping me with the tikanga around the ancestor's body. And to the wider Manawatu whānau: time spent with you all has been uplifting, enriching. I feel lucky to know you all, and I do not take it lightly that it is your name on the books I write. Kia ora for your manaakitaka.

Te Rua Mason, you do so much for this community. I may not be getting much further with my reo, but when I make it to class, I'm learning from you beyond the language. Clayton Cook, kia ora for checking my reo in the book.

Arohanui to Witi Ihimaera for your tautoko. The time we spent together in Tahiti was very special, but one of my greatest memories is when you invited me to be part of your discussion at

Motueka Library. I walked away from that with so much mana. Donna McLeod and Kerry Sunderland, thank you for bringing us together in Motueka – and to you, Donna, for welcoming me into your home, for your manaakitaka and all the kōrero. Briar Grace-Smith, kia ora for having me in Auckland. You and Victor Rodger and the rōpū helped me get my fire going again. Got me out the house.

Kataraina was written with funding assistance from Creative New Zealand. It was also written with the help of *Newsroom*'s Surrey Hotel Writers Residency. I'm grateful to both, and to literary agent Nadine Rubin Nathan and the team at Scribe for taking my books into the world.

To the people I shared a whare with while writing: Tim, Maddox, Siena, Layla, Ariah, Hinearo and Akiwa. It could be too easy to forget how lucky we were to have each other, but I promise not to. Siena, you are so kind, strong and crack-up. I love you, e kare. Maddox, you have your Uncle Kodie's sound compass, a good man. I love you, my boy. I'm so proud of you. Both my kids, honestly couldn't have done it all without you – you've stepped up so much. Ariah, Hinearo and Akiwa: that I ever got the fortune to know and awhi and learn from you will always be one of the greatest blessings of my life. Love you amazing little people, always.

Last, but not least, ever, Tim. I don't know another man who could uncle like you have the past few years. Thank you for all your support and interest in my work. Making it possible for me to take up the Robert Burns residency. Wanting me to write. Love you like in a K-Ci & JoJo song.

You are all astounding. Ka nui taku aroha ki a koutou.

Love yas, love yas, love yas xxx

Glossary for *Kataraina*: te reo Māori and New Zealand colloquialisms

āe – yes
ao – world, Earth
Aotearoa – New Zealand
ara tawhito – traditional travel routes of Māori
aroha – love
ātaahua – beautiful
auē – to cry, wail, howl; interjection showing distress
auē, te mamae – oh, the pain
awa – river

chilly bin – (colloq.) a portable chiller
chooks – (colloq.) chickens
cuz – (colloq.) cousin

haere – go
haere ki o tāua tīpuna wāhine – go to our female ancestors
haere mai – come here, welcome
hākui – (Kāi Tahu dialect) aunty, mother
Hananui – a mountain
hāngī – earth oven to cook food
hapū – to be pregnant, a kinship group or subtribe
harakeke – New Zealand flax
he kimihia – the search or hunt
he pātai nui – it's a big question
hei-taramea – a bag of fragrance made from taramea, worn around the neck
heru – a comb for the hair, often made from carved bone
(e) hine – girl, daughter
hine ngākau – woman of great heart, generous woman
hōhā – nuisance, hassle
hongi – the practice of pressing noses to share breath as a greeting
horoeka – lancewood
hoodie – (colloq.) a hooded sweatshirt
huhu – an edible grub found in decayed wood
hui – a meeting, gathering; to meet, gather
hundy – (colloq.) hundred

Island time – (colloq.) a relaxed attitude towards time, considered derogatory

ka aroha – condolences
ka nui taku aroha ki a koutou – I love you all so much
kā roimata o te wahine – the woman's tears
kahikatea – white pine
kāhu – swamp harrier
kai – food
Kaikōura – a South Island town, literally means 'eat crayfish'
Kairuru – a South Island mountain

kaitiakitanga – guardianship, stewardship
kākā beak – clianthus; the red flowers resemble the beak of a native parrot, the kākā
kanakana – (Kāi Tahu dialect) lamprey, an eel-like fish with a sucker mouth, highly valued food
kānuka – white tea tree
kāore – no
karakia – prayer, grace
karakia mō te kai – grace, prayer before eating
(e) kare – dear friend
Kāti Hinetewai – a South Island iwi (tribe)
Kāti Kuri – a South Island hapu or subtribe
kaumātua – elderly man or woman, a person of status in the whānau (family)
kawakawa – a leaf with medicinal properties
kei te pai – it's fine or good
kei te pai au – I'm good
kei te pēhea koe? – how are you?
kererū – New Zealand pigeon
kete – bag woven from flax
'Ko te Whaea' – hymn 'Ka Waiata ki a Maria' is also called 'Ko te Whaea', meaning 'The Mother'
ko te whaea o te ao – the mother of the world
ko wai ia? – who is she?
ko wai tātou? – who are we?
kōpuru – moss
kōrero – talk
kōrero mai – talk to me
korokī – singing (for birds in this context)
kōtuku – white heron
kōura – crayfish

kōwhai – the colour yellow, native trees noted for their yellow flowers
kuia – elderly woman
kūkūwai – swamp
kūmara – sweet potato
kupu – word
kurī – dog

leaner – (colloq.) a bar in a pub to lean on while drinking

mahi – work
māmā – mother
mamae – pain
manu – bird; (colloq.) to curl the body into a ball to make a bomb when jumping into the water
mānuka – tree
Māori – the Indigenous people of Aotearoa New Zealand
māra kai – a vegetable garden
marae – area in front of the main tribal meeting house for Māori, the buildings around that area
(te) marama – the moon
mātanga pūtaiao – scientist
mātātoka – fossils
Mataura – place
mātauraka – (Kāi Tahu dialect) knowledge, wisdom, understanding
mātauraka o te whenua – (Kāi Tahu dialect) knowledge, wisdom, understanding of the world
matua – teacher, leader
mauka – (Kāi Tahu dialect) mountain
mauri – life principle, life force, the essential quality and vitality of a being or entity
maxies – (colloq.) going to the limit
mere – a short flat weapon made of stone, often pounamu
mimi – urine, stream

mish – (colloq.) going on a mission
moe – sleep
mokimoki – fragrant fern
moko / mokopuna – grandchild or grandchildren
Moriori – Indigenous person or people of Wharekauri, the Chatham Islands

nanny/nan – grandmother
nau mai – welcome
nīkau – a native palm tree
noa – ordinary, unrestricted, to be free of tapu

Ōkārito – New Zealand's largest unmodified estuarine lagoon, home to kōtuku
ōku hākui – (Kāi Tahu dialect) my aunties and mother
Ōtautahi – Christchurch

pā – fortified village or city, stockade
pāpā – father
Papatūānuku – Earth, the Earth mother and the wife of Rakinui – all animate and inanimate things originate from them
parahia – a perennial endemic herb
pātai – question
pātōtara – dwarf mingimingi, a small shrub
pāua – abalone
pīwakawaka – fantail
plasters – (colloq.) sticking plasters
pō – night
pōhutukawa – a coastal tree with red blossoms that blooms at Christmas time
poi – a light ball on string that is swung to music, traditionally made with raupō leaves

pokie – (colloq.) fruit machine for gambling
ponga – silver tree fern
pono – truth
pounamu – greenstone
pūhā – sowthistle, boiled and eaten
pūkana – to stare wildly, dilate the eyes, done by both genders when performing haka (ceremonial challenge) and waiata (songs)
pūkeko – Australasian swamp hen
puku – stomach
pūrākau – stories

Rakinui or Raki – (Kāi Tahu dialect) god of the sky, husband of Papatūānuku – all animate and inanimate things originate from them
Rakiura – Stewart Island
Red Bands – popular brand of gumboots or Wellington boots, often worn by farmers
rātā – large forest tree with red flowers and hard red timber
raupō – swamp grass
rēwena – bread
rimu – red pine
roimata – tears
rollie – (colloq.) hand-rolled cigarette
rongoā – refers to rongoā māori, a natural remedy or the traditional treatment
ruru – morepork

skulled – (colloq.) to drink quickly, often in one go
Swanndri – New Zealand brand of woollen garment for the outdoors

(te) taiao – world, Earth, natural environment

tailies – (colloq.) tailormade cigarettes
Takahanga – marae in Kaikōura
Takaroa – (Kāi Tahu dialect) god of the sea and fish, one of the offspring of Rakinui and Papatūānuku
tāku/tōku – my, mine
Tāmaki Makaurau – Auckland
tamariki – children
Tāne – god of the forests and all forest creatures
tangi / tangihanga – to cry or grieve, funeral, Māori funeral with strong cultural imperatives and protocols
taniwha – a water spirit, monster or guardian that usually lives in the sea, lakes, rivers and caves, and can take on many forms but is often represented as lizard-like; can be a spiritual guardian, a guardian of those who live nearby, or a malignant force
taoka – (Kāi Tahu dialect) treasure
tapu – to be sacred, prohibited, restricted; a supernatural condition where a person place or thing is dedicated to an atua or god and thus removed from the sphere of the profane to the sacred
tangi – to cry, to grieve, a funeral
taramea – speargrass
Te Ara a Kiwa – Foveaux Strait
Te Au Nui – Mataura Falls
tēnā koe – hello (to one person)
tēnā koe i tēnei ata – greetings this morning
te reo – the language, usually used to mean the Māori language
the bone people – the Booker Prize–winning novel by New Zealand author Keri Hulme, with a protagonist called Kerewin
tika – correct
tikanga – the customary system of values deeply embedded in the social context
tikumu – common mountain daisy
tinny – (colloq.) a small package of cannabis wrapped in tin foil
tipuna / tīpuna – ancestor/ancestors
tītī – muttonbirds
toetoe – pampas grass
toikupu – poetry
toki – axe or adze
toroī – pickled pūhā (sowthistle) and mussels
tuatua – edible bivalve mollusc

wahine / wāhine – woman / women
waiata – song, to sing
Waiau-toa – Clarence River
Waitaha – an early iwi or tribe
Waitaiki – the name of an ancestor
we could go hundies – (colloq.) we could go all out
weka – woodhen
wētā – large wingless insects found in trees and caves
whaea – aunt, mother
whakaaro – thought
whakamā – feel ashamed
whakapapa – lineage, to be descended from
whakataukī – proverb
whānau – family (includes nuclear and extended family)
wharekai – building on the marae where food is prepared and eaten
wharenui – the main building and meeting house on the marae
wharepaku – toilet
whenua – placenta, land
wīwī – native plant or rush; sea rush grows in coastal marshes and sand flats